WHAT YOU WANT

Or,
The Pursuit of Happiness

CONSTANTINE PHIPPS

Quercus

First published in Great Britain in 2014 by Quercus Editions
This paperback edition published in 2015 by

Quercus Publishing Ltd
Carmelite House
50 Victoria Embankment
London EC4Y ODZ

An Hachette UK company

A CIP catalogue record for this book is available
from the British Library

PB ISBN 978 1 84866 437 1
EBOOK ISBN 978 1 84866 436 4

10 9 8 7 6 5 4 3 2 1

Designed and typeset by Andrew Barker
Typeset in Sabon LT Std with FrescoSans Pro and Weiss Std

Printed and bound in Great Britain by Clays Ltd, St Ives plc

For Nicky

'. . . a hundred times, my love, than any easier matter'

Contents

Assurance to the Reader

Listener, reader, rest assured,
no benefit would be procured
by cast of characters, or notes:
hearing what the author wrote
is quite enough. No kind of prior
background knowledge is required.

Unhappiness

When I was about halfway through life
(always a cheery moment) I lost my wife
to another man, and as is the natural way
when a woman leaves her man of yesterday,
she kept our child; naturally too
she got our home, and I was the one who
moved out of our apartment; so at a stroke
I found I was a lonely single bloke,
without the intimacy and protection
which family life confers, or its affection.
At this point I should probably have known
there was no going back, I should have shown
some realism at least. Dignity
and guts above all were the qualities
I needed now, rather than wishful thinking
about what might have been, or whisky drinking
and evil hangovers. But something happened:
a mood came down on me which left me flattened,
unable to act at all. My head was filled
with fantasies that we might still rebuild
our marriage, that Louise might still come back,
perhaps out of concern for our son Jack,
perhaps even for my sake – my confusion
fostered every order of delusion.
Does everyone have moments when they feel
like this? Like air out of a wheel
my confidence began to leak away.
At work I found a setback would convey
immediate feelings of defeat, and yet
when things went well I didn't seem to get
a compensating feeling of success.
At home, my confidence was even less:

alone, without even the antidote
of work, depression gripped me in the throat.
Choice was an agony. The smallest act
of daily life would put me on the rack:
even to get the doorbell or the phone
was to be dreaded. Better to postpone
every decision, shut out every friend,
and lose myself in sleep. But even then
disturbing thoughts still woke me in the cold
of night like punches: You are getting old.
Your woman left you, do you wonder why?
This is called failure. Soon you're going to die.
A sympathetic friend would surely say
you've only started thinking in this way
because you are depressed; but you despise
the siren comforts offered by these lies,
however well meant. It is clear to you
you feel this way because these things are true.

Well now, it was about this time I planned
to take Jack on a trip to Themeparkland
in Florida, an outing which would please
him more than anything, and which Louise
could never do because she feared and hated
the rollercoaster rides which fascinated
Jack. So now I stood outside the door
of what had been my home not long before
and where Louise now entertains her new
partner. I rang, the buzzer let me through,
I went up to the flat. My darling boy
opened the door, and now my sudden joy
at seeing him was tainted by the dark
expression which he wore, which was the mark
of everything he'd suffered since Louise
and I split up. I gave him a big squeeze
and said, 'Hey, Jack, we're going to have some fun.'
Louise appeared behind him. She had none

of her former gentle, sympathetic gaze;
instead a steely firmness seemed to blaze
behind those penetrating eyes. She thrust
a box into my hand saying, 'He must
have this three times a day: antibiotic.
He's better, and it may seem idiotic,
but he must finish them. Don't miss your flight.'
Her impatience to have us out of sight
was palpable. It gave the rather bitter
impression that I was the babysitter
for her and her new love. I said, 'Louise,
could I have a moment with you please?'
'What's it about?' 'Just that I'd like a word
alone with you a moment.' She demurred;
so I pressed her, saying it was important,
and tried to show by gestures that I oughtn't
to say anything more in front of Jack.
But she just said, 'We'll talk when you get back.'

The theme park entrance is a lofty gate
festooned with flags, and made to imitate
a crude portal of rusticated stone,
although it's actually made with blown
concrete. Above the massive lintel rise
three words in silhouette against the skies:
'Live The Dream'. I took Jack by the hand,
we passed together into Themeparkland,
and found ourselves upon a promenade
of buildings, smaller than life-size and made
to replicate a street in San Francisco
before the quake, a hundred years ago.
The signs said 'Hatter', 'Bank', or 'City Hall',
but once you went inside it seemed they all
sold the same T-shirts, ballpoint pens, suncream,
and baseball caps, and everything was themed.

Jack hurried us along past these distractions
towards the 'Superhero Stunts' attraction,

which was the thing he most wanted to do,
and here we joined the omnipresent queue;
even inside the building, on it went,
first through a room designed to represent
a banking hall, and then a passageway
in which a giant video display
came suddenly to life over our heads,
showing a guard in uniform who said,
'Attention, attention, security alarm
activated. A group of masked and armed
hoodlums have broken in and occupied
the twenty-seventh floor. Remain inside
your offices.' And then the picture fuzzed
and flickered on and off; the soundtrack buzzed
weirdly as if something had interfered
with the reception; then suddenly appeared
the Joker, a rictus painted on his face
in red greasepaint, threatening to blow the place
to kingdom come unless he got enough
ingots of gold by noon. That kind of stuff.
Next we passed a waxwork of Clark Kent
(amazingly lifelike), and then we went
onwards to where another wax statue –
this time of Spiderman – addressed the queue
and even answered questions as they passed.
Jack listened earnestly to what was asked
as well as to the Spiderman's reply.
When our turn came I thought he'd be too shy –
but not at all: his child's voice was low
but perfectly collected. 'I want to know
if you can make a wish come true,' he said.
The statue's empty eyes looked straight ahead,
and then the voice emerged: 'Before I can,
you have to tell me what it is, young man.'
Jack shook his head and answered, 'I can't say.'
'Go on,' the statue answered, 'it's OK.
You don't have to be shy.' But Jack frowned
and didn't answer. His little head went down,

he took my arm and held it tight. I knew
what he wanted and I wanted it too,
but neither of us spoke.
                              It felt strange
to be this way with him. I thought how changed
he was, by turns resentful or subdued,
as if already given to teenage moods.
Because I was the one who'd moved away,
I think Jack blamed me in his childish way
for splitting up our family, though God knows
I was the very last one to propose
this thing, which came all from Louise's side
and none from mine. And yet, although I tried
to be there for him, still I have to say,
nothing had been straightforward since that day.
It came out in so many ways: his moods,
the sudden fussiness about his food,
the novel reticence and dark expression
and moments of vicarious aggression.
(Though Jack adored all animals, when I
moved out he soon began to vilify
our parrot, even threw things at his cage,
and then – perhaps a natural next stage –
the bird escaped and wasn't seen again.)

We came now to those things like cattle pens
which isolate by means of metal bars
the right number of people for each car,
and got seats in the front row. Now we rode
into a Captain Marvel episode:
witnessed the giant granite boulder slam
and crush the body of wizard Shazam;
we saw the Human Torch, blowing real flames;
the gorgeous Betty Ross, who alone tames
the savage Hulk; witnessed the eerie light
which glimmered in a lump of Kryptonite
displayed upon a plinth like you might find
in a museum. The whole ride was designed

around waxworks arranged in histrionic
tableaux, with a few animatronic
puppets, which gave some movement to the scenes.
Other attractions used other routines:
the 'Pirate Treasure Archipelago'
had costumed actors to compère the show,
as well as for the sword-and-pistol fight,
singing a sea shanty, and cussing lite –
these actors were combined with movie screens
to show the high seas and the battle scenes.
The visitors were borne along a flume
in boats, while all around we heard the boom
of cannons. Then we came to the supreme
excitement of the water chute: we screamed,
the camera flashed, and when the ride was done
Jack said immediately, 'That was fun,
can we do that again?' We had to laugh.
On the way out we bought the photograph.
Now and again, on pavements or street corners,
we stopped to chat with 'streetmosphere' performers –
often as not students in holiday
employment, variously dressed to play
an Inuit villager, or a Zulu,
Rafiki, Pluto, or Winnie-the-Pooh.
And then we came to 'Ride with Terminator' –
a show created by a simulator
which clipped into your helmet while you rode
a stationary motorbike. This mode
of travel gave the rider a sensation
of extreme speed; computer generation
of all your braking, cornering, and jumps
(it tilted, even reproduced the bumps)
contributed a lot to the impression.
The common thread of this diverse succession
of rides was that they started with a queue
and ended in a shop.

When we were through
we went for lunch to Bessie's Country Pies,
where they served only hamburgers and fries,
and this suited Jack well. While we were there
I fell in conversation with a pair
of guys who worked here as 'imagineers' –
young fellows with a childish but sincere
enthusiasm for the Park. These two
had been in charge of fashioning a new
attraction, called 'The Founding Fathers' Hall',
which they said was 'a blast', 'the best of all',
'And seriously,' one said, 'it's not as bland
as you might think; we make you understand
that in the Revolution it was hard
to take a rebel's stand and to discard
the old allegiances and loyalty;
since taking a decision to be free
is difficult, courageous, and requires
we quit the pathways of our old desires.'
His thoughtfulness so took me by surprise
that after lunch I did as he advised,
and took Jack to the 'Founding Fathers' show.

There wasn't any queue. A portico
gave into a large circular hall
with tall ionic columns. Here the walls
had niches cut in them where holograms
in eighteenth-century dress appeared to stand.
Some of them stared blankly, looking through you,
while others smiled and waved, or nodded to you,
and people holding trays went to and fro
with 3D specs to wear during the show.
At last a door was opened and we streamed
into a cinema. The massive screen
was hidden by an arc of corrugated
curtain, lit in blue, and punctuated
by uplighters, in bold chevrons of pink.
Whatever our friends had done, I didn't think

it could have been a big hit: I could see
the auditorium was half empty.
Now an announcer asked us to refrain
from flash photography, and so maintain
the dignity of what we were to see,
and also please to put on the 3D
spectacles, and silence our cell phones.
The programme was a medley. We were shown
some movie clips in 3D panorama,
some real actors in scenes of costume drama,
and interspersed with these, from time to time,
animatronic figures, who would mime
the words, while pre-recorded actors' voices
came through the sound system, with other noises,
like cheering mobs, some scarily realistic
gunfire, or else – slightly anachronistic –
the sound of 'Hail, Columbia' being sung.
First to appear, an actor, tall and young
and dressed in a blue coat, came on the stage
to represent the hero of his age,
George Washington.
                                    'The term "American",'
he said, 'was very certainly not one
we used to describe ourselves. The word was used
by English writers looking to abuse
us colonists, and wanting to suggest
that in America we don't possess
full rights as Englishmen; and naturally
we couldn't hold with that, because you see
we thought of ourselves as British, and possessed
of all the rights and freedoms which the rest
of them enjoyed. Paradoxically,
this was the very faith which set us free
of Britain, with its lords and royalty,
and brought us to a different loyalty.
Hindsight makes it seem destined to be
(because you are Americans), but we

were British, and by God, we had to choose
not to be. History tends to confuse
this issue: you're not struggling to be free
from something new which you don't want to be
but – and it's a harder thing by far –
to be free of the person that you are,
and we did that.'
                              Now on a screen we saw
his life before the Independence War:
an honest soldier loyal to the King,
bravely fighting the French, petitioning
for the acceptance of his regiment
into the British Army, still intent
on an official status as redcoats
with all the rank and honour that denotes.
Franklin was shown next, writing to Strahan
that famous letter: 'Look upon your hands!
For they are bloodied with the slaughtered throng
of your own relatives! Sir, you were long
a friend of mine. But now you have become
my enemy.' But then Franklin's own son,
steadfastly loyal to the crown, protested
against his father's cause, and was arrested
and thrown in jail; and so his only child
was lost to him as well, and the reviled
enemy claimed him, and he emigrated
back to the old country, if not hated
at least lost to his father.
                              On stage next
came Jefferson declaiming from the text
of his 'summary view': 'So I attest
it is neither our wish nor interest
to separate from Great Britain,' he read.
Then turning to the audience, he said:
'My uncle, cousins, and beloved teacher
all lived there, so at first I hoped we'd reach a
compromise agreement of some kind.
I don't think any of us were inclined

to fight our own as we were forced to do.'
All this, although historically true,
sounded unpatriotic, was confusing
and worse than this, I felt, was clearly losing
the audience's attention. I could sense
that what they really wanted was intense
feelings, clear sides, and preferably war.
But this they didn't get.

                    Instead we saw
the movie screen slide noiselessly away
revealing to the audience an array
of puppet men in wigs, sitting on chairs,
with lifeless faces, and immobile stares.
The scene was set as if for one of those
congresses or conventions which arose
to settle business in the Thirteen States
during the early days. The delegates
began unanimously with a vow,
like that of '87, not to allow
a word of what was said within those walls
to reach the outside world; and then they all
took turns to rise on animatronic joints,
gesturing creakily to make their points.
We heard their disembodied voices boom
from hidden loudspeakers around the room,
expressing a variety of views,
until North Carolina member Hewes,
who up till then had always been renowned
for loyalty to Britain and the crown
and a general anti-independence stance,
started up from his seat as in a trance,
staring emptily upward and ahead,
and lifting both his hands above his head
cried out, as if to heaven, 'It is done!
And I will abide by it;' and a stunned
silence follows.

And then, out of his seat

Jefferson rose slowly to his feet;
without anger, and yet without regret,
he said, 'We must endeavour to forget
our former love for them, and only hold
them henceforth as we do the manifold
of peoples on the earth, as foes in war
and in peace friends. Enough. I'll say no more.'

In our hotel room Jack sat on the bed
and played with his toy car, which whined and sped
in little bursts across the bedroom floor;
then stopped, reversed, and shot out of the door
into the bathroom, skirting the TV
console, and back again. As for me,
I lay beside him, drinking Scotch and reading,
trying to concentrate, and not succeeding.
The essay's author seemed to feel he ought
to have a name attached to every thought –
as if a thought required a pedigree
and couldn't function independently.
I felt the irritation which one might
endure at a name-dropping socialite
as eager as a spaniel to disclose
the rich and famous people that he knows,
and laid the book aside. And now I saw
Jack's lip begin to quiver, then his jaw,
and then his face crumpled. I reached and took him
into my arms, and felt the sobs which shook him
against my chest, and said, 'What's it about,
my love?' But he could get no answer out,
just clung to me and wouldn't let me go.
I said, 'I know, my darling boy, I know
it's difficult for you: I'm also sad.
Everyone in a divorce feels bad
when it takes place, but that will disappear
with time. One thing is absolutely clear:

your mum and I still love you just as much,
and that won't change. Divorcing isn't such
a bad thing when a father and a mother
can no longer be happy with each other.'
But even as I spoke, it sounded lame;
and surely to Jack it must have felt the same,
because he said, 'Why can't they?'

There are things you cannot say
to a child: her arm across her breasts,
her hand that pushes yours away;
the months which count their loneliness
in nights; a sudden tiredness

which sweeps upon her, and she yawns,
arches her back, and turns aside.
A deer at daybreak on the lawn,
seeing an observer move inside
the house, canters away to hide.

Many excuses are less robust
than one. Mine were the loveliness
of ample mouth and narrow waist,
the love which they seemed to express;
and when she turns to hang her dress

the vase-shaped loins, perfectly smooth.
Too many reasons. Unhappiness
always turns away from truth
and focuses on something less
distressful, if it can. I guess

I knew that I would never touch her;
and yet I went on open-eyed
as if I might, as if her nature
wasn't really hooves and hide,
a deer running from my side;

as if some human ecstasy
awaited. So what disarray
of heart sustained this fantasy?
What fear, what things I couldn't say,
did I turn from, cantering away?

I took Jack home. Louise opened the door and he rushed by
into the flat; he didn't say goodbye
to me, or hug Louise. She took his case
and stood her ground while something in her face
told me I wasn't welcome. Undeterred,
I said, 'You promised we could have a word.'
She said, 'I have to do the shopping. Is it
something that can wait for your next visit?'
I said, 'It's important.' She gave a look
of irritation, said nothing, but took
me through the kitchen to the front room where
I sat down in my favourite armchair
and she sat opposite me on a pouffe,
so poised and supple she's the living proof
of the effectiveness of yoga classes.
At twenty-nine her loveliness surpasses
what she had been at twenty, when I met her:
perhaps her features now are subtly better
defined; perhaps also in her regard
there's something gratified, something less hard,
which grew out of becoming a mother.
Look at her: it's hard to see how other
women could have offered much allure
when I had her: the skin is very pure
and pale, and very dark her chestnut eyes;
her bird-like gestures subtly catechize
a man's attention. Words cannot portray her
fascination; yet I did betray her,
yes, and often.

'So,' Louise said, 'what
is the important business which you've got
to deal with now, so urgently you say?
I'm listening.' This was the sympathetic way
she had with me these days. I said, 'Nothing
could be more serious or more pressing.
It's this: I'm asking you to take me back –
and Louise, not just for the sake of Jack,
although he certainly would want it too –
no: the reason is that I love you.
Call the divorce off now and I'll agree
to anything you want, I guarantee
you can dictate whatever terms, I swear,
and even go on with your love affair.
I won't object.' A voice, though barely audible
inside me now was asking, 'Is this laudable,
a perfect kind of love, or is it merely
masochism?' She said, 'Now you're really
crazy. Something like that is never going to work for a
    minute.'

Louise, in the social pages of a magazine
I saw you at his side. It seemed that you had found
your childhood once again: the wealth, the world's esteem,
a life inside the privilege compound.

Between us nothing's mentioned. An oath of reticence
restrains the delegates of this congress.
The ecstasy of your revolt, love's vehemence –
to hear that said would be a kind of death.

Please, not a word. But by your silence I am spared
neither the agony of disenfranchisement
nor the political parleying which leads nowhere
and which must now become my instrument.

And yet, don't say it. For death is a taboo subject
in every culture. And you, who became my wife
in sickness and in health, try to be circumspect
and if you must speak, say there is an afterlife.

It doesn't have to be as good as paradise,
but tell me something of earthly life endures: perhaps the halls
of Hades, grim and tenebrous, would suffice
to house the ghosts of happier days recalled.

A wife imprisoned there, a spectre without sex:
for better or for worse, by this solution
we might survive our death: if not the primary text,
with its garden of bangled virgins, then at least the next
best thing to it: a mangled and amended constitution.

I said, 'It could make sense. Call off the divorce and have me back
here in the flat to live with you and Jack.
We needn't share a bed, we'll find a way
forward, little by little, day by day,
we'll find some kind of compromise, a deal
which is acceptable, if not ideal.'
Louise said, 'No,' and then, 'I can't do that.'
Her voice was hesitant and strangely flat,
without the steeliness it had contained
only a moment since. I tried again
to make her see the sense of my idea,
promising her there was nothing to fear
on her side, seeing she would still be free
in every way, and could be rid of me
at any time; but once again she said,
'I can't do that, Patrick,' and hung her head
and fell silent. I said, 'I don't know why
you suddenly can't look me in the eye;
it isn't like you and it doesn't suit
your style to be recalcitrant and mute.

What's it about? Come on, Louise, admit
you're hiding something from me. Out with it!'
And she replied, 'The reason I can't live
with you, Pat, isn't that I can't forgive
your double-dealing and the way you carried
on. It's this: I want to be remarried.'

Happiness

At home, I went to bed and drank some Scotch,
flicked on the TV, and began to watch
alternately a confrontation show
and a biopic on Freud, the easy flow
of each one broken by my restlessness.
First comes a man who's ready to confess
to cheating on his wife. He grins a lot,
showing his gleaming teeth and seeming not
to mind who knows about it; and then a
switch of channel brings me to Vienna,
a family alpine walk, the loving chows
and less loving disciples, and their rows.
Unable to feel tired I took some pills
and I waited for my thoughts to calm, but still
I kept thinking of Jack, how he'd begun
berating the parrot, and how he'd run
into the flat without saying goodbye,
when I brought him back home. (They specify
not to take alcohol with these.) I pressed
the safety cap, twisted it off, and guessed
how many of them I'd taken before.
I shook some out and then shook out some more,
and poured a shot of Scotch and knocked it back.
It made my eyes water.
                                      I thought of Jack
crying, and Louise's head bowed down,
her gaze avoiding mine, her distant frown;
I thought I'd better not die for Jack's sake.
Strangely, I still felt perfectly awake,
the pills perhaps weren't doing any harm;
if anything, I started to feel calm,

though when I leant across the bed to pour
some more whisky, a lot went on the floor
and too idle to move I let it lie.
The actor's nose, his beard and piercing eye,
gave him quite a convincing look of Freud
and the cigars and other props employed
also contributed. We got to see
the house he lived in till, at eighty-three,
he fled the Nazis, also a selection
of shots of his antiquities collection,
and heard his voice-over: 'In many ways
the painful feelings of our childhood days
are like those Greek and Roman artefacts
which time preserved so marvellously intact
because they were deliberately buried
under the ground, inside the many varied
tombs and burial-grounds which men created.'
I thought of how I was initiated
to archaeology, hanging around
beside the excavations as the ground
was dug, and soil was sifted on a tray
with expert care, and then taken away
to designated heaps. And that was where
I met the graduates, among them Clare,
and got to know her. I was just sixteen
and she was twenty-eight. I'd never seen
the point of archaeology before.

Fidgeting with the channels, I restored
the confrontation show. Now its emcee
had brought onto the studio settee
the wife, a woman of uncertain age
who looked uneasy to be on the stage.
Her make-up was too heavy for the lights,
she wore a pair of jeans a size too tight
around the thighs. She told about their life
together, a recital that was rife

with drunkenness and gambling, the effect
on their children, his general neglect
of all the family and especially her.
At this the husband says he would prefer
to sleep with anyone except his wife,
calling her frigid, calling their sex life
pitiful. The show host introduces
the man's lover, but seeing this produces
no real fight, he sits her down and brings
another in, who's pregnant. This one swings
a fist at him, and suddenly they're all
kicking and punching, and a little brawl's
encouraged to take place before they're parted.
The show continued like this till I started
to doze off and to dream that it was me
sitting up there as the interviewee,
and focus of the audience outrage.
Now the presenter brought Louise on stage.
The fanfare sounded, she came through the door
staring at me the way she stared before
when I was unfaithful, a look of pain,
bewilderment and also of disdain.
Something was going to happen. I was braced
for those rebukes which I'd so often faced,
but as Louise came forward to confront
me now, her dress fell open down the front
showing her breasts and pubic hair. I found
myself moving, without touching the ground,
towards her, like my path was preordained;
I wanted her so much it felt like pain.
Louise made no manoeuvre to protect
herself, but spoke softly, with grim effect:
'You raped me.' Now a bell began to toll.
I felt dizzy, began to lose control
of my movements. A crowd was closing in;
I knew at any moment they'd begin

to tear me apart – already I could hear
a voice say, 'Kill him,' and a thuggish cheer
went up around me.

                            Suddenly one man
among them stepped in front and raised his hand
saying, 'Nobody touch him,' and the crowd
at once grew quiet and obedient, cowed
by his authority. I recognized
the beard, the strong nose, and the piercing eyes.
Calmly, he took me by the arm and started
towards the exit, and the audience parted
on either side before us as we made
our way forward, and like this he conveyed
me from that studio into the street.
Still, it seemed my rescue was not complete
because he said, 'Come now, walk by my side.
We have much to reflect on.' I complied,
and went with him, expectant, through a maze
of unfamiliar streets and alleyways
and all the time in silence, till at last
he stopped to let a group of people past,
and as they came, the air seemed to grow colder,
and looking up I saw that on their shoulders
they carried a coffin. A dread suspicion
struck me that this might be a premonition
of my own death, but as my guide maintained
the same determined silence, I restrained
the urge to question him. The coffin passed
and we continued on our way. At last
my guide, unprompted, putting his reserve
aside, threw down his cigar and observed,
'In times of war and famine life is tough.
We don't have freedom, we don't have enough
to eat or drink. Our only pressing task
is to survive. No wonder we don't ask:
"What is the goal of life? How should we live it?"
The question, and our answer, if we give it,

is left until prosperity holds sway.
And when was there more abundance than today?
Even compared to when I was alive,
prosperity is marked, and people thrive
in ever greater numbers. All of those
now freed from starving, are obliged to pose
the ancient question: "How ought I to live?"
Sadly, religion can no longer give
an answer to this, but instead appears
to take its cue from secular ideas,
some scientific, others drawn from those
not-quite-sciences which later arose,
like economics, and psychology.
Religion has borrowed far too heavily
and like a declining family that consumes
its wealth, has leased its palace's great rooms
and moved up to the attics, making sour
comments about the guys with real power
who rent the grand apartments down below.
It can no longer help. But you must know
science can't help you either. How you choose
to live is something it has meagre views
about.'

Course of a car across the room:
circling the TV console,
it stops abruptly, then resumes,
reverses, goes into a roll;
whatever the remote control
held in a child's hand directs
the car is certain to effect.

Immortal gods, you who insist
mankind performs your whims, who spurn
your wives and wrap yourselves in mist
to rape our girls, whose altars burn

with our attention, do we earn
your favour, or is the reeking smoke
regarded in Elysium as a joke?

There are no gods, you dope.
To what cause then do we impute
being a pilgrim or the Pope,
or a temple prostitute?
To what were the schoolmen's disputes
directed? And what do we make
of witches roasted at the stake?

Because after the gods came science,
because no explanation survives;
belief is a nugatory defiance
and so it is with our own lives:
our parents', even our own wives'
love quickly becomes a lie;
our children estranged before we die.

And all you clever men who slaughtered
lowing heifers, and professed
as certain fact that earth and water
were made in seven days, my guess
is no better than yours. Witness
with me the marriage vows I swore,
and a toy car upon the floor.

His eyes, both stern and sensitive,
were fixed on mine. 'The question of how to live
is one of the oldest known to us, as well
as the most crucial. Yes. But I can't tell
you what the answer is. So my suggestion
is that we ask a less ambitious question:
rather than speaking of the one you broach
let's take a more empirical approach
and ask what humans actually reveal
by virtue of their acts to be the real

purpose and intention of their lives.
The answer to this, one easily arrives
at: Men strive for happiness, and clearly show
they want to be happy and continue so.
The project has two sides, of which the first
consists in trying to satisfy our thirst
for every type of pleasure, and a second
whose goal is fighting shy of pain. I reckoned
this programme was transparent and evincible
and named it *Lustprinzip* – the pleasure principle.
The notion swiftly underwent revision,
but for the moment let's just say my vision
accorded it a sovereign, primary status
dominating the mental apparatus;
and yet it's totally at loggerheads
with the whole world. As I often said
in my lifetime, there is no chance at all
of its being carried through. We are in thrall
to an impossible master. There!'
He pointed, and I saw across a square
an archway made of imitation rock.
Its massive lintel was a single block
on which was carved in primitive and gaunt
letters, the terse inscription: 'WHAT YOU WANT'.
We walked beneath it, and across a smooth
expanse of asphalt to the ticket booths
and under the deadpan survey of the clerk
we drifted through like ghosts into the Park.

We walked together down an avenue
until a columned mansion came in view
symmetrically built, though not designed
to look like very much more than a fine
plantation house, the kind of thing that lent
a certain style to a Virginia gent.
Around this dwelling more security
than any palace had is covertly

in operation: cameras scrutinize
the tree-lined streets, and satellites the skies;
the air itself is densely circumfused
with unseen waveband. Well-washed limos cruise
all day and night, in fog, in haze, in snow;
they take their time, they've got nowhere to go.
We walked up to the door and there my guide
produced a pass which let us both inside.
'So here we are,' he said. 'The residence
and office of the US Presidents.'

We found ourselves inside a spacious room
where two men dressed in period costume
were sitting. One was writing at a desk;
the other, marked by a certain portliness,
reclined upon an armchair, immobile
and seemingly lost in thought. After a while
he roused himself and, leaning forward, spat
with practised accuracy in a flat
pewter spittoon which stood beside his chair.
The other man seemed to be unaware
of us, and went on scratching with his quill,
completely buried in his task until
my friend alerted him with a slight cough;
then looking up, he smiled and took off
his wig, and put it on the desk. His hair
was sandy-coloured and a little spare
on top; he ran his fingers through it. The eyes
were frank, intelligent, and worldly-wise,
the face somewhat freckled. He had an air
of fun about him, something debonair.
He seemed to be acquainted with my guide
and greeted him, saying, 'I'm gratified
to see a friendly face because I'm hounded
in all the newspapers. I was astounded
when Callender betrayed me: after all,
I trusted him; and as you will recall

I helped him as a friend. But he, from sheer
malice I believe, set out to smear
my honour, writing publicly about
my slave Sally, and how I came to flout
the taboo of our time. The love I bore her
brought both of us for sure – nothing is surer –
a bounty of that ancient happiness
which fills the heart, though we couldn't confess
it publicly. All humans are confined
in some way by the morals of their time:
as tribal creatures we are powerless
before the herd. How I do loathe the press.
But who's your friend? Not one of them, I hope?'
My guide tapped his cigar and answered, 'Nope.
I found this one being hunted down, like you.
He doesn't have a grievance to pursue.'
'Well,' said the other, frowning, 'in that case
what does he want?' He looked into my face
with what seemed an unnecessary suspicion;
but I could see my singular position
offered a peerless opportunity,
so I said, 'Sir, life and liberty
are pretty standard stuff, hard to confute;
but the other bit you mention, the pursuit
of happiness – what did you mean when you wrote that?'

A heat haze over the plantation;
my study, Monticello, June,
plans for the farm, plans for the nation;
all through the shuttered afternoon
the sound of crickets importunes
like a tinnitus in your ear:
you act as if you didn't hear.

The hours pass. Night comes again.
You lie and wait for her, unsure.
Softly the handle turns and then
here comes your heartbeat, the unmeasured

gift of prehistory, her pleasure.
Darkness confesses what the day
in cowardice has put away.

Morning. I go about my chores
first on the farm, and then confined
to my study. Somewhere a door
is slammed, a voice stays in the mind.
You know she's out there, and you find
you're happy. Crickets are everywhere.
You act as if you didn't hear.

The President sat back in his chair. He said, 'My friend, the
    Declaration
was really just a hurried compilation
of notions that were current in my time.
Nothing in it's particularly mine.
I never felt I was charged to invent
a novelty, and speak no sentiment
which anyone had ever said before.
With this disclaimer, I can answer your
question as follows: I believed that all
men have certain rights. As I recall,
the rights which Locke wanted to guarantee
were life and liberty and property;
and when I substituted happiness
I left it deliberately vague. I guess
I didn't know – and maybe didn't mind –
how happiness was going to be defined.
I wanted people themselves to figure out
what human happiness could be, without
anyone telling them, least of all me –
such is the nature of democracy.
For centuries no one had thought it worth
examining how happiness on earth
arose, since from the Christian perspective
happiness wasn't really an objective

in this life, anyway. The emphasis
in those days was on other-worldly bliss,
with life on earth consigned to misery.
Happiness was a concern that we
men of the Enlightenment revived,
a conception which had barely survived
the centuries of Christianity –
though all through classical antiquity
it had been thought the best and fullest aim.
And since my death, again I see the same
concern with happiness as an objective
and answer to the question "How to live?"
Some people say this is only confusing
and happiness is not the kind of thing
you can aim for at all; that if you strive
for other ends, then happiness arrives
as a by-product. That was not our view.
We felt that it was something to pursue,
requiring both intelligence and will,
to be developed, like a craft or skill.
Perhaps that's also why the ancients say
that happiness is not just for a day
or for a minute or even three weeks:
to call someone happy you have to speak
of a substantial period of time,
like several years, perhaps a whole lifetime.'

He fell silent, and now the other man
leaned out, and spat again into the pan.
He was of mild appearance, with a soft
and plump body. He too had taken off
his powdered wig, and I could see his hair
was going back. He'd something of the air
of a professor, owlish, with a high
crown to his head, rather protuberant eyes
and fine, delicate features which contrasted
with a jowly face. The silence lasted

a minute, before he spoke: 'I practised law –
although in some ways I liked farming more –
and rose to high office. I can't pretend
to new ideas any more than my friend,
in fact less so, since much of what I wrote
consists of (mostly unacknowledged) quotes
from other people. But that doesn't mean
I couldn't think for myself, and wasn't seen
to have sound judgement, even wisdom, yes.
As to happiness, I must confess
I don't believe it ought to be our aim
in life nor do I think it ever came
to us by looking for it.' And his eyes
bulged even more as if to emphasize
his point. 'My friends, I've often speculated
there's nobody to whom I'm not related
in this country. Now tell me, what preserved
this ample family of ours, and served
to multiply and prosper us? I say
it was religion. If you take away
religion we would surely all have been
rakes, fops and sots, drunken and unclean,
gamblers, starved with hunger, froze with cold
or scalped by Indians. As in the old
days when our pilgrim ancestors were guided
here by religion, and the Lord provided
this happy country to them, so today
religion should direct and show the way
in everything we do. Our happiness
is something subsidiary, something less
important than that. Tell me who can say
what happiness consists in, anyway?'
My guide then said, 'My personal preference
is to define it in the strictest sense:
that is, as something very close to pleasure.
We experience it in strongest measure
when a desire is dammed up and denied
and then is subsequently satisfied.

It should be dammed up to a high degree
and then unblocked extremely suddenly
for greatest effect. It can be periodic
but by its nature it is episodic:
the happiness engendered cannot last
depending as it does on a contrast,
and very little on a state of things.
The pleasure which its prolongation brings
can only give rise to the milder state
of contentment.'

            Next in the debate
the fellow with the sandy-coloured hair
leaned forward and pronounced, 'Hold it right there.
You're being over-hasty when you say
that happiness is over in a day
and tell us that a pleasure's being mild
is any reason it should be reviled.
Plenty of thinkers in antiquity
were of the view that, on the contrary,
extended periods of mild content
was very much what being happy meant.
They felt it never came with those acute
pleasures, indulged by very dissolute
people, but rather by avoiding pain
in our bodies, and seeking to remain
as free as we can from troubles of the soul.
Yes, that was a very widespread goal:
exactly the state of mild tranquillity
you're trying to say that happiness can't be.'
At this point my companion interjected:
'In my patients' recitals I detected
a common feature of unhappiness
which at this stage we should also address.
I noticed in their childhoods they had often
experienced painful feelings, and to soften
the blow, they mentally brushed these aside.
They carried on almost like they denied

the pain's importance, even at times the pain
itself – a lie exhausting to maintain,
but one from which they never found release.
By and large, this attitude increased
their chances of being unhappy very greatly:
nothing they felt was felt appropriately.
To deal with this affliction I would focus
the patient's mind on finding out the locus
of ignored pain. But it was not my role
to say what it consisted of. That whole
job was better left to the patient.'

On separate farmsteads the tribe,
not gathered together in one place
but with a single voice, will gibe
and mutter that it's a disgrace
because she's of a different race,
because it's clearly fornication,
because it's really exploitation.

This is the social tourniquet,
the moral code of humankind,
and when you feel it, you will say
Sally's a phantom of their mind,
illusion which can be dismissed –
and they will go along with this.
Go on, say it: ghosts don't exist.

Go on, and keep your gaze ahead,
do not acknowledge with a blush
the woman coming to your bed,
go on with the pretence, the hush,
above all go on with the rush
of happiness, the confidence,
and children, and concupiscence.

Because ghosts do exist. This one,
appearing in your room at night,
you love; but you will also shun

with strategies of oversight
the haunting poltergeists and sprites
which as a child tormented you:
somewhere you know they live on too.

Nourished by your neglect and fear,
they come into the world as wraiths
of living people which appear
and act like them, taking their place.
One of these creatures has your face
and wants your life. I promise you:
if anything exists, ghosts do.

And now my guide, having said what he had to say, turned
on me his gaze, compassionate and stern,
perhaps to ask what I thought on the question,
or possibly by way of a suggestion;
but I was no longer hearing what was said.
My whole attention was focused instead
on something much more pressing: the window
behind him looked onto the lawn below
and there I saw Jack playing, and Louise
watching him, bird-like, with her thighs and knees
bare beneath the plumage of her dress,
a scarlet hair-grip gleaming like a crest
of feathers in her loosely tied-back hair.
Already I was on my way downstairs
to join them, but arriving on the lawn
all out of breath, I found that they were gone.
Had they been there at all? I felt my heart
stop beating for what seemed an age, then start
again. Things round me had become unstable;
the lawn was billowing, I wasn't able
to hold it still, the house as well, the waves
washed through its portico and architraves,
the garden's iron fence was liquefying
before my eyes. I thought I must be dying.

But now I heard my guide's voice close at hand:
'You are in danger now. Please understand
that I can't save you. I can only say
that once in Leyden I spent half a day
walking the streets beside a great composer
whose wife was leaving him. Now I propose a
similar exercise for you and me.
And so, unorthodox as it may be,
walk at my side, witness what I will show you
and speak freely so I can get to know you;
then as we go we'll have a look at what you
wanted for yourself and where it got you.'

Survival

We walked back to the house, passed through the store
selling the souvenirs, and out the door
into the street again. Not far away
I saw looming ahead of us the grey
mass of a pyramid, to which my guide
escorted me. And now, passing inside,
the gloom was such I couldn't see a thing
and stood there for a moment, listening
to a single sound: the crying of an infant
all on its own, an eerie and insistent
voice in the darkness. Gradually my sight
acclimatized, and I made out a light
ahead of me; the outline of a tomb
was visible, the stone walls of a room,
a vaulted stone ceiling; and all around
white lilies lying scattered on the ground.
A pan of oil with a burning wick
stood on this monument, the air was thick
with its perfume. I said, 'So who's in there?'
but my companion met me with a stare
which made me feel uneasy. In my mind
I found myself asking a second time
if I had died already. Or did the tomb
present some kind of preview of my doom?

But now my colleague took me by the arm,
saying, 'The natural feeling of alarm
a threat to our survival can provoke
solves all our other problems at a stroke.
Survival is our ultimate concern
which all others attend.' And then he turned,

and moved on to another darkened vault
while I followed behind. I saw him halt
and drawing level with him, recognized
an image of my grandfather, life-sized
though with an insubstantial quality
which made me understand it had to be
a hologram of sorts. This strange projection
brought back to me at once the great affection
I felt for him; I found myself aware
once more of all the qualities he shared
with my father; recalled how they impressed
upon me that the Navy was the best
of all the services; remembered too
the great unselfish spirit of those two,
the decency and humour which they both
unfailingly displayed. Grandpa was loath
to talk about his trauma at death's door
in Burma, as a prisoner of war,
but now as in the half-light I drew near
to this depiction of him, I could hear
him speaking in his Ulster brogue the few
words which I do remember: 'The likes of you
don't know what hunger is, Patrick. Just pray
you never have to. All that I can say
is that men who are hungry talk of food,
not women. Yes, and even servitude
is better than hunger.'
                              Now the display
flickered erratically and died away,
plunging my guide and me in a profound
blackness. There remained only the sound
of infant crying, which would not abate.
We groped on in the darkness to a gate
which my companion opened and which gave
us entry on a vast and well-lit cave.
And here, rank upon rank before our eyes,
a crowd was drawn up, three-quarters life-size:

that terracotta army which one man
caused to be buried round him at Xi'an
to guard with arrow, halberd, spear, and knife
his coming journey through the afterlife.
'As if an army could allay that fear,'
my guide said, 'for you see it's very clear
that all tombstones, chattris, and pyramids,
as well as all religions, are a bid
to stave off death somehow, or overcome it.
You could say that this man has overdone it,
but then he had the means to. To survive,
at all costs, is the strongest human drive
and so brings happiness, even elation,
but only when we're threatened by starvation,
by thirst, by human conflict or disease,
or other mortal dangers. Without these
we take it for granted. Yet it endures
in that longing men have to feel secure,
to be unthreatened, and to feel protected,
to which so much of our lives are directed.
But someone's caught your eye in this cohort.'
He was correct. The Emperor's escort
contained two figures who were clearly made
to represent my parents, and displayed
standing aside a little from the rest:
my mother youthful, almost girlish, dressed
in clothes well cut to show her perfect figure;
my father upright, with a naval vigour,
a peaked cap on his head, and on his chest a
row of medals, all of polyester
(though painted a vaguely terracotta hue).

I said to my companion, 'See those two?
They are my parents, as you may have guessed.
My mother was a doctor; she was blessed
with brains and beauty. Both were admired
around the hospital where she was hired

in Singapore, where we lived then. Her area
of expertise in medicine was malaria,
and such were her qualities that she was picked
for the research programme. Here she was quick
to fall madly in love with her director.
Even so, my dad didn't reject her
but in the end it was to no avail:
she left him anyway, and soon set sail
for Lagos with her lover, to direct
a university research project
which later made him famous. It was said
by everyone that her marriage was dead.
I still remember her saying goodbye:
crying, she stoops to kiss me and I try
to cling to her lapel, and lose my grip.
She walks along the gangway to the ship
and now she's at the rail, waving to me.
The ocean liner inches from the quay,
a web of coloured streamers torn apart
between us. As I'm waving, with a start
I hear the hooter's terrifying sound
and cling to my father. When I look round
again I see her dwindling in the press
of people on the deck; I see her dress,
then suddenly I can't see her, she's gone.
Soon my father couldn't keep me on
either; his destroyer had to sail;
that was the Navy. Somehow he prevailed
upon his parents back in Ballyclare
to have me, and I grew up with them there
in their white-painted cottage for two years
while both my parents followed their careers.
My dad came sometimes when he had shore leave,
my mother never, but I did receive
her letters, with the drawings of the cats
and monkeys which she found outside her flat

in the communal garden. These dispatches,
with pencil-shading, crayon, and cross-hatches,
perpetuated her in the abstract
long after I'd forgotten her in fact.
And then her lover died. It seems this brought
about in her a wave of second thoughts
about her marriage. Leaving the project,
she went to Singapore now to effect
a reconciliation with my pa,
which she achieved; and having got this far
it was a natural next step to reclaim
their offspring. I remember when they came
to get me. I was only five years old
and naturally enough, though I was told
she was my mother, still she was a stranger.
I had no sort of fancy to exchange her
for my granny. In this anxious mood
they took me, and I vomited my food
for several days. About this time we went
to live on Cyprus, where my pa was sent,
on winning a promotion. We remained
for my whole childhood, which was how I came
to speak Greek, and to learn from Clare
the art of love. And I was happy there.'

And now, leaving the terracotta throng
behind, my guide and I progressed along
another gloomy passage. Still the sound
of infant crying wailed in the background
but now we also heard, nearer at hand,
the voice of Louise's mother, which began
repeating, at the end of her tether,
'Bad girl, Louise, that's naughty. Don't you ever
do that again.' Then more gently I hear:
'Remember the dairy cutlery, my dear.'

Clap handies, Daddy comes
with his pockets full of plums.
Every little girl and boy
gets a sweet and jumps for joy.
Famished infant's monstrous greed
fights off death at every feed.
And neotenous adults,
trapped in this voracious cult,
live afraid to mutiny,
smash the doll's house and go free.
One two three four five six seven,
all good children go to heaven.

Sex

We left the pyramid through the gift shop
and finally the sound of crying stopped,
and we were in the outside air, the sun
upon our heads, the walkways overrun
with crowds, strolling between the Park's attractions
or dawdling at its various distractions,
such as the drink stalls and the souvenir
retailers. Here and there went 'streetmosphere'
performers in their costumes, who would pose
in character while people took photos,
giving the crowd a chance for interaction.
Eventually we came to an attraction
made like a village café you might find
in Cyprus, and attached to it, behind,
a large hangar or shed. I could discern a
stairway at the side of this taverna:
its whitewashed risers climbed to the first floor
and gave access to a blue-painted door.
I said excitedly, 'I know this place!'
My guide seemed unsurprised by this, his face
impassive, as he turned towards me. 'Well,
in that case, please be kind enough to tell
me all about it.'
             'I was just sixteen,
and near our house there was a dig – I mean
an excavation. Here I got to know
some of the people working; they would go
down to the seashore where I hung around –
mainly graduate students. One I found
particularly liked me. By and by
she showed me how to swim the butterfly,

taught me about bronze and cire perdue,
could even be prevailed upon to do
my Latin exercise. This scholar, Clare,
lived over that café, and it was there
one summer evening she took off her dress:
the artefacts of human happiness
exhumed and catalogued before my eyes.
I loved her. Was it really a surprise
that with a Latin tutor such as this
I yearned to be an archaeologist?'

The queue here was a long one, stretching down
the stairway to the street and even round
the corner. As we stood in line my guide
said, 'Everybody wants to take this ride,
for nothing is intense like sexual pleasure.
I studied it as science, took its measure:
my innovation was to see the thread
from adults' personality which led
back to the oral, anal, genital
delights of infancy. Yes, all in all,
an adult lover looks for nothing less
than childhood's first idyll of happiness,
and every girl's a homage to your mother.
You look for that in all your later lovers.
But as a way of living, love is flawed
(or else for any man to have explored
another path for living would be senseless).
The truth is we are never so defenceless
against unhappiness as when we love somebody.'

Royal palms bend in the wind,
believers kneel for their shrift.
Success often enough begins
with a submission: whales shift
in vast oceans, and flocks of swifts

clutter the wires, and on the plains
the herds are on the move again.

They hear, they capitulate.
A secret date, a feted bride,
a mighty summons such as great
migrations answer. Shudders ride
the body, obedient as the tide
is to the moon, the galaxy
to what we know as gravity.

My love, I am afraid. The ties
give, and the vessel slides away
upon the stream, your limpid eyes
are glassy and hooded. The way
down to the sea is silver grey
under the moon, and on the banks
the jungle hides dacoits and tanks.

You lovely women, gatherers
of all men's heed, who, like the free
tentacles of scyphozoa,
linger on invisibly
when you have left, envenom me
with your occult poisons and use
me for the purposes you choose.

Sexual happiness is bought
with jeopardy. No mandarin
who waits in safety at the court
will triumph at the empire's rim.
But gods, preserve us too from him
whose great conquests cannot engender
in foreign fortresses his own surrender.

As I was saying, it was a long wait in the queue to get in here,
yet somehow everyone had disappeared
when we at last entered. We went on board
a punt-like vessel which we found there moored

to a jetty, and set off down a flume
into a tunnel, in the darkest gloom.
Every now and then along the way
a lighted niche showed papier-mâché
figures, combined into romantic scenes
and painted glaringly, like figurines
designed for sale to pilgrim devotees.
In one of these tableaux I see Louise
kissing me at our wedding, on the stair
inside the registry; and in another, Clare
is holding my guitar – the only thing
that I could teach her – while I show which strings
and frets to hold down, and the chords to play;
but mostly, what we saw in that array
of waxworks were the idols of the screen:
Hollywood actors, shown in famous scenes
from their movies.

          At length we moored
the punt and disembarked beside a door
set in the tunnel wall; and in we went.
Inside, I found the room where I had spent
my first night with Louise: a small hotel
run by a Parsee family, where the smell
of cooking permeates the narrow stair.
The décor and the furnishings were spare
by any standards. There was nothing more
than whitewashed walls, a terracotta floor,
a bed with crumpled linen. From a string
a printed tablecloth was billowing
gently across the window, in the draught
caused by the fan. A pair of handicraft
painted puppets hung above the bed
where I lay down, my hands behind my head,
and stared up at the ceiling. Now my guide
sat in a rattan armchair at my side.
At length he said, 'So tell me.' 'Tell you what?'
'Whatever comes into your head. Try not

to censor yourself too much, because the thought
which seems not worth a mention really ought
to be aired as well.'
                    I said, 'On leaving college,
I wanted something new. My store of knowledge
was all Mediterranean, Greece and Rome,
learned in my schools but also from my home
in Cyprus. Now, to change all that, I meant
to understand some other continent,
explore it and discover its delights.
I fixed on India, and caught a flight
to Calcutta, and bummed around a bit
from West Bengal to Rajasthan, then hit
the beach in Goa for some New Year raves.
I found a shack, and frolicked in the waves,
played music with some Spanish guys I met,
smoked chillums with a doctor from Tibet,
drank mango lassi and ate lobster grilled
at the sea shore, and generally chilled
in Goa style.
              'New Year's Eve. The beach
was dotted with bonfires, and next to each
a group had gathered. Somewhere a guitar
was playing: at the improvised beach bar
the sound system, supposed to play all night,
was already broken. In the firelight
not far from me, I now became aware,
a girl was sitting cross-legged; her dark hair
hung down her breast, half covering her face,
and since her skin was tan in any case
the flames picked out the whiteness of her eyes
and teeth in flashes, and this emphasized
such movements as she made; but these were few.
I noticed right away how she eschewed
gesticulation, and how on the whole
her bearing spoke of stillness and control;
but when she looked around, or when she spoke,
it was with an abruptness which evoked

the way a bird moves. This impression
of bird-like poise and bird-like self-possession
was supplemented by the long straight nose
which called to mind the bill of one of those
sandpipers, like the snipe or the godwit.
Her eyebrows had a pure and exquisite
definition; and in all her face
symmetry prevailed.

        'From my place
around the fire I was too far away
to talk to her. I thought I heard her say
something in Konkani to the man who sat
beside her, a sadhu, who hawked and spat
repeatedly in the fire. What I could hear
much better was her laughter, low and clear,
which reached across the hubbub of the party,
a laugh which was surprisingly hearty
coming from such a slender girl.

        'I found
her later on that night, milling around
near to the beach bar, and we fell to talking
of this and that, and ended up walking
along that strand, while little wavelets sloshed
beside us in the dark or sometimes washed
across our ankles. Wading further in,
I felt my trousers billow round my skin,
and sand between my toes. I heard again
her low and hearty laughter; and the hem
of her sarong was floating round her knees.
The water seemed to put us at our ease:
I took her hand and waded out some more
until we were sequestered from the shore –
me up to my shoulders, and her head
rising with every passing wave. I said,
"Where are you staying? Which is your hotel?"
and now it was as if the whole world fell
silent around us and our voices sounded
jumpy, constricted; their timbre confounded

the ordinariness of the words we spoke.
How young we were! She practically choked
as she gave me directions to a beach
some distance down the coast, which you could reach
by bus from here. She said, "My friend and I
are in a shack there. He's the kind of guy
who won't stay in a hotel." Then not long
after this I lost her in the throng
and looked for her until the morning came.
I realized I didn't know her name.

'At least there was no question in my mind
what I should do now. I set off to find
that beach along the coast which she had named,
taking the bus the way she had explained,
and soon arrived there. Sure enough I found her,
with two or three admirers sitting round her,
shaded by a noble frangipani
and sipping from a glass of nimbu pani.
At some stage during this festivity
she told me that her name was Parvati
and she'd been given it in an ashram
where she lived for a while in Kottayam –
her guru said taking a new name meant
she'd made a vow to find enlightenment.
However acquired, I thought it an ideal one
and all that week I didn't know her real one,
though in a candid moment she did say
she grew up around San Francisco Bay,
and that her folks were Jewish, strictly so.
"I couldn't live with all that stuff, you know,"
she told me, "the taboos were way too weird.
Now I've turned into everything they feared
I might become. Thank God, I'm free at last."
In general, if I asked about her past
she was evasive, and so I refrained:
the present was enough.

'Her dress was stained,
her sandals too were in a parlous state
but she was clean, and used a factor eight
protection on her face, and took good care
to paint her nails and wash her inky hair.
Her lover was the sadhu I had seen
beside her on the beach. He must have been
forty years old, with beautiful soft eyes,
and skin of darkest brown, which emphasized
a winning smile. Splendid in physique,
he carries a begging bowl and seems to speak
pretty good English, though sometimes Parvati
talks to him haltingly in Marathi.
This sadhu, known as Siva to the tourists,
though not perhaps among the hard-line purists,
has no possessions, wanders all year long,
loves God, and smokes a very powerful bong.
Holding it up, and calling his own name,
he sucks in, and up shoots a mighty flame.
He is the acknowledged master of this art,
as well as that of blowing a loud fart
almost at will it seems, done to unsettle
Westerners, and put them on their mettle.
Three lines of ash are smeared across his head
in honour of his god.
                              'Parvati said,
"To be a sadhu you renounce your caste,
your family and friends, also your past.
You leave it all behind and lead a lowly
life as a wanderer, but kinda holy.
To live by begging is the archetypal
holiness, as Christ told his disciples:
live without possessions and reject
your families. People do respect
sadhus for this and are happy to give
them stuff to eat and drink, and help them live.
A holy man brings blessings when he begs."
She uncrossed and then crossed her sexy legs.

And so this Parvati and I began
to hang around together.
                           'I had planned
to go to Old Goa and take a look
at some churches I'd seen in a guidebook,
and she, it now turned out, had always meant
to see the same churches. And so we went.
But on the way, arriving at Panjim,
for no very good reason, it then seemed
to both of us an opportunity
to have some lunch and visit the city.
And so we did; and took a stroll around
Fontainhas and Altinho hill, and wound
up in a café eating rice and curried
fish, and then sat on, talking, unhurried,
drinking tea and smoking in the shade
beneath the café's awning. Now she made
some doodles on the table's paper cover
and as she drew I saw among the other
images a yacht, with at its mast
a pennant where she wrote my name. At last
we paid and left. The midday heat was gone
but it was getting late to travel on
to Old Goa. I put my arm around
her waist, and right away her head went down
on my shoulder. We walked along like this
beside the traffic, then we stopped and kissed –
remember, my darling, your tongue and mine,
exhaust fumes pumping into the sunshine,
a rickshaw's klaxon sounding tinnily
as it goes by, and you are holding me,
a whole life taking place: marriage, a child,
our youth.
             'And then we walked on past the tiled
Panjim apartments with their painted shutters,
the sidewalks stained with paan, the filthy gutters,
borne on by our elation and not knowing
where we had gone, or where we might be going

(though in another sense we knew it well)
and in the end we went to that hotel
with painted puppets, run by the Parsees.
She told me then her real name was Louise.'

Lying there again, in the exact
replica of that room, it was in fact
quite easy to remember vividly
the details of that afternoon, how we
had lain together as the blocks of sun
had lengthened on the floor and then begun
to climb the wall. I saw her, in my mind,
the little breasts, the body's flowing line
across her hips, all vividly evoked
by this replica room. I saw the smoke
which, rising from the beedi in her hand,
was sucked across and swallowed by the fan,
and heard the parrots, and the less appealing
sound of rats which scuttered in the ceiling
throughout the night with tireless industry.

'The next day when we woke she looked at me
and said, "Oops. What did we do?" and giggled.
I put my arms around her but she wriggled
away from me and went to the window.
"Come on," she said, "it's getting late, let's go
and get some breakfast." So we went downstairs,
and found a café. Sitting with her there
I sensed she was confused by what we'd done,
untalkative, her usual sense of fun
dissipated, and a little frown
between the graceful eyebrows. Putting down
her beedi, lost in thought, she seemed to stare
intently at the dust upon the air,
her lovely head as balanced as a heron's.
I wondered if her instinct was to run
back to the beach, the sadhu, and his shack,
and get her former life back on its track

where I had interrupted it. If so,
then I can only say she didn't show
much sign of being in a tearing hurry.
She ordered another coffee, and my worry
grew even less when she suggested popping
over to Miramar to do some shopping
and maybe a swim as well. Louise adored
clothes and trinkets, she was never bored
in a bazaar, and always contrived to notice
a textile or an interesting votive
statuette, a bracelet or bedspread;
and later on this visual talent fed
her love of decorating.'

                    Now I fell
silent. It seemed there was no more to tell
and a long pause ensued. At last my guide
whose rattan chair was close to my bedside
(but just behind the level of my head
so he was out of sight) now coughed and said,
'Go on, tell me your thought.' I said, 'That day
she wandered through the shops and came away
with nothing, but later that afternoon
when we regained the little hotel room
she said, "Look what I picked up on the beach
today when we were walking," and she reached
inside her bag and brought out a smooth stone
patterned with spiralled pink and greyish tones
and said, "It's for you, something from the sea.
The colours are special. Look, do you see?
It's got a hole in it." She took a string
and passed it through the middle, fastening
the two ends in a knot behind my neck.

'That night we sat outside a café decked
with strings of coloured lights. Louise began
to tell me how at just eighteen she ran
away from home. "I couldn't take the rules.
It wasn't that I thought my parents fools,

because they aren't at all. But what I hated
was having my own life so dominated
by a religious faith I don't believe;
and in the end I knew I had to leave
to get away from that. I gave them the address
of a schoolfriend in Washington and, yes,
even went there briefly. But I was clear
about where I was really heading: here.
As soon as the required visa came through
I bought a ticket, packed my bag and flew
to Bombay, and yay, freedom at last!
I finally busted out and left my past.
I texted Mom and Dad with one of those
warnings after the fact, which I composed
while waiting for the train at VT station.
It felt like I'd written the Declaration
of Independence. Things could never be
the same from now on. I was truly free.
I teamed up with some girls from Mississippi
and travelled down the coast, to all the hippy
coves and beaches, having the best time.
When I was bored of that I took a shine
to a Brazilian boy, but he was gay.
I thought I'd travel with him anyway
and went southwards as far as Kottayam
and there I spent some time in an ashram
which helped me, like a spiritual time-out . . .
but what I think you want to know about –"
a teasing smile appeared on her lips –
"is my sadhu and our relationship."
I looked at her: her beauty didn't lie
just in her long nose, or the coffee eyes,
but in her intuitions and the way
she acted on them too without delay –
everything she did had this distinctive
immediacy, and seemed to be instinctive.
I said, "Well, since you mention it, I guess
I would prefer to have that clear. So yes."

to bring the adept to spiritual health
without forbidding sex or worldly wealth.
The girls were very pretty, but at heart
I wasn't interested. I did take part
in meditation classes and the rest
but something had happened: I was depressed.
Not just unhappy that Louise had gone
but more than that. I couldn't carry on
with my travels, or even socialize
with the sannyasin. I was paralysed
with indecision, and the end result
was that I stayed much longer with the cult
than I'd ever intended.'
                                    Once again
I lapsed into silence a while, and then
my guide said, 'Well. Perhaps we've done enough
in here. But there's a lot of other stuff
for us to see. Shall we be on our way?'
Personally, I would have liked to stay
here in the hotel bedroom in Panjim:
to leave it was like waking from a dream
of someone dead.
                              I walked behind my guide
back to the flume, where our vessel was tied,
and getting in, he cast off, and we drifted
onwards with the current. Darkness lifted
only once, revealing a tableau
of lovers kissing in a gazebo;
behind them was projected a lagoon
and in the sky there hung a neon moon.
And after that we floated in the dark
as far as the next place to disembark,
and here we found a kind of replica –
half life-size – of an ancient cinema.
A lighted panel ran above the door
which in detachable black letters bore
the title of the feature coming next
upon the screen inside, in this case: 'SEX'.

The store here sold the cheap paraphernalia
you find in sex shops: plastic genitalia
and fishnet stockings, rubber underwear,
and so on. But we didn't linger there,
and passed between the shelves of this emporium
into a small and dingy auditorium
with rows of seating and a battered screen.
At first there was nobody to be seen
and so we hung around. My colleague lit
a cigar and we chatted for a bit,
and then a man, appearing from nowhere
with piercing eyes and springing curly hair
came up to us, and shook our hands in turn,
greeting us with ebullience in these terms:
'I have no predecessors. Before me
nobody had the honesty to see
what love is really – although plenty since
have seen it well enough.' (My colleague winced
a tad I thought, but exercised control
and let the stranger carry on his role.)
'All love, however ethereal its tone,
is rooted in the sexual urge alone;
for love is nothing else, I realized,
than sexual impulse individualized.
To have sex is the most urgent of goals
and more than we admit, this urge controls
a thousand other acts that we perform.
For sex, social disruption is the norm;
it stimulates the marital imbroglio,
slips letters in the minister's portfolio,
embarrasses the dry-as-dust professor,
cajoles the wife, and defrocks the confessor,
demands the sacrifice of loyal friends,
destroys the senator and quickly spends
the savings of a lifetime. I saw
beneath this anarchy an iron law:

the object of our love affairs transcends
the petty goals of other human ends
since what's decided here is nothing less
than the next generation: they possess
existence by it, also their nature;
so flirting is a solemn legislature;
fashion and parties, jewellery and dance,
are grave negotiators who advance
the interests of a child not yet conceived.
When people are attracted, they're deceived
into believing it's about each other:
in fact the inclination of two lovers
is nothing but the growing will to live
of the offspring which their affair could give,
and the more suited that they are to fashion
this child of theirs, the stronger is their passion.
My next discovery, also correct,
was that a child inherits intellect
only from the mother, while the will
comes from the father. Both parents fulfil
a role in forming other attributes
where each of them is able to commute
the defects of the other, and supply
qualities of their own. And this is why
love marriages are very highly prized
by our society, and generalized
sexual appetite is not. Such lovers fix
on qualities in their beloved which mix
perfectly with their own, so love takes place
as if by special order of the race
and in comparison with this great charge
the lives of individuals don't loom large.
They're wrecked without a thought, or else abandoned,
and any resulting happiness is random.
The work goes on, in busy offices,
in pillared halls with gilded cornices,

in huts and igloos and among the dwellers
of godforsaken and stinking favelas,
in war, among the craters and the bombs,
during outbreaks of plague, during pogroms,
when people cast their votes or when they roister,
in lepers' colonies and in the cloister,
the work's relentless and it's everywhere.'

He stopped, and motioning us to take a chair
walked over to a ramshackle antique
cine projector and made as if to tweak
a switch; of course, the thing was just for show
and didn't really function, but a glow
of light somehow appeared upon the screen
before us; then an image could be seen
in black and white: two people with briefcases
walking a corridor with measured paces,
a man and woman, both of them well dressed
in business suits. Neither of them expressed
any emotion. Coming to a door
they went inside. And now, almost before
the door is shut, they fall into profuse
kisses, and her hair comes tumbling loose,
impatient hands go underneath a shirt,
he in a tie and she still in her skirt,
they lie down and have sex upon the rug.
We witness an ungainly kind of hug,
the wobbling of a cellulitic bum,
some grunting, and then pretty soon it's done.
And while this strangely charmless scene was playing,
the curly-haired projectionist was saying:
'It seems a humble act; yet they contrive
through this to keep the human race alive.
So many rooms like this exist behind
a fastened door, a window with a blind;
hardly a building stands where sexual acts
are not occurring, and yet these contacts

are nearly always private. It's a trait
of Homo sapiens that when we mate
we do it privately and out of view,
unlike the lion, the dog, or kangaroo.'
He touched the old projector at his side
and on the screen came up a colour slide:
a man and woman having oral sex,
their naked bodies intertwined; and next
there followed on the screen a whole series
of slide-like images, and all of these
portrayed a type of sexual predilection.
This medley and the speed of its projection
was baffling. There were whips and rubber tubes,
men with huge pricks, and girls with massive boobs,
people handcuffed or tied up to a chair,
people in gags and leather underwear,
oral, anal, genital penetration,
bondage and cunnilingus, masturbation,
a girl lifting her skirts over a man,
another gang-banged on an old divan,
women with women and then men with men,
threesomes, foursomes, and still more again.

I felt a trifle awkward sitting there
while this went on – a discomfort not shared
at all by my companions, who displayed
no more unease than if the show portrayed
the mating rituals of an insect.
But members of the public, I suspect,
may have been more like me, since at the end
the house lights came back on, and now our friend
admitted, 'Sometimes customers complain
about the slide-show. But I should explain,
they'd like it still less if we could make clear
the social rank of people featured here,
since all of them are members of Congress
or Senates past and present. Limitless

are the impostures of the human race,
for we don't wear our sex-lives on our face,
nor are they as we'd like them to appear.
And though the aim of love is very clear,
our sexual nature can be complicated,
is rarely changed or even modulated,
and almost never gets to be dismissed.'

Leaving the curly-haired projectionist,
we took a fire exit which brought us out
inside a passageway. I looked about
for signs of life, but nobody was there –
only a tapping sound made me aware
of someone's presence. Then, from an intersection
a man emerged, heading in our direction,
dressed in a chlamys, and also wearing shades.
This person seemed to stumble as he made
his way towards us, tapping with his staff
in front of him, as if to find his path.
And yet in spite of being blind he waved
to us from far away, which rather gave
the lie to his performance. As we drew
level he bowed and said, 'All hail to you,
O hoplites!' – just the type of phoney greeting
which actors in the Park give on first meeting –
'Hear what an old blind man reveals to you.
I have the gift of prophecy. I knew
the future of Odysseus long ago,
Oedipus too, and now today I know
that you are here to ask about the pleasure
that comes from sexual passion, and what measure
of happiness it can bring in a life.
Some years ago the lord Zeus and his wife
quarrelled about which sex derives the greater
pleasure in intercourse. The arbitrator
they chose was me, since I had the unique
experience of being equipped to speak

for both sexes. You see, I have been both
a man and woman and, though I was loath
to take sides, I was willing to admit
women have more enjoyment out of it
than ever men do, in fact ten times more.'

Even as he recited this I saw
a screen light up behind him which displayed
a photo of Loretta. It portrayed
her standing in a characteristic pose,
at one of her own parties I suppose,
though which I can't at this point recollect.
She holds a champagne bottle by the neck
and swigs from it. Her elegant forearm
is strong, and calls up to my mind the charm
of that athletic body, full of grace
and elegance. Her slightly freckled face
is tilted up in profile, and her nose
is well defined; abundant red hair flows
about her shoulders. I cannot forget
her sexual duplicity, and yet
in making love how generous, how free
was her surrender, how thrilling the spree
of that upheaval, and its aftershocks;
the flush upon her face, the tangled locks;
and then the way her limbs all found their place
and softly fell asleep in my embrace.
How good it was!

Sex is ungainly on the whole,
its psalms are grunted more than sung;
you can't say that this rigmarole
looks very different from the fun
of dog in ditch or hog in dung.

Every language is protean,
transformed out of an earlier one;
even ur-Indo-European
itself comes from an earlier tongue
spoken when speech itself was young,

a language lost, although the thread
down to the present day holds good.
The Buddha used a flower instead
of words to bridge this interlude;
and the disciples understood.

A hotel room, an old divan,
a million years gone from my mind –
didn't we know and understand
the flower in the Buddha's hand,
the dance of dogs, the songs of swine?

The vision of Loretta faded away as fast as it appeared.
'And so in the myth,' the robed stranger went on,
'I gave my answer. The phenomenon
seemed simple then, but actually is not.
The truth is, sexual pleasure's polyglot:
people have very different appetites
and very different quotas of delight
which they take from it. Surely nothing is
more wonderfully various than this:
some quick as napalm, others slow to kindle
as fire when you make it with a spindle,
while others won't ignite at all. Did you –'
he asked my guide – 'suppose it was to do
with upbringing? That childhood events
could cause it to be stifled and prevent
the orgiastic joy of the adult?
This scheme of things, if true, has the result
that therapy of some kind might effect
a change in it. It offers the prospect

that one who doesn't burn could be ignited.
But my view is that such a soul is blighted,
that some are born to sweetest joy, and others
to sexual sadness and frustrated lovers.
It is the fatalism of a world more ancient than your own.'

This changes everything. You feel
a sudden, easy confidence.
Beneath the sea a clipper's keel
goes unobserved, but brings balance
and speed. A certain innocence
has entered you; and looking back,
defeat seems only a setback.

Sometimes it seems as if a muse
speaks through you, like an ancient bard,
uninterested in your views,
thoughtless, immoral. Should she depart,
the singing stops, and though the heart
goes on beating, you can recall
notes indistinctly, if at all.

And then, with inspiration lost,
decline begins. Your city's blocks
of elegant apartments rust
and crumble, as the streets are blocked
with rotting refuse, and the docks
are blighted by repairs not made
or edicts in restraint of trade.

Cities of the sexual cult,
your ships are sound, your streets are thronged,
the fragile happiness of adults
is born out of your muse's song.
Hear and pass easily along,
you who are able to. These lays
are not for everyone, or always.

My guide was not immediately drawn by what the blind
prophet had said. He held his peace and smoked
in silence for a moment. When he spoke
it was to say, 'A healthy person's able
to discharge tensions bred from the unstable
impulses of sex by gratifying
the urge in regular and satisfying
orgasms. And all the evidence
is that this person will experience
emotions such as hatred or despond
appropriately; that is, they correspond
to something real and proximate. Not so
the poor neurotic, who declines to know
the cause of his emotions. These address
material which he maintains repressed,
and so his feelings seem to overstate
the case, and aren't at all commensurate
with their apparent cause. This way his rage
seems disproportioned on the little stage
where it must play; or maybe he discovers,
to his confusion, that with all his lovers
the very abandonment he always dreads
is fully where his chosen steps have led;
or else perhaps a sudden love infects him
virulently when a girl rejects him,
whom previously he'd held in small account.
You see, he never has the right amount
of sentiment, but always an excess
or a deficiency: the gift of happiness
seems to be less in such people, and they
were ones that I was able to convey
to a more happy life by my technique.'

And now a spotlight lit an Ancient Greek
statue, or so I thought it anyhow,
until it stepped forward and gave a bow;
I realized then that he was one of those
drama-school mimes that do living tableaux

and earn some dough in the summer recess
by working in the Park, in period dress.
This fellow now declaimed, as though on stage:
'I lived in Athens, in the Golden Age,
and many problems interested me,
but none more so than what I took to be
the central quest for everyone alive
which is: "What makes a human being thrive?"
My answer was to balk at all the extremes,
and this came to be called the golden mean.
We can be angry too much or too little,
be over-confident or else too brittle.
The same applies to every disposition
since every virtue finds a mean position
between two shortcomings. And this applies
in all cases: for instance, courage lies
midway from rashness to timidity;
desire for wealth between cupidity
and thriftlessness; desire for honour too
must hold a middle path. That was my view:
measure in everything should be our aim.
Too much or too little will not attain
that happy path which is the middle way
but signifies a life in disarray.
Now, on the contrary, to have these feelings
at the right time, about the right things,
and in the right amount, all this I say
is the mean and the best, and is the way
to happiness.'
                    He bowed again and stepped
back into his alcove where he kept
his vigil, and his spotlight was extinguished.
We walked on, and before long I distinguished
the melee of the gift shop with its throng
of dogged shoppers. Hurrying along,
we slipped between them out into the glare
of sunshine, and the torrid open air.

Marriage, Fidelity

Strolling together on the promenade,
we came to the three-quarter-sized façade
of that town hall in which Louise and I'd
been married. Pausing now outside,
my colleague stated, pointing to the door,
'The Park does love a cliché,' and I saw
suspended from a nail a sign like those
in shop windows which say 'Open' and 'Closed'
on either side, but in this case it read:
'Forsaking All Others'.
                                    My colleague led
the way inside, and down a corridor
without a word; but then we heard a roar
of thunder deafeningly loud, the lights
flickered the way they do on stormy nights,
and then went out. After a little time
a spotlight came on, picking out a mime
upon a pedestal. The man was dressed
in clinging silver lamé tights and vest,
and wore a cape like Superman's on top.
He held aloft a couple of stage-prop
thunderbolts, and struck a macho pose.
As we approached, this work of art unfroze
and spoke to us: 'Mortals, listen to me:
immortals marry for eternity
and I was no exception. With my wife
Hera, it's been eternity of strife.
Fidelity was never my strong suit,
I always had a weakness for a cute
eighteen-year-old (I didn't want them older),
who'd come and lay her head against my shoulder,

and if she was unwilling I would drape her
in seemly clouds of turbid mist, and rape her.
I loved goddesses, mortals, nymphs, and dryads,
I have lost count of all the girls that I had.
From my experience, I can reveal
that serial infidelity's ideal,
provided that your wife is stuck with you –
which in my case undoubtedly was true.'

And now without warning, the lighting died.
In such moments of darkness I had learned
to trust my guide to steer me, and I turned
at his prompting, adopting in the dark,
this way and that, the alleys of the Park,
his hand upon my arm. Pretty soon
a lamp came on to simulate the moon
and I distinguished in its silver light
a low-built house, all shut up for the night.
We crossed a lawn and then a bridge of stone,
and came closer. In front of us a lone
shutter stood ajar, as if by chance,
and through this gap I saw as we advanced
a youthful woman sitting on the floor.
Behind her was stretched out, six feet or more,
her black hair, which a maid was occupied
in dressing with a comb. The girl had dyed
her teeth black, and had whitened up her face,
her eyebrows had been shaved and in their place
she'd painted on another block-like pair
about an inch above the level where
they'd normally appear. This apparition
was lost as someone shifted the position
of her blind. Someone giggled. My guide
gave me a sign to come and sit beside
the blind, and whispered, 'It's for sure they know
we're out here. Speak to her. Ask her to show
her face to us.' And so I did.

But she

replied, 'It is dishonourable for me
if you can see my face; please, just remain
out there beyond the blind, while I explain.
The world I lived in practised and respected
polygamy; in fact it was expected
of men who held a place in the elite.
In all my long story you never meet
a man of any status who forbore
to take a concubine or two, or more.
And, strangers, don't go thinking we were freaks,
since we were far from being a unique
example of this kind; in fact I'd say
that most societies have been this way.
Polyandry and polygamy
might seem a blessing or an infamy:
in fact they're neither – just a social norm
to which the individual must conform.
The women of my time wholly accepted
the double-standard, and we all expected
our husbands to take up with other wives,
and make us share our houses and our lives
with concubines as well. What was the same,
then as today, was the emotional game
we played out with our husbands: on our side
cancer of jealousy, atrophied pride,
and on our husbands' side prevarication
and duplicity. The situation
doesn't change at all simply because
according to our country's moral laws
emotional betrayal is condoned.
Jealousy's in our nature, it's been honed
by evolution (or some other means) –
however inconvenient it seems,
it's always painful. But I won't go on.
Although a thousand years have come and gone,
sexual jealousy and married bliss
still go together. Nothing has changed in this.'

The 'moonlight' cut out, and I heard a rumble
as of a scene shifting. We both now stumbled
to our feet in total darkness. Then 'sunshine'
came on, but there was nowhere any sign
of that garden or that Heian mansion
endowed with shingle roofs and wooden stanchions
or the embroidered screens with their forbidden
cargo of women, whispering and hidden.
Instead we saw an empty loft-sized space
with several different doors, the kind of place
where in computer games you have to choose
without knowing what lies behind. Confused
by these alternatives, I asked my guide
to help me now, but he only replied,
'It makes no difference. There can be no doubt
at all that marriage can exist without
fidelity to one person, to wit,
the many cultures which dispense with it.
They don't concern us here. What is germane
to our investigation is the pain
and pleasure we experience. In this
we have a bedrock which we can't dismiss,
a nature which we cannot rise above.
This is about fidelity and love.
Choose any door you want, and you will find
the same charade is going on behind.'

I picked one out at random, and my guide
followed without a word. We found inside
a kind of flimsy stage-set which portrayed
that office in the town hall where I made
my vows to Louise. I sat in the chair
I had that day, my guide took his place where
the registrar had been. 'In this context,'
he said, 'I want to focus in on sex.
And since there's no one here to take offence,
I will speak frankly and without pretence.

What makes sex good? I've had plenty of time
since I was dead to ask what is sublime
and what is . . . well, less so. The mere act
of sex is not so great. It is a fact
that being raped is no pleasure at all
and similarly the rewards are small
from having sex with somebody you're not
attracted to. What does make it a lot
more pleasurable is to feel the sway
of love for your partner; and I would say
(although it isn't something you can measure),
the more you love someone, the more the pleasure
you can have from sex. A king may know
dozens of wives, a whole seraglio
of concubines, and yet there still may be
a favourite of the moment, one that he
loves more, and all the other women less.
She will bear most upon his happiness.'

And in my recollection, as he spoke,
the memory of Loretta was evoked,
of all the girls I'd known the least constrained,
the most generous, and the most unfeigned
in pleasure; and it's true with her I found
some happiness. But still my most profound
pleasure in sex was always with Louise.

As if he read my mental processes,
my guide went on: 'But since we have discovered
that what people call love is nothing other
than sexual impulse individualized,
we can't pretend it's really a surprise
that sexual fidelity's entwined
so closely around love; in fact we find
the greater the love, the more it has a focus,
and greatest love must have a single locus.
Fidelity's not something to disparage:
love is monogamous even if marriage

often isn't. Look at the evidence:
wherever passion is experienced,
fidelity's an easy vow to keep;
the truth is that you only want to sleep
with one person, the thing is effortless.
It's obvious too that jealousy's no less
a natural hanger-on in the affair:
where we love most, we least accept to share.
Vile though jealousy may be, it's written
in our souls. You know: you have been bitten –
when your Louise went back to the sadhu;
and also now that she's divorcing you.
These days jealousy tends to be explained
in terms of evolutionary gain,
but whether you believe that stuff or not,
you really can't give credence to the rot
that was talked at the ashram in those days.
You must remember what they used to say
about how people should aspire to love
without possessiveness, and rise above
their jealousy by exercising mental
discipline, and learning transcendental
meditation, and so on.' I said:
'Certainly, I'm with you on that head,
and really, when I look back on the choices
I made in my marriage, my inner voices
loathe me and decry me. And in fact
I am surprised at just how many acts
of my past life arouse this sense of shame.'
My colleague met this comment with the same
attentive silence he had used before
to hint he was expecting something more
from me, but now I felt I'd lost the thread.
Focusing on my narrative, I said:
'However silly some of the advice,
I did discover something of great price
inside the ashram: namely, her address
back in the States. I saw, I must confess,

I'd been an idiot, glumly sitting round
achieving nothing in this strange compound,
feeling at once depressed and slightly bored,
when all the time the sannyasin records
held this address that might have told me where
she was. Who knew? She might even be there.

'A phone call would have done it, I could see;
but so great was my curiosity
to see the place she'd grown up as a girl
that I preferred to travel round the world,
even if in the end she wasn't there.
I had enough money to pay the fare,
and took the train to Bombay, and a flight
to Rome and San Francisco, overnight.
Arriving there, I found to my surprise
a beautiful mansion of such a size,
I must admit I felt a little daunted.
I rang the bell, explaining what I wanted
into the intercom. A voice replied,
"Louise no here." Another voice inside
was barely audible, and they conversed
a little while together, then the first
spoke once more in the intercom: "Plis wait."
I stood a little longer at the gate
until a maid in uniform arrived.
She let me in, and showed me up the drive,
across the portico, into the home,
to where Louise's mother sat alone
arranging flowers and leaves in a display.
I saw the family likeness right away
and felt a rush of blood: the mother's face,
her long straight nose, and the familiar grace
and bias of the eyebrow all foretold
Louise's features, though she lacked the bold
darkness of Louise's eyes and hair.
She told me Louise wasn't living there:

only two weeks ago she'd left to start
a three-year course at Chelsea School of Art
in London, in photography and style.
And as we talked I saw the mother's smile
was like Louise's too.

                              'She must have had
a striking beauty once, but something sad
now hung about her which I understood
when she explained about her widowhood.
"It was so unexpected when Saul died.
The terrible thing was, that though I tried
to find Louise, I'd really no idea
where she might be. The Jewish rules are clear
that burial should take place very soon
after a death, and the next afternoon
we buried him. So when Louise at last
contacted me, nearly two weeks had passed,
and everything was over." There were framed
photos of him all round the house.

                                  'Her name
was Candy, and she'd been a second wife,
much younger than he was, just starting life
and working as a model when they met.
It wasn't passion from the first, and yet
she liked him, and the course of it ran smooth.
Clever and always cheerful, she could soothe
the sadness which he felt at his wife's dying.
He was the married type. How gratifying
to be pampered by such a lovely creature;
and as for Candy, it was a novel feature
to have as her admirer and protector
a powerful tycoon in the retail sector.
And now she was the owner of the firm.
She said their family lawyer was concerned
about the risks involved. He had suggested
she sell the firm and get the funds invested
more widely in the stockmarket, but she
felt that the business was Saul's legacy

and wanted to retain it if she could.
This loyal strategy was well and good
until the chief executive died too.
And then she had to find somebody new
to run it, which was not an easy task.
"What could I do? I felt I had to ask
our lawyer to advise me, which he did.
We found a young hotshot. He seemed a kid
to me but there's no question that he had
the right qualifications. I'm just glad
to feel I've done the same as Sauly would."
The sadness of her recent widowhood
was very evident.

               'She took me round
the house, showed me the chambers underground
where Saul and she had kept their modern art
collection, or at any rate a part
of it because, she told me, they stored most
inside a nuclear vault on the East Coast.
We saw his portrait and we saw his bust.
She had preserved his desk and study just
the way it had been on the day he died:
the chair and Torah still at the fireside,
the family photo albums bound in leather.
And in the garden they had made together,
and where his turtles were allowed to roam,
we visited the geodesic domes
in which he housed his notable collection
of cactuses. We made a close inspection
of his beehives and saw the honey store;
and then the screening room where the décor
had been redone in an Egyptian style
after their honeymoon along the Nile:
murals of dancing women in the buff,
some pharaohs and Luxor, that kind of stuff.
"That's Cleopatra," Candy said, "and there
is Charmion, her servant. Quite a pair

they were, those two. Do you know the story?
Caesar had reached Egyptian territory,
and Cleopatra needed him to kill
her brother, and make her queen. Her real skill
was in the way she played her cards. She knew
if she could only get an interview
with Caesar in person, her sex appeal
and devastating charm gave her a real
chance. And so she had Charmion roll her
up in a carpet; and carried on the shoulders
of footmen, past the unsuspecting sentry
on duty by the door, she made her entry
into Caesar's presence, was unwrapped
in all her grace and charm. Caesar was zapped,
completely stunned by her. She had her way
with him, and when he snuffed it, made a play
for Antony; nor could he resist her.
And then of course she also killed her sister,
who might have been a rival to the throne of Egypt."

Oh no, Charmion, please don't say
I didn't love him. I was using
all my wits to find a way
to get him – that needs no excusing:
something shameless and amusing
was needed to become his wife
and, doing so, to save my life.

And, Charmion, don't go and tell
the world I couldn't stand her sight.
We might have got along quite well
had things been different. I admit
she had good qualities: some wit,
a certain savoir-vivre, a sense
of humour, and intelligence.

And let's be frank, she was quite pretty
in a horsey sort of way.
Even the Roman mob took pity
on her and spared her life that day.
She definitely could convey
to shaky claims a bit of glister.
After all, she was my sister.

Really, I had to have her killed.
She would have done the same for me.
I see her in my nightmares still –
the torn carotid artery,
the blood upon her finery,
when like a puppet in collapse
she crumples on the temple steps.

Does it strike you as unrefined?
Perhaps a little. Let's just say
my charm was of the adult kind.
And men are children in a way:
sweet, but inclined to disobey.
I find that once a man is bitten,
it's best to get the contract written.

Caesar went under at a stroke,
Antony, poleaxed, took a dive;
I smiled and listened while they spoke
about their art, or their beehives.
I knew what men liked. I contrived
to coax from their concupiscence
the barest shreds of common sense:

babies, soldiers, gold, and land,
and even life itself. We use
what naturally comes to hand
in this life; we don't get to choose
the times we live in. Yours accuse
the murderer, but mine repay
a monarch who resolves to slay.

When I was young, men were aghast
to see me, they endured desire
like pain; but now my youth is past,
they walk on by. People admire
the name of a retail empire.
Money, the ownership of art
and PR also play their part.

So, Charmion, this is my dower:
a certain deference and respect,
the loneliness, arranging flowers.
And, Charmion, please don't suspect
my love for him was not perfect.
The bargain struck was a good one:
my love was surely worth this throne.

'The tour ended back in Candy's flower room and there,
among the blooms, on maple slatted chairs,
we sipped our Cokes and picked at a cascade
of kosher salads brought us by the maid.
Being with Candy, I had the impression
that flower arranging was her great obsession,
and several times during the course of lunch
she got up from her chair to take a bunch
of blossom and put it in the arrangement.
After the many months of our estrangement
I wanted to talk about Louise, but all
Candy was interested in was Saul.
"To tell the truth," she said, "before he crossed
my path, as a young woman I was lost.
But he showed me the spiritual side of things,
the added dimension religion brings.
He was punctilious in the way he kept
shabbat and kosher, and could not accept
Louise rejecting this. But Saul's concern
was more with making life holy. I learned
from him the value of community
(another thing Louise could never see)

and family life. That's why, now he is gone,
it means so much to me to carry on
the business in his memory." She took
a plume of carex with a wistful look
and placed it in the arrangement. In her tense
and hesitating gestures I could sense
a little of the tedious loneliness
of her existence, and the flavourless
season of widowhood. Still, I was pleased
to have at last a number for Louise.

'In London straight away we fixed to meet:
a pub near her college, on Marsham Street.
I see her still, arriving through the door,
her hair worn shorter than it was before,
her skin far paler now without its tan.
Instead of the hippy clothes from Kottayam,
she wears a roll-neck pullover and seems
relaxed, but less exotic, in her jeans.
Though I am nervous, she is confident:
perhaps her usual bird-like stillness lent
a look of calmness, and perhaps also
that hearty, almost manly laugh bestowed
an air of self-assurance too. The place
was crowded but we found ourselves a space.
I knew at once nothing needed explaining.
Later, with little daylight still remaining,
we went to her apartment. As she peeled
her Levi's off and once again revealed
that curving figure, caught in the half-light
of dusk outside the window, I caught sight
of something at her shoulder, something new
inscribed upon her arm: a green tattoo
of Siva's name.'
               I ceased as I recalled
the ugly lettering, and how appalled
I was to see it. My guide sensed an unease,
his eyes narrowed a couple of degrees,

and, settling back into the registrar's
chair, he tapped and relit his cigar
but said nothing.

          'I asked about it later,'
I said, 'but it just seemed to irritate her,
so I didn't insist. She said, "Oh, that.
Yeah, I did it when I left you, Pat.
I went to Mapusa, I wanted to get
the Siva thing done with, but it upset
him too much, I felt sorry. In the end
he talked me into trying it again.
We did the tattoos as a kind of pledge;
to me it felt more like a sacrilege.
Pretty soon after that I got to learn
about my daddy's death, so I returned
to California. That changed things for me,
him dying. I no longer want to be
a vagabond, or live with a sadhu.
The only thing I want now is to do
something useful, and to have a skill
which I'm good at. Photography's a thrill
that way, because there's so much stuff to learn."

'Now that I was back I had to earn
some money fairly quickly. And immersed
as I was in archaeology, my first
idea was to work in that. I tried
the various agencies, and then applied
for a junior position with Highways,
and then a better one doing surveys
for a developer. Without success.
And then, because I was still penniless,
I played the piano for small change and beer,
backing a friend in pubs. Soon his career
was going well, he managed to secure
a record deal and got himself a tour
in the US; but this rapid progression
didn't include myself. He hired some session

musicians over there, and we lost touch.
I went on job hunting. I hadn't much
else I could do for now, so I just played
music when I could get a gig, and made
a little money and had lots of fun.
That time of life, when all is said and done,
is when you can do largely as you please.
Art school asked almost nothing of Louise
and as for me I was barely employed
and so it turned out that we both enjoyed
plenty of free time we could spend together.
For once, the English summer brought good weather.
We sat out on the pavements after dark,
drank vodka, took acid in Richmond Park,
spent nights out on our roof, heard Nusrat sing,
stayed up all night at Chanctonbury Ring,
saw lots of dawns, saw little of our friends,
lost touch with world events, spent lost weekends:
those summer days without a thought or care
were I suppose what our friend back there
has called an engineering of precision,
a step in life's most important decision.'

I broke off now, remembering the day
we went for breakfast to the Sun Café,
and as I ate my egg and toasted cheese
at last got round to broaching with Louise
something I'd been wanting off my chest.
I said, "When we first met, I did my best
to be honest about myself, but you
told me nothing. I never had a clue
about the multi-million-dollar home,
the retail empire that your father owned,
or anything like that. You hid it all.
But Louise, I don't own a shopping mall,
I get work here and there as a musician
while I look for a job. My sole ambition

is to become an archaeologist,
and all my education's been for this.
Even if I succeed in my career,
there's no way I could come anywhere near
the kind of social world where you belong."
She took my hand and said, "You are quite wrong
if you think I want that. I'm not impressed
with money, social status, and the rest.
I grew up with that stuff, it was expected
of me. But, Pat, you know that I rejected
worldly things and attitudes like those."
And now she told me how her parents chose
to break with what their friends did as a rule
and send her to a local public school,
which by a quirk of geography was rougher
than most, and drew on several of the tougher
housing projects in the city. "All
the rich folk living round us were appalled.
Their own kids had the best money could buy –
in the event, a private school nearby –
but that had no appeal to my dad.
He wanted me to study like *he* had,
and know the life of ordinary kids,
learn the hard way, and do the things he did.
As for me, I liked the place, although,
as his daughter, I did have to lie low
and take care not to stand out from the crowd;
but I was good at that, and kinda proud
of how accepted I was. Certainly
it never entered my head to envy
the rich kids down the road or to subscribe
to their amusements. They were not my tribe.
One day a crazy boy, he was a preacher's
son, flipped out and knifed one of the teachers.
My mom went nuts, she pulled me out of there
and put me in the private high school where

the kids I got to know all seemed like snobs.
After school I hung out with the mob
from my old school. But slowly, in the end,
I did acquire another gang of friends,
although inside I still felt a rejection
of them. Later, I took a new direction
away from them, away from home as well.
Really, I only wanted to rebel –
which brought me to the India episode
and living with a sadhu on the road:
no synagogue, no club, and no rupees."

'If I was not in love with her, Louise
might have seemed just another spoiled kid,
wasting it all; but, feeling as I did,
I saw her only as original,
shedding her family's tutelage in all,
going her way and making her own life,
the ideal child of our time – or wife.
The time had come. It must have been around
the middle of September, and I found
a country house hotel where we could spend
the warm days of a late summer weekend
between some watermeadows and the downs.
A painting of Diana and her hounds
hung on the panelled staircase, and the theme
continued in our room with hunting scenes.
Louise loved the four-poster and the food,
but that weekend she wasn't in the mood
for love. And though I wanted to propose,
somehow I couldn't do it. I suppose
the moment lacked passion, something like that.
It wasn't till the next April in fact
that we became engaged.'
                                My guide caressed
his beard without speaking. His eyes expressed

no judgement, but they looked straight into mine
with an unflinching gaze, not quite benign
but frank and realistic. 'So it's clear,'
he said, 'that sex was something very near
your heart.' I said, 'Perhaps. But anyway
nothing was really lost by the delay,
which influenced the timing, not the choice.'

Suddenly now, I heard my father's voice
and looked around the chamber. But although
there were some conference chairs aligned in rows
behind me, as there had been on the day
of our wedding, no waxwork was displayed
on them, nor any actor. Still the sound
seemed to be issuing from all around:
'Patrick, my boy, to go through married life
and be completely faithful to your wife
is rarely easy; but to disregard
fidelity and be happy, that's the hard,
the really hard thing. Marriage is blessed
as long as sexual passion is expressed
and when sex dies it always dies too soon.
Yet even then, marriage is still a boon
for happiness. I will be candid, son:
a man should never let his life be run
by his willy. That's never been the way
to happiness, to tumble in the hay
with every pretty thing you take a shine to.
Fidelity's something you put your mind to
consciously. Value it above
the cravings that you have for sexual love,
it will reward you.'
                        I heard this speech
originally walking on the beach
with him in Cyprus, by the very sea
where Aphrodite, naked, had stepped free

of the water; and listening to it there,
ecstatic as I was from sex with Clare,
he sounded ludicrous; hearing it now
a second time reminded me just how
novel it had been to hear him speak
of sex at all. Had it been an oblique
allusion to something we'd not discussed –
the period when his own marriage was bust,
my mother gone to Africa, and he
dreading his shore-leave, with its all too free
leisure, the feelings of humiliation,
the empty house, the secret medication?

'Sir, I am of your opinion.' The sound
came from behind me now, and looking round,
I saw the General had materialized
behind us in the corner. Had my eyes
deceived me? Had he been there all along?
Or was he a hologram they'd just switched on?
He was got up in boots and a blue coat,
a white scarf neatly tied around his throat,
and taking off his tricorn greeted us
with a low bow, formal but courteous,
the image clear though slightly wavering.
'Yes, love is a mighty pretty thing,
which no man in his senses would disparage.
But more important to a happy marriage
is both parties' good character and sense,
and if you are a man, the affluence
you need to support a wife. It is a fact:
these are the qualities which will attract
in later life both esteem and regard.
Value this esteem and this regard.
It is the very stuff of happiness
because, if lovers' passion, growing less,
is not transmuted into these, it must
perforce resolve itself into disgust.

When I married Martha, did I love her?
Certainly not; in fact I loved another.
And yet we have been happy. And in fact,
in my life, marriage was the single act
which most contributed to happiness.'

His image froze and then, still motionless,
it vanished in the air. And now I saw –
how had I failed to notice it before? –
upon a stand, inside a perspex case,
that watering can. And though of commonplace
enough design, this object was the key
into another vivid memory.
I said, 'One time in India I stayed
with a raja. This charming man had made
a guest house of his family home, a vast
palace in marble, relic of the past,
which dominated all around. This king
was ex-Army, patrician, welcoming
to everyone. He'd laboured all his life
to keep the palace going, while his wife
had made a garden, choosing as her ground
the great courtyard. One day she took me round,
carrying that old watering can you see,
and as we went she pointed out to me
her favourite plants. Now and again she stopped
to give some special bloom an extra drop,
or parse on my behalf some subtle beauty,
and analyze its singularity.
Caught up in her excitement, I became
more and more astonished, and it remains
one of the loveliest gardens I have seen.
Her knowledge was compendious. In between
this work and her programme of propagating
certain pinks, she was collaborating
with breeders in Japan and Germany.
I asked her if she'd studied botany.

"Oh no," she said, "I never went to school.
My tutors, though quite learned as a rule
in languages and letters, were pathetic
in science. I had to teach myself genetics
by correspondence since, in the old days
one lived in the zenana. Going away
to school or even university
wasn't an option for someone like me.
My brothers went, but we girls had to stay.
Then I came here. My family chose Vijay
because he's from a family like mine:
you know, distinguished, from an ancient line,
and all that stuff. I didn't get to choose,
or even meet him. We were introduced
shortly before the wedding, that was it.
Clearly we were not in love. That bit
came afterwards." I couldn't help but say,
"But how? How could you fall in love that way?"
"I don't know. But we did." Really it went
without her saying, it was evident
both in the intimacy of their looks
and in the obvious pleasure which they took
in one another. Then she said, "In most
cultures and ages, marriage was imposed
by parents, property, or diplomats;
but do you really think because of that
that love didn't exist?"'

                         And now my guide
stood up from where the registrars preside
over the ceremony, and showed the way
out of that office of our wedding-day,
along some corridors, and then an alley
with dustbins on each side. We didn't dally
here, but swept along, and yet to me
it felt uncomfortably leisurely:
posters on either side of us displayed
the faces of girls with whom I had betrayed

Louise: not just Loretta, though there were   /85
certainly plenty which depicted her –
the strong and freckled arms, the scarlet curls –
no, not just her, but also the other girls
who made me happy for a night or more.
Disloyal pleasures, pleasures to deplore:
that angel with the beautiful grey eyes;
the prostitute with bruises on her thighs;
and then those girls, of whom there were a few,
whose company was given impromptu
on trips away from home. Some to my shame
at this remove I couldn't even name.
And also there were girls who I had tried
to get to bed, but failed: undignified
reminders that even a rank betrayal
can be a task in which a man may fail.
My guide said, 'Patrick, you have slept around
in your marriage, but let's say you had found
Louise to be unfaithful. How would you
have felt about that?' I replied, 'The true
answer is this: nothing could hurt me more.'
My guide made no reply. We passed the store
which sold the sodas, souvenirs, and sweets,
and came out to the sunshine of the street.

Children

Strolling beside me, my companion said,
'During the long decades of being dead
I've had no pain, nor any satisfaction,
in any of the Park's diverse attractions.
You who, unlike myself, are still alive
experience sex as the decisive drive,
but there's another prompting which you feel
more subtle, quieter, but no less real:
an urge to reproduce, which is distinct
from the desire for sex. I cannot think
it so immediate as lust, and yet its laws
are still very insistent and may cause
the homosexual to want a child,
the childless spouse of years to be reviled,
make husbands of the most egregious cynics,
send the infertile hurrying to clinics.
A thousand new duties of every sort
are taken on without a moment's thought.
The life where it's easy to go away,
changed for a yearly family holiday,
the life of fashion, festivals and bars,
for changing-bags and child-seats in the car,
for helping with the homework after tea,
then staying in and watching the TV,
and always governed by the iron dictates
of babysitters, and the half-term's dates.
How onerous is this indenture, and yet
how the freedman is burdened with regret!
During my lifetime I managed to vex
practically everyone by giving sex
so openly the most important say
in governing behaviour. (Though today

it's certainly the thing people prefer
about my work, back then it caused a stir.)
I stretched its sense from simple copulation
to cover wider family relations,
and shocked the world by daring to suggest
that infants sucking on their mothers' breast
enjoyed with them an erotic relation;
or that a child's act of defecation
could be erotic too, a source of pleasure
which they should learn to master at their leisure.
The idea I was trying to get across
made family life the crucial omphalos
of human satisfaction, and therefore
the realm for my profession to explore.
That intimate life which is centred around
getting and raising children is the ground
on which the towers of happiness must rise
or fall; and looking back, I realize
that though this happiness may prove elusive
my view of it was wonderfully inclusive:
it meant the fullest happiness in life
is everyone's to have, in fact is rife
as much among the hovels of the poor
as for the billionaire and senator.
And just as in the old days they queued up
in church to drink the same Communion cup,
equal before God, so what I had done
affirmed a common ground for everyone,
where everybody has the same access
to what little there is of human happiness.
Not much, it turns out, really rates above
the satisfaction of this family love;
and all the world's opulence, fame, and glory
are only subplots of the personal story.'

While he was speaking, we had made our way
along a bustling, serpentine pathway

which now debouched into a spacious square,
almost a little park. I noticed there
the hospital where in that summer dawn
I brought Louise, and where our son was born.
Mounting the steps, we went into the hall
and found nobody there, but on the wall
there hung a poster of Louise undressed,
with swollen belly and the bigger breasts
and the dark line which pregnancy drew there
below her navel to her pubic hair.
Beneath this image was a washing line
pegged out with photographs which called to mind
the hours of pregnancy she spent enclosed
within the dark room, working on photos.
'My brain won't function in my present state,'
she told me then, 'but I can concentrate
on visual things all right.' And so she'd stay
shut in the darkened room day after day
working on her craft.
                        We didn't linger
here for long, my guide's impatient finger
had straight away summoned the lift, and now
its metal doors slid open to allow
our passage, and we rode up just the same
as she and I had done that day, and came
into the room of her delivery.
The place brought back the vivid memory
of that expectant night within these walls
when she was giving birth. And I recalled
the kindness of the midwife, his scrubsuit,
the obstetrician in her rubber boots
encouraging Louise, and looked again
upon the metal bed where she had lain,
remembering the moment Jack came out,
unbundling like those paper flowers that sprout
when dropped in water, and the plastic cot
where he had lain wrapped in a polka-dot

sheet, like a tiny mummy. As I peered
down into this cradle, there appeared
a hologram of him, a baby boy.
Once more I was so overcome with joy,
instinctively I bent down to his face;
but as I did, without leaving a trace,
the image disappeared.

                        My guide asked me,
'Being a parent's never trouble-free,
and most couples experience some stress,
but did it also bring you happiness?'
'The greatest possible. Yet it remains
somehow elusive, tricky to explain,
shot through with other pleasures forfeited:
the baby all too often in our bed,
and yet adorable to hold; the nights
I woke reluctantly, and yet the sight
of him would surfeit me with happiness.
Childhood's tastes are cute and obvious,
its scenes appear as cliché and gimcrack
as theme park exhibits; whereas in fact
they're very pure, also very profound.
Nothing that I can say is going to sound
particularly wonderful, I know;
and yet the truth is I did find it so.
Why in all honesty would someone tend
this ugly bundle leaking at both ends –
the bawling in the night, the sick, the poo?
But somehow Nature comes to your rescue;
your love for your own progeny is boundless.
Often at night, abandoned in the darkness,
Jack was afraid and couldn't get to sleep;
so when he went to bed I used to keep
a watch beside him, in the luminescence
of the nightlight, and I could feel my presence
wrap itself around him, and overcome
all his anxieties until his thumb

fell from his mouth. And I experienced
in those unspeaking vigils an intense
feeling of happiness, a happiness
more easy to achieve than to express,
not of my own engendering, but rather
arising simply out of being a father.'

We left the birthing room, and as my guide
led me along the corridor outside,
I was thinking how vignettes of this sort
about parental love always fall short,
and like descriptions of the act of sex
sound faintly ludicrous: they don't express
the bit which is important to the soul.
That bit was very simple, on the whole:
just coming home and finding Louise there,
maybe cooking, maybe in an armchair
with Jack in her lap, watching the TV –
nothing special. Then it would fire in me,
a boiler lighting from its pilot flame
well out of sight, something I didn't name
or even think about that much: a wife,
a son, some satisfaction out of life.

And now, as if commanded by my thought,
we stopped beside a door, and my escort
ushered me through to that familiar scene
where all our family happiness had been:
the perfect likeness of our living room
laid out like I could walk in and resume
that life which I had lost. But now a sole
extraneous figure jarred upon the whole
reconstruction: there, on the settee,
sitting with a paper on his knee
doing the crossword, was Louise's dad.
This was a pleasure I had never had
in real life, since Saul was dead before
I married and became his son-in-law;

but all the time we lived here, his photo
hung in our bedroom and I'd come to know
those features, at the same time dignified
and sympathetic.
                    Now I told my guide
who this guy was. At once, as if my words
had thrown a switch, the animatronics stirred,
he laid his pen down, and began to speak.
The voice was very quiet, almost weak,
which seemed incongruous in such a man
so used to giving orders and who ran
a retail empire, but I now recalled
Louise saying his quietness held in thrall
whole meetings, forcing those at loggerheads
to shut up and listen to what he said,
and how he never spoke a word in anger.
So now with calm, even a certain languor,
he spoke to us:
                    'Poor Candy. Being pregnant
was something she found utterly repugnant;
not every model feels that way about
losing her figure, but there was no doubt
that Candy did. The poor girl was forlorn;
and sadly, even when Louise was born,
her spirits were no better, I could tell.
From the beginning things were never well
between the two of them. The tragic fact
was that she didn't have a real contact
with her own child, and so couldn't provide
the comfort which she needed. When she cried,
somehow the nanny always got there first
and did what Candy couldn't do. The worst
part of it was her coldness made the child
angry, and so they went unreconciled
because Louise would push her mum away
and Candy, overpowered by dismay
at this rejection, ceased to even try
to comfort her. I think perhaps it's why

she had no natural authority
with Louise later. The majority
of mothers find it easier to show
love for their children . . . maybe, I don't know;
people assume these things are automatic
but Nature's rarely quite so systematic.
In many animals the progeny
is reabsorbed or eaten; and though we
in mankind tend to go not quite this far,
mixed feelings or depression often mar
the happiness of childbirth and beyond.
Not everyone immediately bonds.
Candy did love Louise, I'm sure of it,
but somehow couldn't make her actions fit
the feelings. They refused to testify
when they were called. I can't tell you why.
I only know the anguish and distress
it caused her, and her great unhappiness.
What could she do? Being able to love
is something given us by God above.
No force of effort or tenacity
can make increase in that capacity.'
The puppet ceased and, picking up its pen,
reverted to the crossword once again,
whereon it froze, sitting with lowered head
back at its starting point.
                              My colleague said:
'Capacity for happiness depends
hugely on family. I see that men
have simple souls – for here the cleverest
and most refined are just like all the rest.
When patients talked to me they always thought
they had all kinds of problems. But the short
of it was in the end, no more than this:
mother, father, child. The edifice
of human happiness is nothing more.'

If he had more to tell me, he forbore,
and so an awkward silence fell, until
I found myself saying, 'It was a thrill
for both of us to have a child. And she
was radiant, it was beautiful to see
how close she was to him. The earliest sign
of it had been apparent at the time
of Jack's birth. He had lain beside her bed
inside the little plastic cot, his head
emerging from the polka-dot bundle,
and when she fell asleep the midwife trundled
this vehicle with Jack sleeping on board
along the corridor into the ward
where all the new babies were kept in rows
to give the burned-out mothers some repose.
But when Louise woke up, and Jack was missed,
she called the nurse a cunt for doing this,
became so furious I thought she'd strike her.
It was so violent, and so unlike her,
but it signalled the visceral closeness
she felt to Jack, and her protectiveness.
Right from the start that's how she was about him.
She never would go anywhere without him.
It was a whole new life she had discovered.
I noticed that her way of being a mother
was the exact opposite of the brittle
and distant love she'd had, when she was little,
from Candy; and of course I had a sense
that this might not be a coincidence.
Seeing her so loving with our boy
was satisfying to me, in fact a joy.'

Still standing in the cloned interior
of our apartment, I approached the door
to our bedroom, driven to see that space
which surely more than any other place
was central to our family life, since there
Louise and I, in love, without a care,

conceived the thing most beautiful to us,
most meaningful of all, and most precious.
But now instead a far less welcome scene
arising in that bedroom supervened;
a scene which was the unlooked-for result
of having Jack, which like a catapult
ejected us: I see our marriage bed,
and on her side of it, Louise's head
lies calm upon the pillow; her thick hair
and fine eyebrows appear to be etched there
against the paper whiteness of her skin
and the unruffled cool of the linen.
How beautiful! Yet no trace of desire
stirs in the perfect features, and no fire
inside her is betrayed by a sudden deep
intake of breath. No, this is a sleep
which didn't trouble her, but troubled me:
a sleep of utter self-sufficiency.
How lovely she is! No one can deny
Louise is God's promise to gratify,
written in flesh – a pledge no sooner spoken
by God than most unscrupulously broken;
because from this point on, no one was less
inclined than she was to voluptuousness.
As months went by, the truth appeared to be
that having Jack, she had no need for me.
I thought I heard my guide say, 'It appears
some women cease their sexual careers
almost entirely once a child is born.'
And certainly our marriage was deformed
from this time on; and I recall with shame
how I was always finding her to blame –
my love born like a monster, all askew.
What things I said to her, true and untrue!
How apt I was to nag and reprimand,
and to deliberately misunderstand!

Frustration with a husband or a wife
comes out in every part of married life:
like superpowers fighting proxy wars,
everyone else's cause becomes your cause.
And on those rare occasions when we start
to make love, I feel nothing on her part,
no broken breath, no movement of response,
no sense that this is something which she wants.
Where did that go so soon? And where, too,
that subtle distillation, residue
of sex: the feeling of closeness, our happiness in each other?

What ghost was that I saw slipping away?
Was it a cloud's shade scudding across the park,
unnoticed by those boys between the goals?
Or was it the lengthening shadows of our day,
the distance filling up with mist like weakened eyes,
the bluish hills forgetful of their own details?
Decline sets in like drought upon our souls,
like it or not. And in the end all vigour fails
and love's recorded as the highest-water mark.

The music of our youth! Its hold on us was sure,
yet no one taught us to appreciate it.
Our parents hoped we'd grow into maturer
tastes, our schoolteachers could barely tolerate it.
But it was natural enough to us, God knows.
I still recall discovering that sound:
the kids were all elated, wedged in the windows,
their legs dangling outside. In the playground
some girls began to dance. It never counted as 'cultura'.

The moment doesn't last. The founders who created
a city-state have perished. First the supply of crops,
and then fighting of wars, is delegated.
Later the gods are swapped, the armoury
mutates into a ballroom and then into gift shops,
and finally only a name remains, a memory.

Our history itself is patched like some sublime
fresco on a convent wall, corrupt with damage,
restorations, and overpaintings; in any case an image
of somebody else's time.

Nowadays, anger was mostly what I felt towards Louise:
it left me with a poisoned, racing heart,
unable to sleep. Then for the most part
I was exhausted when morning arrived,
and getting out of bed, still sleep-deprived,
I'd see her nightdress on the bedroom floor
and kick it. But what I dreaded far more
than anger was the feeling of dejection
which always followed on from her rejection,
leaving me listless, racked with indecision,
something like half a man. This glum transition
was as remorseless as those fogs which roll,
like ghosts, on sunny days into the bowl
of San Francisco's Bay, and now you know
that nothing you can do will make it go.
It was the same depression that I knew
in Goa, when she followed her sadhu.

Suddenly, in my mind I see the stair
of my grandmother's house at Ballyclare.
My grandmother is with me; we are standing
beside the bookcase on the upstairs landing
and she is saying, 'Come on, dear, let's go
downstairs together then, and say hello
to Mamma.' And I'm saying, 'Mamma? Who's
Mamma?' And when I meet her I refuse
to kiss her. The grown-ups radiate unease
and talk in high voices, but I am pleased
to find she's someone I could like. I say
to my grandmother, 'Granny, can I stay
with you, Granny?'

And so it is that every mortal
city has an origin:
it starts at a bridge or harbour, portal
to commerce, and there it begins
in infancy, with souk and inns,
where merchant caravans can enter.
Childhood is its historic centre.

And sexual character takes form
in trails across the open grass,
to which the streets later conform
with lines of wattle, then surpass
in brick, and later towers of glass:
fleeting embodiments, and yet
those routes, how resolutely set.

Work

We left the hospital and walked along
the pristine asphalt street, among the throng
of visitors, stopping upon the way
to buy some sodas from an ice-filled tray.
Eventually in front of us we saw
a scaled-down version of the flagship store
of Louise's father's company, which stood
in the Embarcadero neighbourhood
of San Francisco. It all looked the same
except the sign which bore the family's name
above the door, which in the present case
was stamped instead with heartening clichés
typical of the Park; for now it read
'World of the Workplace: Earn and Get Ahead!'
and underneath, in cursive neon letters,
'It's Loads of Fun – the More You Do, the Better!'

Curious to inspect, we went inside
and, as we stood in line, I told my guide,
'Soon after Jack was born, in all the ruckus
of early parenthood, disaster struck us:
Louise's family company went bust.
Because Candy had always felt she must
hang on to it at all costs, she had never
sold a single share. This wasn't clever:
it turned out that her total wealth was sunk
in this sole enterprise, sadly defunct,
so there was nothing left. Louise as well,
instructed by her mother not to sell
the shares she got under her father's will,
lost all her money. Strangely, we could still

live pretty much as we had lived till now:
we'd never spent much money anyhow;
we didn't own a cottage or a car.
The only luxuries we had so far
were eating out in restaurants, acquiring
some not very expensive art, and hiring
a cleaning lady, who we now let go.
For Candy, though, it was a real blow:
she didn't feel she counted any more
in social circles where she moved before.
She had to sell her art off in a hurry
to pay the debts, and now began to worry
she wasn't really wanted on the board
of the museum. More or less ignored
by many of her so-called friends, she might
have found herself in even graver plight
had it not been for Hew, who years ago
had been Saul's right-hand man and CFO,
and who, on hearing of the firm's demise,
contacted her.
                    'He helped her organize
the wreckage of her life, dealing with banks,
preying professionals, shareholder cranks,
lawyers and art dealers and other crooks,
helping her sell assets and balance books.
He flew out many times to San Francisco
to do all this for Candy, even though
he had his own retail business to run
in England (this was something he'd begun
himself when he left Saul).
                                      'In the process
of sorting out this vast financial mess,
he visited Louise and me. A large
fellow, and clearly used to taking charge,
he had a tousled mane of silver hair,
a rather florid face, and general air
of bonhomie and generosity.
He said, without the least pomposity,

how shocked he'd been to ascertain the shambles
the management had made, and by the gambles
they'd taken with our own shareholder funds.
He was astonished that they could have shunned
all Saul's directives, right after he died.
The way he spoke of Saul now testified
to the real warmth of their relationship;
in fact for Hew it seemed almost worship.
He spoke with fondness of the hives of bees
and cactuses, and used to call Louise
the cutest child he'd seen before or since.
"Saul changed my life," he said. "I was convinced
by his example."

                'Something about Hew
was very likeable: he was a true
enthusiast, and there was nothing shifty
or double-dealing in him. Nearly fifty,
he was as optimistic as a boy
and always seemed to manage to enjoy
whatever life threw at him. He would say,
"What I like best is work, and next best, play –
my cars, my racing dinghy, and what-not.
One day, you'll see, I'll get myself a yacht
and when I do, it'll be down to Saul
and what I learned from him. He had it all,
knew it instinctively."

                'Seeing as Hew
was parted from his wife, I took the view
that now he must be looking for another.
And why look further than Louise's mother,
who was both lonely and completely broke?
Hew would resolve both problems at a stroke.
And was she not appealing? After all,
she wore an aura of his hero, Saul,
which he might well have relished, and I knew
he was about her age, and Jewish too.
I said to Louise, "Could you hope to find
a better husband? He's generous and kind,

pretty good looking, sense of humour too –
surely he's made for Candy. Wouldn't you
be tempted by him?" But Louise appeared
upset, and said, "I think that would be weird
to have Hew for a stepfather." I felt
I'd been untactful.

'Indigence dealt
a whole series of problems to us now.
First and most pressing was the one of how
the three of us could live. Louise's share
of our joint earnings was no longer there,
and though I did have work as a musician,
sadly I was not in a position
to make it up. Before long we had spent
all our reserves, and not having the rent
was now a real possibility.
A quarrel with Louise brought home to me
that it was up to me to find this cash.

'There was a woman called Loretta Ashe
who I had seen a few times around town.
Her much-abused husband was a renowned
publisher of art books, very rich,
who snapped her up but who was quickly ditched,
and now she lived, in some bohemian state,
in a large mansion in Notting Hill Gate
with her two kids. She hung out with an arty
café kind of crowd, and loved to party.
She had a great figure, striking red hair,
and was well known for having love affairs.
One day she rang and asked if I would play
a party at her house for her birthday.
I told her yes, and found a pair of friends
to do the gig with me. I can't pretend
we did much preparation, but we played,
and everybody danced. I think we made
a good showing. Loretta was enthused
and danced right at the front, her face suffused –

doubtless from the Ecstasy she'd taken –
with beatific smiles. Her hair had shaken
loose from its ties and hairgrips, to frondesce
in maple colours on her velvet dress,
and drew attention to how well she danced.
We played until the night was well advanced,
and all in all it went down pretty well.
Louise was there, but somehow I could tell
she wasn't having fun. I also think
she must have seriously hit the drink,
although with her you never could be sure,
she'd such a head for it.

                                    'She sat in dour
silence as we drove home in the van,
but once at home she said, "Well, Superman,
what did you earn for that?" "Nothing," I said.
"Whatever put that idea in your head?
It was Loretta's birthday after all.
It would have been a bit stingy to call
for payment, and especially since I knew her."
"And then again, maybe you want to screw her.
Well, and why not? Seeing it's her birthday
and everybody else does anyway."
"Louise, what are you saying? Are you mad?"
"I can't believe we need money so bad
and you played this for free. She isn't poor.
What did you have to make her a present for?"
I said, "I think you're making a big deal
out of nothing." "You're an imbecile!"
She shouted this; I urged her to be calm,
assured her that I meant no kind of harm
and didn't want Loretta in the sack.
I warned her she was going to wake up Jack –
the sitter, too, was sleeping in his room –
but she was wholly unimpressed, and fumed,
"Christ! If you weren't so sad, you would be funny.
I just wish you could earn some fucking money,"

and stormed out of the room, slamming the door.
I followed her into the corridor
but found the bedroom locked. I had to spend
the night out on the sofa in the end.

'We sold the works of art which we had bought
and tried to live on that. I felt we ought
to move house, and began to look around
for somewhere cheap; but everything I found
just seemed depressing to Louise. I saw
the cost of having Jack, and how much more
that would be in the years to come, no doubt.
Things we had done quite happily without
till now – such as a car, adequate plumbing,
and health and life insurance – were becoming
less optional, and even recommended.
I saw too that from now Louise depended
on me in ways she hadn't when I met her.
Something inside me may have liked this better;
because although her wealth was a lifeline
in other ways I felt it undermined
my role, made me irrelevant, almost.
Whereas before it seemed OK to coast
along, enjoying life, my new concern
was simple: I was desperate to earn.

'Up until now I'd always tried to find
a job in archaeology of some kind,
and though I sent out endless applications,
I met with no success. The situation
was getting serious when, off the cuff,
I made a call to Hew. He was as bluff
and positive as ever. "Patrick, my boy,
there's sure to be somebody who'll employ
a guy like you. Press on, and you'll succeed.
Just think: how many jobs does a man need?
Eh? How many, when all is said and done?
Jobs are like girls: you're only wanting one.

Now listen: only today I heard they're hiring
at Beston's Bank. I know you're an aspiring
archaeologist, but even so,
I think you should apply. You never know,
you might get lucky and the money's big.
There's no technical stuff required – the gig
only requires a little oomph and brain;
in any case the firm prefers to train
everyone themselves. They have their own
way of doing things. Get on the phone
and call them."

       'Well, I did as he advised,
and not long after, much to my surprise,
I was summoned to go for interview at Beston's.'

And then, after the interview,
with nothing left to do but wait,
we went up to the cabin. You
sat up reading till very late.
I went to bed. I lay prostrate,
then supine, and then on my side;
studied the clock; identified

some of the noises from next door:
your cough again, the biscuit tin,
and then your footsteps on the floor,
the taps, the lid of the waste bin;
but each time you did not come in,
and each time your absence recast
itself as silence. Hours passed,

and when you slipped into the bed
the mattress barely moved. Your hand
gently put mine away. Your head
lay motionless, as if embalmed
on the pillow. Your breathing calmed,
and almost at once you were asleep.
Now it was my turn to keep

a vigil in the room next door.
I took the bathrobe you had worn,
added to your ashtray more
butts of my own, and watched the dawn.
A deer came out onto the lawn,
saw me, and ran away. I knew
that I had flunked the interview.

Sleeping beauty, this is despair:
a lawn with hoof-marks in the dew,
an ashtray full of butts, a chair
where you had read the half-night through,
a cabin in the woods. With you
defeat hangs in the morning air.
Beauty, I see you everywhere.

'I was convinced I'd flunked the interview. But now I see
that was only depression hitting me,
arising from the weekend at the cabin.
In fact, when we returned, a genuine
surprise awaited me – the job was mine.'

So far we had been standing in the line,
but now we came at last to where the queue
entered the turnstile gates, and we passed through.
I found myself again inside that hall
with trees in tubs, the fountain, and the walls
of highly polished slate, and the array
of elevators where, day after day,
I'd ridden in the smelly and congested
cubicle. Reluctant, I protested:
'But do we really have to go in here?'
He nodded. 'Work is definitely a sphere
where every man or woman can go out
and get fulfilment. Yet, seen as a route
to happiness, we have to recognize
it isn't in itself especially prized.

Humans don't hanker after this attraction
like other avenues of satisfaction;
the greater part of mankind only work
out of necessity. This urge to shirk
raises some most perplexing social issues.'

I thought, 'You're not kidding!' For who would choose
of their free will, long hours, having to work
for someone who in your view is a jerk,
who tries to catch you out, or bears a grudge,
the need to take the rap for him, or fudge
his figures, all those niggling disputes,
the office with no window, the commutes
with nowhere to sit down, the whole palaver . . .
For my part, I'd a hundred times rather
engage in having sex or drinking beer.
The elevator halts.
                  We get out here,
and walk the corridor of frosted glass.
Various of my former colleagues pass,
appearing not to notice us at all.
Nor is there any sound from our footfall;
we are like ghosts, walking around unseen
in the locations of my old routine.
The secretaries' room is on the right,
and through the open doorway I catch sight
of Kate, who did the admin work for me
and several other people. I can see
her standing at her desk, as she was prone
to do, laughing and talking on the phone,
her body swinging as she shifts her weight
from foot to foot. Her skin is desiccate
but still corrupt with acne – it's a shame
because she was anyway rather plain –
but she is very good at looking after
us who use her, and her constant laughter

cheers us up. And even her straight face
appears to have a hint, the faintest trace,
of laughing. This helpful and sunny girl
had found a job in the investment world
through her disabled brother, who took care
of all our dealing-IT and software.
Kate loved to go dancing. At the weekend
she went to clubs and raves with all her friends,
and weekends in the summer found her heading
for Glastonbury or Bestival or Reading.
She kept budgerigars. One day she brought
a bird into the office which she'd bought
nearby in her lunch hour, and the absurd
Peter Marsh, who always was a nerd
for health and safety, swiftly sent her home.
She had a budgie's scream as her ringtone.
This Kate did all the little things I asked –
like parking permits, booking flights, the tasks
which otherwise eat up the working day.
All of these chores were swept out of the way
by her efforts, but more than that, she lent
a note of humour and encouragement
to my workday. I even could depend
on her for after work or the weekend,
and often she came over to our flat
to bring me air tickets or stuff like that,
and later on she helped with babysitting.
She was a godsend, I don't mind admitting.

A little further down the corridor
is Clint (my boss)'s, office. Through the door
we see and hear him, on the telephone
to someone in a far-away time zone,
his deep, rich voice issuing down the line.
The body is still – though whether by design,
or else because its mechanism is broken,
I cannot tell. And, as to what is spoken,

just from the tone of voice you understand
this person has the habit of command,
even when he is speaking to his wife
or stepsons. In the later prime of life,
he still has all his dark and curly hair –
though a few threads of grey have crept in there –
and keeps himself in good shape at the gym.
His wife, a widow when she married him,
arrived with three stepsons, on whom he dotes
as if they were his own, and he devotes
a lot of time to them. The boys all share
his taste for classic cars – he owns a pair –
and love to go out with him for a cruise
or strip the engine at the least excuse.
He spends a fortune on their education
and takes them all skiing in their vacations,
so good natured he doesn't seem to mind
the teenage moods. You couldn't hope to find
a better stepfather.

          His own PA
here in the office is the blonde Jane Day;
she is his mistress, everybody knows.
Jane is radiant. She seems to glow
with health or youth or natural vigour
of some kind; and she has an hourglass figure.
Perhaps to counteract her great allure,
she has adopted rather a demure
style of dressing: hemlines on the knee,
low heels, and high-neck sweaters seem to be
the favoured combination which she wears
to the office. But everyone still stares.
Her eyes are grey, her manner is direct,
her yellow hair is cut bang on the neck
(always a good idea if, like Jane,
your neck is long, and white as porcelain).

Had I been speaking this? Or was my guide
reading my mind? His voice came at my side:
'And you? Be truthful, did she catch your eye?'
'I noticed her, of course, I can't deny.
My love life with Louise was so inactive
that I'd begun to find women attractive
who wouldn't have appealed to me before,
and if ordinary women, how much more
a paragon like this? For everywhere
among the office folk her yellow hair
would somehow catch my eye. I have to say
it made me feel good in a restless way.
After a week at work I told Louise
tactfully, as in parentheses,
that if we could make love a little more,
it might enhance our marriage. What a bore
a husband is who has to ask for sex!
If love is felt it looks for a pretext,
it doesn't try to reason or be fair,
and if you have to ask, it isn't there.'

We left Clint's office, and the lovely Jane,
and next along the corridor we came
into my own office, and here I found,
sitting with all my work-fellows around,
my mother, at my desk. 'Patrick,' she said,
'foolish and loved offspring that I have bred,
let me explain it to you once again:
work represents a whole society's claim
on you. Of course, this isn't a contract
you signed as some kind of deliberate act,
but in your nature as a human being,
binding you to its law as well as freeing.
It doesn't just give you whisky and cigars
and central heating, clothes and sushi bars,
but also science, music, and the law,
religion, language, games, friendship, and more.

The herd is beneficial and complex;
and work is the social counterpart of sex:
exchange for what society's supplying –
and as such it is truly satisfying.'
My mother ceased, her body was quite still.
And though her mouth stayed firmly shut, I still
could hear her voice, now with an echoey sound
and distant, seeming to come from all around:
'No, love, I have to work. Mary Lou
will give you lunch and take you to the zoo.
I'll come and kiss you in your bed tonight.'

And now coming towards me, I caught sight
of a new actor. He was dark, with dashing
looks, and at his neck he wore a flashing
bow tie. This fellow said, 'I never knew
a day of melancholy. Quite a few
things have made me happy: much the best
was wife and family; as for the rest,
religion has been deeply life-enhancing;
good, too, were swimming pools and Scottish dancing,
charades and board games, too, in any guise.
My students liked my jokes, also the ties
I wore, like this.' He must have pressed a switch,
because the flashing tie began to twitch
and then revolve. He laughed. 'My own design.
It's always been a favourite of mine.
At work I was admired, even revered
for boundless industry. I pioneered
the field of body language, and invented
the whole idea of social skills, fomented
their teaching in a way that came to be
quite commonplace throughout society.
As time went on, I felt that my profession
had concentrated too much on depression
and academically, perhaps this theme
was in reality a worked-out seam.

So I began to study happiness
instead, a subject which had got far less
attention from psychologists. I found
that marriage was the most important ground
for happiness, and that the number two
was work. So think about it, what have you
enjoyed about your work? What's the attraction?'
I said, 'I had a lot of satisfaction
as a musician, though I never made
much money doing it. But when I played,
it was intense, a pleasure of its own,
myself on piano, Joe on saxophone,
Raoul on drums. I used to come away
feeling happy then, despite the pay.
Then in my banking job, I felt a spark
of happiness in beating my benchmark –
not huge, but it was definitely addictive.
And though for sure the lifestyle was restrictive
(not much time off at all), it was a blast
to feel so powerful, and spend such vast
amounts of money. You were not a stooge.
The prestige that goes with this stuff is huge,
it's hard to do without once you have had it.
The feeling of self-worth becomes a habit,
and also it feels good to be connected
to other people. Often I detected
my job was thought boring by arty people
such as Loretta. But these party people
just annoyed me. I was never bored –
just happy I could pay off the landlord.'
The fellow with the bow tie said, 'I found
in my research that people have profound
happiness in mastery of tasks.
But not just this. We like a job which asks
that we combine with team mates and connect
our skills with theirs, and work on a project

jointly with them, and share our information.
Sometimes it seems it's this communication
above all which promotes our happiness.
You found that too in music, I would guess.'
I said, 'It's true it feels good to be linked
to other people. Maybe an instinct
exists to make us love our social bonds,
akin to the sex-drive, but which responds
to social groups and their co-operation,
rather than sexual acts and propagation.'
My guide looked dubious. He said, 'That view
was never mine.' And now there came a new
awkwardness in the air, and he refrained
from saying more. The atmosphere was strained
as we stood there, observed by all my other
fellow workers, not to say my mother.
And then, recalling that my guide had said
to speak whatever came into my head,
I found myself saying, 'I quite enjoyed
the first fortnight of being unemployed,
of having time to dawdle and ignore
the clock, the date, and even to get bored.
But later, with the novelty abating,
I felt my self-esteem begin deflating.
Without a job, I sensed I'd no respect
and seemed like half a man. I recollect
a kind of vacuum that I couldn't fill:
my social value had collapsed to nil,
and I was miserable with it. Oh yes,
work is important to our happiness.
And yet . . .' 'Go on,' my guide prompted. 'And yet
I keep remembering a guy I met,
a doctor who had worked with AIDS. This guy
told me, "I've seen a lot of people die.
At that stage they've no real desire to hide
their true feelings, and many will confide

in their doctor. The most common lament
by far is they regret not having spent
more time with their children. Many are vexed
because they didn't get sufficient sex,
or lost their wives, or lovers they preferred.
But this is a regret I never heard:
nobody said to me, 'I feel a jerk
because I didn't spend more time at work.' "'

Leisure

My colleague led me back onto the street
and there we strolled on through the midday heat –
pausing only beside a soda vendor –
towards the next display on our agenda.
The line here stretched ahead towards the door,
a various and good-humoured bunch. They wore
flip-flops and bathing shorts, with towels slung
across their shoulders; some had aqualungs
or golf clubs, pairs of skis and tennis rackets;
a group of hunters dressed in combat jackets
had rifles, hippies carried their guitars,
old folks had guides to restaurants and bars;
people wore hiking boots or high-heeled shoes,
or carried bedrolls, cigarettes, and booze,
their purses stuffed with foreign coins and bills,
packets of condoms and malaria pills,
and all of them in glad anticipation
of some excitement or some relaxation.

My guide said, 'Here we hope to get away
from normal working life for several days
and do something society won't employ
us for, a pastime, something we enjoy
for its own sake. Though leisure is adored
by most people, by others it's abhorred;
but on the whole too much of it will test
us more than not enough. When we assess
the leisure of societies in the past
we find that hunter-gatherers had vast
amounts of it, as far as we can say;
at any rate, we know that present-day

hunters and gatherers, who live like those
of Arnhem Land, appear to dispose
of leisure four or five days of the week.
And likewise in antiquity the Greeks
had lots of leisure – that's if they were free.
Leisure is bound to interest you and me
since by its very nature it's revealing
about what human beings find appealing
when left to their devices. In my day
there was a leisure class who lived this way,
people of means who didn't have to earn
but could afford to live on the return
from land or capital. They occupied
themselves from year to year with a wide
range of pursuits, like riding hard to hounds,
going to spas, or following the rounds
of luncheon, dinner, coffee, social calls,
or charitable work and sumptuous balls.
It was a life of culture and festivities.
Other unsalaried activities
were soldiering and government, which drew
the courage and the skills of quite a few.
Nowadays no class like this exists.
Though privilege and riches still persist,
society's regrouped and changed its measure.
A life of unapologetic leisure
is no longer admired in quite the way
it used to be.'
          Without further delay
my guide ushered me forwards to a hall
with row on row of desks, and they were all
equipped with screens. In here we meant to find
what leisure could provide to humankind
and what fulfilment's found in a vacation.
We took our places at an empty station.
My guide held the remote. Up on the screen
the range of leisure options could be seen

laid out in tiles with colour-coded text:
'Religious faith, intoxication, sex,'
my guide intoned, reciting the top three
attractions on the list. 'It's plain to see
how vital leisure is. And yet I'll skip
past those because we're going to come to grips
with all of them later. They have their own
divisions in the Park, which you'll be shown.
What else is on the list? Yes, let's explore
this one for a minute.'

                    And now I saw
the screen had been transformed into a chart
of where I'd gone in India. The start
was at Calcutta, and a wobbling line
traced out those random wanderings of mine
as I was travelling westwards that November.
Seeing it here, I couldn't but remember
the scenes along the way, the mighty wealds
of jungle, the sun-hammered patchwork fields,
the whitewashed temples with their flags and bells,
and women standing at the distant wells,
flamboyant saris like a semaphore
calling the eye, the chaotic uproar
of motorbikes and rickshaws in the street,
the plangent horns and tinny songs which greet
the traveller, all conjured in my mind
and charted through the map along this line
which led to Goa.

                  'Here's another way,'
my guide said, 'to keep wretchedness at bay.
Just as a journey structure always gives
momentum to a movie narrative,
so too in life a journey gives a sense
of purpose where through wealth or indolence
that purpose has been lost. For I have found
that leisured people often move around

to give their lives some meaning, and supply
direction to a life that is awry,
and maybe it's a part of the appeal
of travelling for everyone to feel
this sense of purpose.'

                              Now my memory skips
back to Loretta, and the endless trips
she used to take. Arriving home from Bali,
she'd take off for the Venice Biennale,
or else to Formentor for the weekend,
or hang out in Manhattan for a friend's
gallery opening night. But, as I watched,
the map of India on screen grew blotched
and dim, its colours fading till it bleached
to white; and in its place we saw a beach
on which I saw a thousand people sprawl,
wearing not much, and moving not at all,
lined up in rows like fillets on a grill.
'Not exactly practising a skill,'
my guide said, 'but how popular this is!
Fifty weeks a year these people whizz
about, obeying dictates of their work;
but here for once they have the chance to shirk
effort of any kind. Since nothing's asked
of them on holiday they simply bask,
asleep or not asleep, it frankly makes
no odds at all. They travel here to take
a well-earned rest. And yet when they retire
and don't work any more, they still desire
this holiday. You have to wonder why.
What kind of thrill, what kind of special high
do they get? What can be their motivation?
Even the briefest pause for meditation
reveals the answer: people want a change.
We're drawn to something new and even strange.
And so, to get a fix on this mentality
we're going to visit virtual reality.'

He handed me the visor and headphones.
With these I moved inside a virtual zone,
and walked a trail, not by my own intention,
but by the headset's cyber-intervention,
which guided my advance until I reached
a little cove with pine trees and a beach.
Here the exhausted wavelets gently plied
the sand and pebbles at the water's side
which barely shifted in its listless flows.
As I looked on, a woman's head arose
out of the sea, and then the virtual figure
waded towards me, growing always bigger,
a mythic birth I could identify:
not Venus, but Loretta, somehow dry
and wearing once again the dress she wore
that evening when she opened up the door
beneath her portico and let me in.
I followed her along to the kitchen,
she handed me a bottle to uncork,
we settled onto stools.

At first the talk

was strained in spite of all the jokes. She flicked
her cigarette a lot. The air was thick
with her perfume, it tasted in the wine.
Whether by accident or by design,
the way she sat, her lower back was arched
provocatively. Now my mouth felt parched.
I poured another glass and tried drinking
a gulp or two of that. And I was thinking,
'Why am I doing this? I don't desire
Loretta, even if I do admire
her figure and her verve.'

And yet it seemed

I did want her, since now, as in a dream
where all unfolds without a conscious plan,
I saw my hand move out and touch her hand.
We went on with the chat, but now our words
struck me as being ever more absurd,

the conversation faltered, rudderless,
and later on there was an awkwardness
in making love as well.

When first she let her dress fall to the floor,
and the light from the lamp fell on her freckled skin,
that was a country I'd not visited before,
a rumour from beyond the ocean's rim,
a sailor's tale which I could not ignore.

And shameful as betrayal was, I kept on going back
to trade in that territory, and travel among its strange
flora, and feel with her its freshets and earthquakes;
because, given so freely, nothing sates like that exchange
of unobstructed barter, which she and I could make.

Let me pretend betrayal helped. For after all,
even pretence may bring relief. I took that tack
but how consoled was I really? As I recall
I was fooling myself, more than forgetting you.
Louise, only a cold caress of yours and I was back
where I had been before: longing for you, not getting you.

The great love of Loretta's life so far
was Anton Sholnikov, the ballet star.
From him she had picked up all the confused
talk about art, and movement, and the muse
(doubtless a feature of the ballet corps),
which candidly could be rather a bore:
for borrowed talk is always irritating
when heard enough from somebody you're dating.
Like him, she used to say 'one and a quarter'
instead of 'one fifteen', and he had taught her
to use 'good, passionate feeling' as a plaudit.
Its opposite was 'frauding' or 'defrauded',
or else she spoke of 'cheap feelings'. Likewise
from Sholnikov she'd learned to dramatize

relationships, to row with violence,
screaming obscenities and 'Fraudulence!'
and then make up with reckless sexual passion.
They used jealousy also in this fashion.
She used to lock him out and make him shin
the drainpipe to her bedroom and come in
that way instead. She told me with some pride
how once she'd lain in wait for him inside
and then, as he was making his appearance,
she whacked him with a chair. This gay ebullience
caused Sholnikov (now lying on the floor)
to grab the nearest article of war –
in the event, one of Loretta's shoes –
and hurl it at her head. His aim was true.
'Look here –' she pointed, pulling back her hair
and turning to me. 'That's the scar from where
the heel got me that day.' And I could tell
she'd like me to come on that way as well.
'One night,' she said, 'Anton got mad, and threw
me out onto the street, and my clothes too,
and I remember lying on the ground,
and people going to work were stepping round,
and I was screaming, spitting like a cat.
It was a good, passionate feeling, Pat.'

But now the image of Loretta faded,
the virtual beach location was invaded
by quite a different scene, this time a town
in Rajasthan where I had sat around
beneath a shady awning, getting high
on Himalayan charas, drinking chai,
and chatting through the long hot afternoon.
How exotic it seemed! But pretty soon,
as I observe some more, the elements
which made it quaint begin to re-invent
themselves as commonplace; the garish sweets
are metamorphosed into Mars and Treats,

beedis grow fat and turn into cigars
while rickshaws morph into electric cars
and sadhus into suave ecclesiastics;
fruit peels itself, and wraps itself in plastic,
the sound of vedic hymns booms out as rap,
and turbans wither into baseball caps,
and generally whatever had been strange
and new to me, now underwent a change
to something familiar which I knew at home.

How can a ring of menhirs end up seeming suggestive,
mysterious as a woman? What quality has drawn
the tourist to this henge, to a broken, useless vestige?
Is it enough that meaning and purpose remain unknown?

It seems that in this figure, in these monstrous limbs of stone,
you find a flawless body where fantasy can play,
a woman unalloyed with soul, except perhaps your own:
this is the tourist's playground, the globetrotter's byway,

shallowest of all men's loves. For when its meaning's lost,
an icon stands no higher than any work of art;
the canticles and scriptures are literature at most,
the old gods' place of pilgrimage no more than a resort.

Intoxication

Emerging once again into sunshine,
my colleague paused, then put his arm through mine
and led me to a café for iced tea.
Then, both of us refreshed, he guided me
along that leafy broadwalk which connects
the fleeting charms of leisure with the next
attraction.
             Here the set was dressed to show
an Irish pub of fifty years ago,
its windows curtained to above eye-level,
the ample panes of glass frosted and bevelled.
Italic lettering proclaimed the sale
of finest whiskey, cider, stout, and ale.
It was, like everything the Park devised,
too clean, too cute, and smaller than life-size;
but once inside, the quaint old-fashioned style
gave way. We found a minimalist aisle
where walls of white partition alternated
with lengths of perspex and delineated
a row of variously proportioned stalls
to hold exhibits. Somehow these recalled
the glass compartments of a rodent house
in zoos; but here, instead of some rare mouse,
it was humanity we found displayed
arranged in living tableaux to portray
the different methods of intoxication
employed by folk of every class and nation.
Some merely tipsy, some out of their heads,
some animated, some collapsed on beds,
but all were in the process of abusing
intoxicating substances, or boozing.

Here there were scenes to represent the dopers,
giggling or staring blankly, the no-hopers
on methamphetamine with rotted teeth,
Bolivians chewing on the coca leaf,
the drinkers' endlessly repeated jokes,
the junkies' needles, silverfoil, and smokes,
the crack addicts, with their paraphernalia,
the feast of Holi, and the Saturnalia,
the spliff, the bong, the hookah, and the bottle,
the curandero with the fresh peyotl,
Siberian shamans with their amanitas,
the ayahuasca and datura eaters,
a hundred others which I couldn't name.

And as we walked on, here and there we came
upon a scene which I would recognize
from my own life; for now before my eyes
Louise's sadhu sat in padma-asana:
in one hand he was holding a banana
lassi, in the other a large spliff.
He grinned at me and I inhaled a whiff
of charas as we passed him. Further on,
we came to the ice-cream van where I'd gone
with Louise on that day in Richmond Park
when we were tripping; also to the dark
tavern in Cyprus where I first got wasted
drinking ouzo, since I'd never tasted
liquor in my life before, and passed
out on the floor.
                My guide said, 'In the last
analysis, drugs are a very crude
short cut, acting directly to elude
life's pain or briefly helping us to capture
a feeling of contentment, even rapture.
You might call them a sledgehammer corrective,
but of all means they are the most effective,
and so to me, at any rate, the most
intriguing. Physiology can boast

an understanding which has hugely grown
since I died, and whole continents are known
which were only the subject of conjecture
when I attended Herr von Brücke's lectures.
Music, food, and sexual attraction
have all been analysed in terms of action
of chemicals inside us. Dopamine
and endorphins can easily be seen
as kinds of drug. We find that natural highs
induced by dancing or by exercise
are big contributors to happiness,
according to research. And more or less
whatever drug our bodies may produce
organically, can also be induced
by Pfizer and Novartis.'

What is this wonderful feeling?
The elixir has set you free
from hawking and from parroting
the words of others. Now you see
the way that lovers do:
a heron perched on cages at the zoo.

My room is chilling to the bone;
I watch the lovers pass outside:
when did I feel so all alone,
so trapped, so punctured in my pride,
as now? Barely alive
and waiting for that feeling to arrive.

The next door we came to gave entrance to a salon, tall and
 wide
and lit by chandeliers. On every side
lilies and roses teemed in jardinières.
Pinpoints of light picked out the gilded chairs
where people sat playing at dice and cards,
costumed in coloured silks, the women starred

with jewels, the men with wrists of frothing lace,
and sometimes a beauty-spot upon their face.
My guide admonished me: 'Now have regard
to how the turning of a piece of card
can seem to be enough to fill a life.
On every continent the custom's rife;
mankind loves wagering in any form.
In the *ancien régime* it was the norm
for those whose means permitted it to play
at dice or cards a good part of the day
(the other thing they liked to do was hunt).
And see here at the tables near the front
how noble men and women use their leisure
to win a bit or lose a bit, the pleasure
coming with the luck.

          'Beyond, sitting apart,
you see their present-day counterparts,
yourself among them, sitting at their screens:
the money managers. In your routine
a lot of pleasure comes from making bets
against a client's benchmark or index.
And you must surely be aware of it:
you have a win, you feel the benefit,
a buzz of genuine gratification.
What counts here is the moment of elation.
Repeated intermittently, it gives
some meaning to a life. The gambler lives
in expectation of success, his game
confers the gift of hope, confers an aim
in life, which brings a satisfaction with it,
answers the puzzle of life and how to live it,
as people in this room can testify.
And yet, though gambling is a natural high,
it is addictive too, like many drugs,
and then it will destroy the hapless mug
who takes that path, as much as heroin
or any other misused medicine.'

And now we walked through those depressing places
where gamblers' and the junkies' desperate faces
barely turned to look as we passed by:
the rich man with the syringe in his eye,
the girl selling herself outside the station,
and many other scenes of degradation,
until we came at last to the hotel
where Robbie Norton lived. I knew him well:
he was my oldest friend from Cyprus days.
Later, an inheritance came his way,
he settled in New York. I tracked him down
to this untidy hotel room downtown
where we stood now, exactly recreated
and placed in the theme park. The simulated
view from the window was the one I'd seen
that day, the buildings' outlines very clean,
and here and there the vapour rose in wisps
from off their roofs, ascending in the crisp
fall air; I saw again the water tanks
and shining glassy towers of distant banks
against the cyan sky. His Walkman lay
upon the table with a metal tray,
a roll of silver foil, and some burnt matches,
and on the soundtrack I could make out snatches
of a Nirvana album which he played
that time.
       Now I remembered his tirade
about the music business being dead
and how it could be remedied. He said
he might rent space in the basement below
to set up a recording studio
somehow different from the industry's.
He had a project to sell jewellery,
too, something about the internet,
and some Jamaican rastas he had met.
Now he launched into a rambling spiel
about how opiates protect and heal

the body's cells, retarding the process
of ageing. 'Shamans used them to suppress
symptoms of cancer and as a specific
against the plague. It's very scientific
and all the best authorities agree.
Opiates aren't bad for you, you see.
You maybe think that I'm a total loser,
as seedy and abject as any boozer –
admittedly this room's a total mess –
but what you don't see here is the matchless
feeling I get, despite this habitat,
of being secure – no, better than that.'
He died in a car accident one night
in Hoboken.
          I got onto a flight
as soon as I heard the news – his family
asked if I would give the eulogy –
and barely had checked in to my hotel
when I heard sound the chimes of my doorbell.
Opening the door, I thought that I was dreaming:
Loretta stood outside, her red hair streaming
from underneath a cap of sable fur.
Stunts like that were typical of her;
but though she often did materialize
from nowhere, so bewitching in surprise,
she was equally liable to vanish –
the way she did one evening at the Spanish
Contemporary opening at the Tate.
I couldn't find her, and since it was late
I drove to her house, thinking she'd gone there;
but there was nobody but the au pair.
That was my first experience of the way
Loretta was.
          And then there was the day
we went to a party that a friend of hers
was giving, a well-known restaurateur:
I found her in the bedroom, making out
with his sixteen-year-old. There was no doubt

that she deliberately engineered
these situations, so we always veered
from crisis to crisis. And then the night
when we'd been having something of a fight,
Loretta, flushed with wine, her lovely hair
breaking loose from its ties here and there,
shouting as if I wasn't sitting near her
(the taxi driver couldn't help but hear her),
'Just fuck me now! Come on, why don't you, Pat?
Just fuck me!' It was many times like that
with Loretta – exciting in its way,
but I was very conscious that one day
her love of danger, and her recklessness,
would in the end discover us. I pressed
her to be more discreet but she was bored
by circumspection. 'Patrick, you're a fraud.
When you have passionate feelings, you can't keep
them hid forever. You are not a creep
because something gets out you don't intend:
it happens to most people in the end.'
And I was thinking, 'I had better break
this off right now, or else she's going to make
Louise discover it somehow.'
                                    And yet,
rather like smoking one's last cigarette,
I always put it off a little longer.
The truth was, her appeal to me was stronger
than I was willing to admit. And there
was one more thing, unspoken in the air.
I had been growing conscious by degrees
of this: that though I surely loved Louise
more than Loretta, more than anyone,
Louise gave me the feeling I had flung
a pebble in a void. Not an echo
came back out of that chasm. And so
that was the other thing: I was lonely in my own marriage.

At last we ran aground there, on the island of the witch;
as soon as we found her cottage, my followers like thugs
drew lots for who would have her. But that all-seducing bitch
was too clever for them. She gave them drugs.

At once they metamorphosed into beasts.
Some were turned to piglets and squabbled in the trough;
others, cackling with laughter, mutated into geese,
hissing and flapping as she drove them off.

Those who drank from the great flask turned to panthers
and hunted her as quarry beneath the bright moon's beams,
others swarmed as bees against her anthers,
filling her combs with honey, and learning to work in teams.

To me she gave a different drug. I fell for her,
I was her slave around the farm and in the sack,
I grew her corn, and made a child as well for her,
but after three years' labour, I wanted to go back.

She said: 'Do not imagine I mastered you with drugs.
That is a fantasy. You met with no shipwreck,
you never had companions, there were no helpless mugs
transmuted into junkies, indentured or henpecked.

'This slave-driver woman is of your own creation,
this island you envisage as lost in the salt foam
is not a compass-error, or a lapse of navigation,
this is no island at all: it is your home.'

Walking onwards now, my guide and I approached a hologram
which showed a meeting I had had with Sam:
me in the business suit, wearing a clean
shirt and a tie, and Sam in dirty jeans
and fleece, with a designer-stubble beard
upon his face and headphones in his ears.
This was the firm's most wealthy client by far:
the sole heir of his father, avatar

of a global patent. Here the image fit
the whole scene just as I remembered it:
his zippered folio was on the table
just as in real life; and I was able
to hear the scratchy, tinny sort of sound
which came out of the headphones. Now I found
the memory of that day came back to me
in all its points, with total clarity:
he pulled the headphones out and scratched his stubble.
'Patrick, I gotta tell you I'm in trouble,'
he said; his voice was indolent and hoarse:
'Josephine is filing for divorce.'
I said, 'I see. I didn't know you two
were having problems. Maybe you could do
some marriage guidance.'

                               Sam just sat and stared
blankly at me like he was unaware
that I had spoken. Then he said, 'I guess
there's something else I really should confess.
I am a sex addict. I just returned
from Southern California where I learned
about my illness in a special clinic.
And though you know I've always been a cynic
about these programmes, it made perfect sense
the way they spelt it out. All my defence
was stripped away, for thirteen painful weeks,
and I was kept exposed to their techniques;
a part of this process was coming clean
about my addiction with Josephine.
I had to tell her how I'd screwed around
incessantly, with anyone I found,
however unattractive, though I guess
I did tend to prefer the powerless.
Prostitutes especially were my bag,
and also both women and men in drag,
transsexuals, the homeless, and so on,
I told it all to her. And now she's gone.'

The hologram dissolved. Now a spotlight
came on ahead of us, and I caught sight
of a sideboard on which there lay a letter.
I saw at once that it was from Loretta
since on the envelope I recognized
the black ink and the oddly different-sized
words she always uses when she writes,
smudging her ink the way a child might.
'Patrick, you are a foul, disgusting creep,
a total fraud. Your kind of love is cheap.
I don't hate you because you're not worth hating . . .'
And so it went on, always execrating
and always spelt all wrong and freely dotted
with lewd obscenities, and well ink-blotted.
These letters, strong in their vituperation,
often didn't raise an accusation,
but once we got to talk, it soon came out
what the whole argument had been about:
that I had found another girl attractive.
Then after I had gone through a protractive
explanation she would soften her insults
and be appeased and make up. The result
was always sex in which she took extreme
and lively satisfaction.
                                    Now the beam
of the spotlight was suddenly extinguished.
I groped my way, unable to distinguish
anything in the dark where I was led,
until we saw the bright light up ahead
of the gift shop, with its array of tat;
only this time, besides the usual hats
and theme park T-shirts, fizzy drinks, and mugs,
there were displays of imitation drugs
of every category. Lines of speed,
and phials of coloured pills, and bags of weed;
the shiny cans of beer; the brands of liquor,
and wine and so on, all in replica.

And here among the objects to be sold
upon the shelf, I saw Louise's gold
evening purse, lying as it had lain
in the pub bedroom on the counterpane.
Out of our window we could see the hulls
of boats at anchor, and we heard the gulls
yelping above the harbour. When we kissed
there was no warmth in it, and she dismissed
me with 'Not now, Pat; later. I must dress.'

Later, at the party, we recessed,
and sat together on a littered lawn
and watched the lamplight narrow, as the dawn
lit up below a vista of the sound,
and nearer to us, couples walking round,
the girls in party dresses with their hair
dishevelled from the dancing, their feet bare,
and carrying their high heels by the straps,
their boyfriends with bottles of beer or schnapps –
men in tuxedos with their bows untied
and collars undone – walking at their side.
From time to time someone we knew would say
a few words to us; others walked away,
perhaps from delicacy, since Louise
was lying with her head upon my knees,
which spoke of intimacy and closeness.
But then Louise, while pulling down her dress,
would call out, 'Hey you guys, don't go away!
We want some company, it's quite OK
to stay and talk, there's nothing untoward
happening with us, in fact we're getting bored
'cause everyone's avoiding us. So stay!'
I said to her, 'Darling, let's be away
to the hotel now.' But Louise just gazed
blankly as if she hadn't heard, a dazed
expression on her face; then with a frown
she took the golden evening purse and found

her cigarettes and lighter, took a drag,
and then went back to looking in her bag
until she found the coke, laid out a line
and snorted it, saying, 'I feel just fine.
Now that's good stuff.' She seemed to have no yen
to have and hold, no fondness to expend.
Inside her nothing stirred, nothing was there,
while I was filled with aching of despair
even remembering.
          I turned away
from the gold handbag on the shelf display
and said to my companion, 'All the rage
I felt towards Louise and which rampaged
through me for so long vanished in the air,
now that I had embarked on my affair
with Loretta.' 'And did you have the feeling
Louise on her side might have been concealing
a deep unhappiness, equal with yours –
about your carnal life?' 'Louise forbore
to speak of sex except on the occasions
when I raised it. And even then evasion
was more her style. So it was hard to guess
whether this was from guilt or tactfulness.'
My guide made no comment. I said, 'Louise
now got a part-time job which by degrees
she grew to love. It was a humble post,
but in a leading gallery, the most
well known for photographs. Here the director,
though exigent, came quickly to respect her
for her acute intelligence and taste.
As time went on, increasingly he placed
his more important clients in her charge,
and once Jack started school she had a large
part of the business in her hands, and dealt
with everything quite easily. I felt
maybe she was discovering satisfaction
in other things, and sexual attraction

had grown senile and passed away in peace
without being much mourned – by her, at least.
But family life continued, and I think
we still felt close because we had that link
which Jack provided. Yes, we could have fun
with him at least. In that we were as one.
Were we happy? In a way we were.
Of course, before, we had been happier,
but still we had a life, a home, and Jack.
It seemed better to live, and not look back;
untroubled by delight or misery.'

My guide remained silent; he seemed to be
waiting for me to go on, and another
longish pause ensued. 'You had a lover,'
he said. 'So did you never feel a yen
to leave Louise behind and start again
with your new friend?' 'Not in my wildest dreams,'
I said immediately. 'Perhaps it seems
perverse on my part, but the truth is this: I was in love with
    Louise.'

Fishing the archipelago,
the cormorant goes on a string,
but even so it might swallow
the fish it finds. And so a ring
is placed around its neck,
and now it brings its catch onto the deck.

Well, this is not the way to heaven
but nor is it the way to hell;
the little chunks of fish you're given
will fit through. It's just as well
you know your role: to dive
and bring these fish to deck is to survive.

I came to Asphodel meadows,
where all those people come who died
without being either jocose
or miserable. The gods provide
a special recipe
to keep at bay these people's agony.

Beauty

We left the house of drugs, and made our way
blinking into the fierce light of day,
and walked along the central promenade.
On either side of us were the façades
of those 'Victorian' houses, always fronted
with moulded polyester, and always stunted
to less than real-life-size. It must have been
washed nightly, it was so supremely clean,
and as my guide and I sauntered along
this well-scrubbed thoroughfare among the throng,
I said to him, 'Louise adored to go
to Camden Market and to Portobello
looking for junk. And just as in Panjim,
exploring the bazaar, she always seemed
to find something special, so here as well
she'd uncover a length of brocatelle,
a fine engraving, or a lacquer chest
for our apartment. Truly, she possessed
a talent for interior design.
Her style was quite eccentric but refined;
I loved the way that our apartment looked.
While she was out shopping I often took
Jack to the zoo, since he was passionate
for animals; occasionally Kate,
my secretary at work, invited us
to see her birds, and then we'd take the bus
to Clapton, to the little ivy-clad
terrace where she kept house for her dad.
Jack was always happy on these visits.
Kate would unlatch the cage and her exquisite
budgerigars rushed out and flew around
the room. By keeping very still we found

the brilliant-coloured birds would come and land
on Jack's shoulder, or take seed from his hand,
and he loved that. And then we'd have to catch
them up again. One time we saw chicks hatch
and as the weeks went by their skin and bone
developed feathers and became full-grown,
and Kate made up stories and gave them names.
She had a fondness for inventing games.
As well as these, she had a mynah bird
which mimicked everything, not only words
but also sounds such as the telephone,
the doorbell, or her father's baritone
humming a snatch of tune.

                         'This father cherished
music above all things. Impoverished
and ineffective, too, he edited
a music journal. Katie credited
her dad with every human quality.
She worshipped him, though in reality
she had to cope with all the practicalities
of their existence, since her mother died
when she was only sixteen. On his side,
her father, almost childlike, depended
on Kate for everything. She cleaned and mended,
cooked and did the shopping, leaving school
and finding work in Bestin's typing pool
to earn money. She had a natural bent
for looking after people, and this lent
maturity; but she was still nineteen
when I began to work there and she seemed
at times nearer in age to Jack than me:
they liked the same programmes on the TV,
the same jokes, and the same computer games.
On one occasion she remarked, "That Jane
who works with us is really quite a cow.
She's pretty useless really, but somehow
she never gets the blame for anything.
We all know it's because she has a thing

with Clint. It's clear she thinks she's quite a beauty
but that isn't a reason to be snooty,
is it? It doesn't do her any good."
I said, "I think she is misunderstood."
She stared at me and then said, "Oh my God,
you fancy her. Of course, it would be odd
if you didn't. All of the others do." I said, "You're quite
    wrong there."'

Goddess of beauty, where you go
petals appear upon the floor,
a car waits in the street below,
the first-class lounge opens its door.
Goddess, I think you know the score:
when you arrive the guys look happier,
money is spent, the tempo's snappier.

You're not particularly clever,
I couldn't say that you are blessed
with wealth or culture or whatever,
your sense of humour's not the best,
you're not even very well dressed.
The nightclub greeter points to you
and lifts the rope and lets you through.

Going in at the next attraction, we walked along an enfilade
    of halls
where, hung gallery-wise upon the walls,
were clumsy replicas of works of art
from museums of the world, for the most part
by famous masters. These my guide ignored,
although I quickly noticed that he wore
a pained expression, and eventually
he told me, 'Beauty meant a lot to me,
but what about for you? Did beauty count
for very much?' I said, 'A huge amount.

Music is where I come under its sway.
It makes me feel good, I could even say
it makes me happy. Playing at weekends
along with Joe, Raoul, and other friends
I feel fulfilled; no, more: I feel elated.
And yes, beauty has had me captivated
in women too, sometimes it was so strong
I felt it like a pain.'

               And now, headlong
into my memory there came the shock
of passing that familiar office block,
as usual after work, when from the door
emerged a girl I'd never seen before,
so beautiful I stopped. She passed, I turned
and followed her. I'd like to say I burned
with quick thinking, but actually my brain
was empty, and a lump akin to pain
stuck in my throat. I followed in this fraught
and zombie-like condition, then I caught
her bus and rode, robotic, through the city,
and she, exotic, heartrendingly pretty,
was like a magnet dragging me along,
across the crowded streets, and through the throng
of traffic to her stop. There she descended
and I followed on foot to where she ended
her journey at a tall apartment block.
And there she put her key into the lock,
the door closed, I was left upon the kerb
of a remote and unfamiliar suburb.

I walked by my companion as we made
our way together through the enfilade
of picture galleries, all much the same
as one another, till at last we came
into a theatre. Here upon the screen
a figure from the Ancient World was seen

with flowing beard and wearing a chiton
against a backdrop of the Parthenon.
Despite the background, he at once began:
'Welcome to ancient Croton, where I ran
a school of mystical philosophy.
My adepts swore an oath of secrecy
and vegetarianism; we abjured
bean-eating too – that helped to keep us pure –
and talked philosophy. Girls could belong
as much as men, the sect was very strong
on non-discrimination for its day.
If anyone got sick we used to play
the lyre to make them better; and we believed
that when you die your spirit is received
into another body. And yes, we banned
private property. You can understand
that we were thought of as eccentric. You
yourself are very likely thinking, "Who
hired this guy? What in his tutti-frutti
of cranky notions throws a light on beauty?"
The answer's this: it was disclosed to me,
the inmost nature of reality
is mathematical, and I revealed
numerous cases where this is concealed
from first inspection. Though at first there seemed
to be no obvious ratio between
a triangle's three sides, yet still their squares
revealed one. All of Nature, unawares,
was constituted out of such relations
and could be made subject to computation.
Even beauty, always enigmatic,
revealed itself as made with mathematics:
I showed that harmony in music springs
from ratios of different lengths of string
and how in other instruments the sound
relates to volume. Ratios are found

for every instrument and every pitch.
The history of aesthetics has been rich
in theories which derive from my surmise,
for ratio exists in every guise,
whether as a symmetrical reflection,
as distribution, or the golden section,
or any of the other ratios
which thinkers down the ages have proposed
in architecture, painting, and in verse.
A little probing always disinters
proportion of some sort which lies behind
their beauty. It's the same with humankind,
'cause human faces also seem to be
more beautiful when they have symmetry.
Since me, I'm bound to say, aesthetic theory
was mostly pretty poor and often dreary,
so what I've done is cull the very best
ideas and make a short beauty contest.
Enjoy!'
      The actor's face faded from view
and now the screen divided, and its two
sections slid back, to show an esplanade
on which a line of models could parade
as if on a catwalk; and not just girls
in bathing costumes with their fresh-done curls,
but men wearing historical costumes
with swords or frock coats, togas, ruffs or plumes,
from every period. This oddball mix
of fancy dressers and half-naked chicks
all wore a ribbon draped across their chests
as is the norm in these beauty contests;
and on the girls' were written 'Harmony',
'Repetition', 'Rhythm', and 'Symmetry',
'Proportion', and other concepts of aesthetics
which readily relate to mathematics.
As for the men in costume, they all wore
the same sashes, only the legends bore

the names of thinkers throughout history
who sought to unravel the mystery
of beauty, what it is and how it came
to be so valued; men who found their fame
in architecture and philosophy,
the Church and perceptual psychology
from earliest times until the present day.
Of these men, some believed that beauty lay
within the object; others, as astute,
conceived of it as being an attribute
of their perception. Truly, I confess
that my attention was enraptured less
by this distinguished band of heavy-duty
thinkers than by the wonderful beauty
of the girls, which no one could repugn.
The whole parade was over all too soon
without a winner having been declared.

And now my guide, who seemed to be aware
that I'd learned little from it, turned to me
and said, 'The difficulty's this, you see:
aesthetics has been unable to explain
the nature of beauty or its urgent claim,
whether in naked girls or ancient prayers,
in works of art, or in the Himalayas,
in choral symphonies or human faces.
And as usually happens in such cases
where much is said and little is revealed
lack of success is artfully concealed
beneath a sonorous flood of empty words.
None of the aesthetics that I've heard's
tremendously convincing. Yes, and sadly
psychoanalysis has also done quite badly
in parsing beauty. All that I arrived
at, really, was that somehow it derived
from sexual feeling which had been submerged
by civilization. The basic urge

is to have sex, but this way being blocked,
the disappointed libido is locked
on to another mark. Beauty exhibited
the classic trait of impulses inhibited
from capturing their aim. In this context
it's worth remarking that the actual sex
organs themselves are hardly ever judged
as beautiful. Instead, the thing is fudged
and beauty is attributed to faces,
to eyes and hair, to noses and to graces,
to secondary features, in a word.'

We left the theatre now, and soon I heard
a voice ahead of us calling my name.
We went towards the sound and quickly came
on Dougie, my professor, having lunch
in the canteen. He looked up from a bunch
of papers and said, 'Listen here, young buddy,
it seems psychologists have done a study
which shows statistically that most men rate
the physical appearance of their date
more highly than intelligence. The churls!
And more than that, apparently the girls
think money's more important than good looks
when they select a man.' And here he shook
his head and tutted in mock disbelief
and laughed, and then setting aside his sheaf
of papers, he went on, 'Of *course* a guy
is going to be strongly attracted by
a youthful woman's beauty. Let's assume
a man – say, me – is shown into a room
with twenty Harvard graduates, all plain,
and two ravishing babes without much brain.
Do I go over to this sexy pair?
Don't stop to think, I am already there.'
He held a finger up in just the way
that Dougie used to do. I have to say

the whole effect was utterly convincing,
the voice, the gestures and the laugh evincing
the real man I remembered.
                                        He went on,
'But let's consider the phenomenon
a little more closely. We can agree
that someone's beauty's absolutely *the*
pre-eminent reason for wanting sex
with them. And so its role in the context
of human evolution has supreme
importance; yet, oddly, it doesn't seem
that any real advantage is conveyed,
except the likelihood of getting laid,
and this leads to a circularity.
Is beauty then a singularity
developed out of chaos? Is it just a
self-perpetuating random cluster?
Scientists have tended to propose
reasons why it isn't. Among those
is the idea that some characteristics
of girls – such as their own vital statistics –
identify them in a microsecond
as being female, childless, young, and fecund.
Science reveals that swelling breasts and hips,
a little waist, a pair of pouting lips,
gleaming white teeth, masses of glossy hair,
a fresh complexion, a taut derrière,
are signs of being young. It also finds
these are the very features which define
beauty in a woman. So in truth
beauty may only be a souped-up youth
exaggerating signs which indicate
a girl is young and apt to procreate.'

When a man must go away to worship, farther
than some thought possible, and sailing with the Dutch,
half starve and shiver in the cold at Plymouth harbour
to seek God's mystery, will this seem to him too much?

And will he complain when he is sent away
from the loved home to uncharted wilderness,
to seek a fertile soil by analysis and survey –
will he complain then that his labour is endless?

Or will he go forward ungrudgingly to found
a colony of the righteous, like none that has been before?
And will he then discover at the end of the trail, a ground
fertile for crops and timber, or rocks that are rich in ore?

Boy, my beauty is the promise of this continent,
my hot mouth is a survey of minerals to despoil,
my young breasts are my certain indication of God's covenant,
my thick shiny hair the nutrient analysis of my soil.

At this point in his speech the sound cut out
quite suddenly in mid-chuckle, without
the laughter coming properly to an end;
and as it did the waxwork of my friend
picked up its papers jerkily and froze
in readiness to start again for those
who followed after us through the attraction.
My guide said, 'Tell me, what's your own reaction
to beauty in a woman? For example,
Kate, your secretary, possesses ample
qualities, and has displayed a real
kind-heartedness towards you; can you feel
attracted to her, though she's not a belle
in any sense, and has poor skin as well?'
I said, 'In office hours I couldn't pay
much heed to anyone except Jane Day.
I have to tell the truth: her lovely eyes
had cast a spell, and she monopolized
my glances and my daydreams. I was caught.'

Now, as if prompted by my train of thought,
a famous artwork flashed onto a screen:
the three dissected rats which I had seen

beneath a spotlight at the museum party.
Here a crowd of cool and rich and arty
people had been invited to the show
(clearly the mailing list didn't yet know
about Louise's family disaster).
The exhibition coupled the old masters
with new contemporary art, and here
beside these rats and a serene Vermeer
I found myself conversing with Jane Day,
in a familiar and flirtatious way.
She was standing unusually near
and looking up into my face, her clear
grey eyes had me again under their spell.
I thought to myself, 'This is going well,'
and then, to make the chain of thought complete,
wondered if she was ever known to cheat
on Clint with anyone.
                              To my surprise,
Loretta quietly materialized
from nowhere, and at once I felt constrained.
Of course I introduced her now to Jane
but something in the atmosphere was altered
on Jane's side too. The conversation faltered
(I wondered suddenly: so does Jane know?)
and we began to talk about the show.
Loretta laughed her silky laugh, mocking
the three dissected rats. She found it shocking
that a museum would be content to give
a place to something so derivative,
and thought that, far from being new or vital,
they were a fraud with a pretentious title.
Jane disagreed. What had appealed to her
was how well made all the exhibits were.
Loretta gave a peal of insincere
and musical laughter. 'Love that idea.
You mean the real art of this creation
somehow resides within the fabrication

of its perspex or its ironmongery –
most likely by some bloke in Hungary
or Poland. I love that.' This little sally
had its desired effect. Jane didn't dally
and when she'd gone Loretta said, 'Patrick,
don't tell me, let me guess: she's dull, she's thick,
and she's conventional, she has to be
some kind of low-level employee
at your bank. Tell me I'm not right!
Go on, you know I am.'

                        Later that night,
Louise and I were lying in our bed
reading our books, when suddenly she said,
'Tonight Loretta Ashe was always there
beside you. Are you having an affair?'
'Of course not.' 'I'm glad, darling, I would hate
it so much if you were.' I felt a spate
of blood surging inside me at the danger.
But to myself I thought, 'Dog in the manger.'
Louise went on, 'She stuck to you like glue.
The strange part of it was I felt that you
were kind of bored by her and liked the other
girl, you know, that bombshell who's the lover
of your boss. Loretta had the look
of someone vexed, like somehow they both took
a fancy to you, and she was losing out.'
That was the way she was: even without
real evidence she knew by intuition.
But now, as if provoked by her suspicion,
something was taking place: her hand caressed
me gently in the hairs upon my chest
and suddenly she was all over me.
God knows it had been long enough since she
had wanted that. But she wanted it now.
What happened? What had altered to allow
this sudden burst of sensuality?
Was it a simple sexual rivalry?

I'll never know. It came out of the blue,
like so much with Louise. I only knew
it was as wholehearted as it was sudden.

Soon after this re-entry into Eden,
she stunned me by suggesting that we take
a holiday without Jack. For his sake
she'd never done it, even for a night,
and even I was doubtful it was right
to leave a child so young without his mother
or father. But Louise was of another
mind. She said, 'It's no big deal, you know.
We leave him with my mom in San Francisco
and drive along the coast for a few days.
It'll be fun. Come on, Pat, I always
said we should do that journey. So let's go!'
Who is this potent impresario,
for whom the actors work with perfect ease?
Some people call him Mephistopheles
and others talk about a god of love;
whatever name we use, we will observe
the fluency of his performances.
In his productions, life's perplexities
are much the same as ever, yet on the night,
we improvise, and no one has stage fright.
I said, 'Well yes, of course!' That was the way
the trip was settled on. And the next day
I asked Kate at the office to reserve.

And now, having had leisure to observe
the case of rats, my guide and I resumed
our path, and ambled onwards in the gloom.
My colleague led the way and, following
his lead, I came upon a kind of hollow in
the passage wall. A blue illumination
flickered in this space, like fulgurations
from off a welding iron. The stuttering light
at last composed itself and we had sight

of Stella, as a hologram, portrayed
just like in the days when we had played
poker at school: a placid girl, and plump,
at sixteen she already was a frump.
Her father was a chemist who had fled
the dark Norwegian winter for the Med
and ended up on Cyprus. Now she spoke:
'Patrick, you're a kindly sort of bloke
but even you can't help showing surprise
to find me here. No, don't apologize:
you're right. I am not beautiful at all;
but cast your mind back and you will recall
the spirited reception I enjoyed
at the lyceum with the Cypriot boys.
That was entirely down to being blonde.
My hair was a magic Scandinavian wand
which turned me from a troll to a princess
and made me the siren of the school recess.
Do you remember? I even converted
our village café, up till then deserted,
into the meeting place of local boys.
It was a change for me to know the joys
of being beautiful, I who had always been
a plain Jane. Now, in an unforeseen
reversal, I was swiftly made aware:
beauty is rarity, and I was rare.'
She paused, before continuing, 'Behind
your colleague, if you'll turn around, you'll find
a poster of some girls in Calabar,
Nigeria. In this province there are
women like these ones, of the Efik tribe,
women that you and I might not describe
as beautiful because they are so fat.
But here in Calabar there's none of that:
there's nothing they love more than flesh like jelly
and rolls of fat around a virgin's belly.
Good thick wrists and ankles, log-shaped thighs,
and wobbly buttocks are what Efiks prize.

In this society a girl who's svelte
is not considered pretty; and it's felt
she'll be unlikely to attract a date
unless she does something about her weight.
So when she comes to marriageable age
she goes into seclusion to engage
a process called Nkuho. What this means
is fattening her up with a routine
of feasting: copious pepper soups and stew,
porridge and plantain, ekpang, yam fufu;
plenty of sleep enhances the digestion;
no exercise – that's quite out of the question;
she is condemned to inactivity
until this gluttonous captivity
has made her big enough for Efik men
to think of her as beautiful and then
Nkuho's over and they set her free
to marry and to start a family.
That such a curious practice should exist
is interesting to social scientists.
It illustrates with some flamboyance how
contrasting cultures manage to endow
beauty with very different attributes –
make brutes of angels and angels of brutes –
and generally lends credence to the line
that beauty may be socially defined.'
Stella ceased, and now her pudgy face
and slightly sour expression were displaced
by flaring light in three spasmodic bursts.
She leaned towards us, as if unrehearsed,
and in a low voice said, to my surprise,
'I loved you, Patrick, did you realize?'
and then she disappeared. We left the place
and I walked on, still haunted by her face.

Then suddenly there surges from the past
a different memory, in flat contrast

with that of Stella. This time at my side
I had Jane Day with me, blond-haired, grey-eyed,
and she and I were walking through the door
of Cesto restaurant. All round I saw
the faces turn to look in our direction –
a gesture redolent of genuflexion,
conscious perhaps for some, for others more
an automatic thing. We crossed the floor
as talkers paused, and listeners wavered
in their concentration; and I savoured
the moment, because to be identified
with such a stunning girl flatters the pride
of any man . . .

The craftsmen have gone away. Their door
bangs in the wind, their dustbins roll,
their tools lie broken on the floor
and auction catalogues extol
virtues of their undying soul.
The face you knew at twenty-five
will haunt your dreams in middle life.

The waist so small, the skin so fresh –
little remains of them today;
the perfect arms and legs, the flesh
which gravity seemed not to weigh,
the richly coloured hair which lay
across the sheet, your slender waist,
the flush of youth upon your face.

Where are the notes you used to pass,
the things that were done for a dare,
the legs that ran in the long grass,
the urgency of the affair?
Great masterpieces become rare,
creation falters. A sublime
tradition goes into decline.

And now you're left with the best houses
and works of art and cars and jewels
and closets of expensive blouses,
great hairdressers and swimming pools,
diets with complicated rules.
Defeated nations must defer
to values of the conqueror.

The generals nod, they all attest
pleasure in the museum display.
You have their medals on your chest;
yes, works of art confer cachet
but when the love is gone away
will beauty be enough? It seems
a tainted and quisling regime.

Louise once said, 'Beauty's a thing a woman has no option
    but to show:
a force of nature, like a volcano
erupting when she comes into the room.
The gods bestowed it to her in the womb,
but it's unlike the other things they grant:
despite ingenious ploys, a woman can't
enhance her beauty very much. In this,
being a beauty's different from success
in things like business or photography –
in fact in most things where a mastery
is gained through practice and experience.
That is the curious life-predicament
of the bewitching girl; she does feel prized,
massively so, and yet in her own eyes
it almost seems this isn't about her.
Often, some part of her will register
the world's attention as a cold neglect
which goes to undermine her self-respect.'

My guide and I pressed on, making our way
towards the gift shop; but a last display

awaited us before we went outside.
It showed a low hut, nestling in the wide
bend of a river. A banana tree
stood in the garden there, and we could see
a lonely figure sitting on the ground
in lotus posture, sunk in a profound
meditation. Birds pecked happily
about and even hopped onto his knee
as if he were a statue; but they flew
away when we drew near.

       He said, 'I knew
the world and its ways once, so don't deduce
that I was always this kind of recluse,
seeking to free myself of every tie.
My father was a minor samurai
and I was in employment to attend
a powerful family, and became their friend.
I could have had a more conventional life,
made a career, had children and a wife
and a position in society.
But none of this meant anything to me;
instead I studied poetry and read
the classics, learned calligraphy, and led
a life in what is called the floating world –
experienced beauty, and the love of girls,
and grew to be a poet. This regime
succeeded and I came to be esteemed
for what I wrote; but though I tried to feel
happy, this happiness was far from real.
There was something inside me which rebelled
against my pleasant life; I felt impelled
to leave it; and to seek out solitude
within this humble cabin, and exclude
whatever might distract me from the way
of understanding.

      'Here, day after day,
I wrestled with the hardest work of all:
zazen. The wind would blow, the sun would crawl

across the sky, but I sat wholly still,
surrendering emotions and the will.
Gone from the world, I only would return
to seek in it the truth which I could learn
from beauty. Truly, nothing else was worth
my scrutiny, for nothing else on earth
could help me in the arduous process
of realizing total consciousness.'

Money

Leaving the attraction we emerged
into the sun and joined the crowd which surged
along the roadway, caught up in its flow
and following where they all wanted to go.
Ahead of us there loomed that high-rise tower,
symbol of money's privilege and power,
whose gleaming windows make a clear landmark
from everywhere you go inside the Park;
and now I was impatient to be there.
I think my colleague must have been aware
of this, because to speed up our progress
we took a service alley which was less
used by the public; luckily he knew
the layout of the Park and short cuts through
the crowds at each attraction.
                                           As we went,
I spoke about the holiday we spent
in California visiting Louise's
mother, Candy. 'Holidays like these
were naturally a personal expense
not chargeable to work, but it made sense
for me to have the admin done by Kate,
and they encouraged this, to concentrate
and focus our attention on our work.
She, by exploiting some mysterious quirk
of airline systems, got us all upgraded
to fly in First and somehow she persuaded
the airline to throw limos in as well.
Louise was thrilled about it, I could tell.
She tipped her seat and stretched out, revelling
in all the space. "This is like travelling

with Dad," she said, "when I was just a girl,
and he and Mom and I went round the world
like this. Later we had the private plane.
Ah, those were the days." She sipped champagne
and looked in the newspaper. There she saw
the news that Hew had won his bidding war
to take over a massive retail chain.
"My God," she said, "he's making quite a name
with this affair. He really has been clever.
Even a couple of years ago, who ever
would have imagined this? Now I'm betting
he'll buy that yacht he's always dreamed of getting.
I hope he asks us on it! I could use
a week or two of Caribbean cruise."
I said, "Whatever happened to the friend
of the sadhu?" I didn't quite intend
the bitterness which this seemed to evoke,
and laughed to make it seem more like a joke.

'In San Francisco we put up two nights
with Candy. She was full of the delights
of having Jack entrusted to her care,
but there was an aggression in the air
between her and Louise. When I mentioned
something to Louise about this tension,
she seemed pensive, and said she missed the old
home of her childhood days, which now was sold.
She thought maybe emotionally she blamed
her ma, and felt her childhood was profaned,
and doubtless that was true. But I suspect
she also was on edge at the prospect
of being away from Jack for the first time.
The bankruptcy was on all of our minds
as well; for now the family home had proved
too costly to keep up, Candy had moved
to an apartment with a single spare
room which Louise and I and Jack all shared.

Candy was plucky, she didn't complain,
adopting an ironic, jokey vein:
"Frankly, going bust has brought a lot
of benefits, I find. Being shot
of rubbish friends is one of the appeals.
And no staff problems. Really, the ordeals
of being ordinary are overstated."
The truth was that she felt humiliated.
Without her wealth, she found she was ignored
by most of her acquaintance from before.
People at the museum respectfully
suggested she step down as a trustee;
and there were also unintended snubs.
Now she found she couldn't afford the clubs,
and even friends who hoped to stay in touch
discovered they weren't seeing her as much,
moving in different circles as they did.
All these were things she generally kept hid.
I think she was relieved to have Louise
and me to talk to; also she was pleased
to be with Jack. "More than she ever was
with me," Louise said drily. But because
of this rapport we could abandon her
and Jack in town, and take off to Big Sur.

Our stay there was in some ways like Panjim;
we seemed as happy as we'd ever been,
and yet, though we were getting on so well,
Louise was also anxious. I could tell
she didn't like being away from Jack
and part of her now wanted to go back.
One time, when I could see that she was fretting,
I said, "Why worry when you know he's getting
your mother's full attention?" She replied,
"That's why I worry." But, joking aside,
there also were plenty of happier features
of days we spent alone, and none was sweeter

than feeling close to her again. It seemed
to come up like a mushroom crop, pristine
and edible one morning in the grass:
so had this thing out of the ancient past
quite suddenly appeared for us unbidden,
from nowhere. How mercurial and hidden,
Louise's sexual personality!
This country had the same duality:
for one moment a fog is on the air
and cools the forest, hanging droplets there;
the next it rolls away and hangs its pall
across the ocean where the combers crawl,
leaving the glaucous oaks unblanketed.
Now the hot sun hammered upon our heads,
reflecting like a furnace off the stone
pathways, and there were glimpses of the foamed
breakers of ocean, with the smoky curtain
of fog banked up behind them, still uncertain
of its position, constantly shifting –
five miles out, five hundred yards, or fifty.
On our first day we went out for a stroll
and came on a deserted water hole
high in the live oak forest. Here we stripped
and, holding our breath and counting three, we slipped
into the icy pool and splashed about;
and then, elated by the cold, got out
and lay spreadeagled on the scalding rocks
to dry off and recover from the shock.
Now in the hot air, resinous with pine
and redwood needles, as the noon sunshine
bedazzled on the waters of the creek,
I heard Louise's voice begin to speak,
saying she wanted another child . . .'

The path snaked down towards the shore.
We walked across the hot grassland
and through a shady corridor
of bearded oak trees, hand in hand,

down to the ocean. On that strand
the fog moved in, setting a lace
of tiny droplets on your face.

I go down to that littoral
of sun and mist and ancient oaks;
I walk upon the chaparral
hillside and where the spindrift soaks
the headlands; standing where we joked
and flirted in the fog among
that grey driftwood, when we were young.

It is a path like any other,
a beach like many on that coast.
Like youth itself, those two lovers
have walked on; but their laughing ghosts,
so carefree and yet so engrossed,
like wisps of vapour linger on
the cold side of the canyon.

Perhaps all of us have a song
which we can hear and comprehend,
a written score where we belong,
not given to us to transcend.
Perhaps I for a moment, then,
heard it above the ocean's roar
with you beside me, on that shore.

'After that holiday Louise and I spent on the coast, I knew
that, going home, the first thing I must do
was break off my affair with Loretta.
I went round to her house. She took it better
than I'd imagined, claiming she'd a strong
presentiment that something might be wrong
while I was absent. I did not believe
the bulk of this, but I did feel relieved
that she had heard me out without creating
the drama I had been anticipating
and which I knew she loved.

'I hurried back
to our apartment and Louise and Jack,
and made a carbonara which we ate,
and then put Jack to bed and sat up late.
A happy time: it seemed a simple thing
to be like this – why shouldn't the future bring
more of the same, and then again still more?
That night there came a ringing at the door
of our apartment. Louise let her in
and left me with her. Now her freckled skin
was grey with cold, God only knows how long
she'd been down in the street below. Her strong
athletic legs appeared suddenly frail,
her whole demeanour seemed to tell a tale
of shivering weakness, dressed in just a skirt
of thinnest cotton, and a black T-shirt.
Her pallor, and the stark intensity
of her expression as she stared at me,
had lent to her arrival something ghoulish
which otherwise might just have seemed foolish.
I said, "Loretta, did you have to come?"
but she just carried on like she was dumb,
staring around the room in utter silence.
Her look was one of traumatized defiance
and spoke of love we undoubtedly had
for one another, but which now with sad
finality, was being set aside.
I felt regret, but also couldn't hide
my anger that she had to make a scene
here with Louise, who up till now had been
ignorant of the affair in every way.
Loretta seemed to have nothing to say.
When she was gone, I went in to Louise,
propped up in bed, a book upon her knees,
reading, or at least seeming to read.
She kept her eyes cast down and paid no heed
at first when I came in, then raised her head
and in an almost casual manner said,

"I know you're having an affair with her."
I said, "It's over." She didn't demur,
but from that moment all the intimacy
between us drained away, the obduracy
and sexual chill returned.
                                    'When we discussed it
she'd only say that I couldn't be trusted
and that meant everything. Time and again
I promised that in future I'd remain
faithful to her. And I meant it too:
the very last thing I desired to do
was disappear on Jack, the way my mother
had disappeared when she left with her lover
for Africa, when I had been a child.
But more than that, since we were reconciled,
and since the time together at Big Sur,
I knew how little tenderness from her
it took for me to break off my affair.
Without a doubt, Louise's love, once there,
was utterly commanding: when it spoke,
marriage could be rekindled at a stroke.'

We came now to the entrance of the next
attraction. On the gate a single text
spelt out the word 'Money'. We passed beneath
and made our way towards the centrepiece
of the display: the gleaming office tower
which radiated status, wealth, and power,
and which we'd seen from far off. Here a throng
of people queued in snaking lines, so long
they filled the square in front of it. 'This ride
is pretty popular,' I said. My guide
smiled weakly to himself. 'One of the most.
Now walk behind me, try to stay as close
as possible.'
                        We cut across the square,
slipping like ghosts between the people there

who took no notice. When we were about
halfway across it, suddenly a shout
was heard above us and a murmur ran
among the crowd, and now I saw a man
at one of the high windows. He hung there
for half a moment, toppling in the air,
then tumbled like a ragdoll to the ground.
People were screaming, and the crowd around
drew back to make a circle round the place
where he had fallen; and we saw his face
crushed to a pulp, as if it were as soft
as peaches' flesh. And now, carried aloft,
the corpse was borne away, and though the floor
where he had died was puddled with his gore,
people still crowded in and filled the space
in eagerness to get into this place.
I said, 'Guide, when visitors witness
a suicide, are they not slightly less
anxious to get in themselves? I mean,
at times like this when customers have seen
a person actually defenestrate,
does it have no effect upon the gate?'
He said, 'See for yourself: this suicide
has not dispersed the clients for this ride.
They all still want a go, and rightly so.
In this attraction most of us will know
unhappiness at times; but this alone
will rarely cause a suicide. No one
is put off worldly goods by what a few
unhappy plutocrats decide to do.'

Once through the door, we found ourselves inside
an atrium some forty metres wide
and circular in form. Around the walls
stood plinths of polished granite. They were all
empty. He said, 'Those pedestals you see
around the room, they were supposed to be

for teachers and philosophers who would
propose possessions as the greatest good.
But as you see in fact they couldn't find
anyone prepared to take that line.
But though the pedestals in here are empty,
out in the square there's always more than plenty
of punters in the queue to come inside.
In all the Park this is the busiest ride –
which says something about humanity,
and also about moral philosophy.'

We passed into the next room where a scene
of gold prospecting had its place. A stream
of water trickled through it and, beside
a pool, animatronic figures plied
their repetitious task, jerkily lifting
the pans, then holding still like they were sifting,
before lowering them back into the brook
to pan some more. Now, as we looked,
I saw an actor had been planted there
among them, an old fellow with white hair,
dark eyebrows, dark glasses, and flashing teeth.
He said, 'I loved money; it's my belief
I had more dough than anyone had got.
My interests were vast, so was my yacht.
I had charisma, I was loved by girls,
I could do what I wanted with the world
and yet (and I'm well known for saying this),
for certain, if women did not exist,
the money would mean nothing. Its allure
originates from women, that's for sure.
Enjoy this ride! Keep on beside this stream
until you find a member of our team,
and he will be your guide to the delights
of the next two attractions, and their sights.'

We did as he said; and to our surprise
the escort was someone we recognized

from earlier on: the same corpulent frame,
the owlish face and bulging eyes, the same
grizzled mutton chops and balding crown,
the same habit of spitting on the ground –
that President who doubted happiness
to be a good objective, and expressed
confidence in religious faith. And now
he greeted us, and started telling how
he'd been commissioned to negotiate
loans for the newly formed United States.
'I spent some time in Holland, and came out
appalled by how the Dutchman thought about
nothing but money and its acquisition.
I thought this a contemptible ambition
at which I hope my children never aim;
but I am bound to show you, all the same.
What is the real purpose of worldly wealth?
That money is of no use in itself's
a commonplace in all philosophy.
We men of the Enlightenment agree
its usefulness is to facilitate
exchanges between men, and arbitrate
the welfare and resources of the earth.
Left to itself, money cannot make dearth
or plenty but, by fostering exchange,
vastly increases both the ease and range
of specializing in our social roles;
and so it has made possible a whole
new way for Homo sapiens to live.
It also offers an alternative
to brute force as a method of directing
human interchange, and of subjecting
the selfish urge to the collective good.
Its settlement is clearly understood
without recourse to arms or piety.
Money's the signal of society,
the messenger which says, "Do that", "Do this".
And when, as happens, the instruction is

unwelcome to us, people tend to blame
the messenger and say it is a shame
that no one cares for anything but money
in modern times. But this is sanctimony
concealing a resistance to the change
which money signals. And it isn't strange,
in fact it's natural that people mind,
since change is difficult for humankind.
And yet we've changed a lot. We've come to dwell
protected from the elements in cells
of concrete, far from our hereditary
habitat, inside a termitary
we call a city; you could almost say
that urban-dwellers have evolved away
from what we were before, and christen us
a new species: Homo denarius.
Now step right up, choose one of these elite
sports cars you see lined up, and take your seat,
and I'll come with you, so I can explain.'

The 'cars' were more like wagons on a train –
parked in a line and running on a rail –
although they did adopt in smaller scale
the bodywork of various famous cars.
We started off, and hadn't travelled far
along our way when I made out ahead
the entrance of a tunnel, which we sped
towards and entered. Here upon the walls
were hung posters of men and women, all
people whose money I had managed. When
we came at last into daylight again,
who should be waiting there but John O'Reilly,
the M&A tycoon and all-round wily
operator.
      When we met, he'd said
that in a year or two he would be dead,
and he was. Generally, we'd do
the business in a brief moment or two,

and then he'd sit me down to have a glass
of whisky, and the two of us would pass
an hour chatting in his library –
which usually involved him telling me
about himself, his life, and his impressions,
his business deals, even his indiscretions.
He also spoke of death. So many things
were touched on that it left me wondering
whether the real reason he asked me round
was loneliness. Perhaps in me he'd found
a better listener than his attorney.
He said, 'My life has been a constant journey.
I've had homes everywhere – San Francisco,
New York, Fiji, Nassau, Monaco,
Paris, Gstaad – you name it, I've lived there.
But, you know, the darned thing is I never cared
for moving house, and never really rated
resort life either; in a way I hated
those rich men's ghettos and their cul-de-sacs,
but more than I hated these, I hated tax.
I had a yacht – it wasn't just a boat,
the thing was a monster, it could barely float –
and when we came to shore we had to anchor
miles away. Then I began to hanker
after a private jet – another whopper,
an aircraft that would be a real show-stopper,
parked on an airfield. Take my word for it:
it was one heavy-duty piece of kit.
All these toys were really a lot of fun
to play with. But, when all is said and done,
the point of all this pricey apparatus –
the real point, as I'm sure you've guessed – was status.
People believe that money's their object
but what they're really wanting is respect
from other folk. So money comes to be
the medium by which society

enforces on us its imperatives
and coaxes us into its narrative.
With little bribes of status and respect,
the complicated termitary directs
our lives within itself. This was as true
for wealthy men like me as guys like you.
We feel the same.' 'Mr O'Reilly—' I said.
'No, please, just call me John now I am dead,'
he interrupted. 'OK, John then, tell me,
seeing you left it all to charity,
why were you so averse in your lifetime
to paying a dollar or even a dime
in taxes?'

So tell me, when the taxman is taking half your gold,
who doesn't feel reluctance to hand him the obol?
Everyone's first instinct is to shelter it, to hold
his property intact. Those T-bills and consols
are stockpiles of respect, their indicated presence
speaks to the world, commands its acquiescence.

The prophecy was clear: his grandson was to slaughter him.
To forestall this he framed the stratagem
of stopping one being born, and boarded up his daughter in
the tower, and held her prisoner, beyond the reach of men.
For like a miser now he's come to feel inside,
despite the prophecy, that death can be denied.

She lies upon the mattress and idly masturbates.
The sound of distant music drifts in upon her bed
across the barred-up window, a relentless bass. It's late.
The dance won't last forever. Her skinny thighs are spread
and her young blood hammers in her arteries like a drum.
Locked in like this, how did she manage to succumb?

The fairy tale which is widely believed
is that a shower of gold entered her womb.
How foolish to imagine that gold might have conceived

life in that nubile body! Should scholars then assume
the story symbolizes the force of affluence
with which an old man bought her acquiescence?

It didn't work like that. Also, you must discard
as fanciful the notion that gold refers to a deft
distributing of kickbacks among the palace guards.
No. The god himself kicked in the door, and as he left,
filled full with sexual pleasure, laughing aloud,
threw coins from his chariot, to the crowd.

After the fatal time Loretta came to our apartment, grey
and shivering with cold, and put an end
to everything which we had found again,
Louise and I drifted without direction:
no sex, no intimacy, no affection,
our marriage gradually falling apart.
Now quarrelling was all too quick to start
and disagreements neither of us cared
anything about abruptly flared
in angry quarrels, ludicrously so
in many cases. Now I came to know
how any pretext is enough to vent
one's anger, and how much we may resent
being the one to go and fill the car
or put out rubbish, things which were by far
too trivial to matter, and anyway
everyone has to do them every day –
they're nothing at all. How dismal to live
as we did, grudging always what you give
in terms of money, succour, and the whole
supposedly wished-for duty of the role
of spouse to one another.
                                        One night
I went into our room, switched on the light;
Louise was lying prostrate on the bed,
and when she lifted up her lovely head

I saw the sign of tears upon her face
and welling in her eyes. I took my place
beside her saying, 'What's it all about?
Tell me.' At first she could get nothing out,
and then she answered, 'Patrick, can't you see?
It's everything that's wrong, it's you and me.
How did we get to where we are today?
I never wanted it to be this way.'
I put my arms around her but her face
did not turn up to me, and the embrace
felt awkward and unwanted. At this time
no tenderness or blandishment of mine
was welcome to her, or advanced my cause.
Rather, repugnance showed itself like claws
which come out in a cat, instinctively.

One day a girl at work remarked to me
with what appeared to be a telling look,
'You should thank Kate, you know, she really took
a lot of trouble with your holiday,
got you that stuff you didn't have to pay,
like ticket upgrades, limos, and the rest.'
This struck me as a fairly strange request,
seeing as actually I had thanked Kate
some months ago now. But I made a date
to give her lunch. When all was said and done,
I felt at ease with her, and she was fun
to be with. At this tête-à-tête I learned
that she was giving most of what she earned
directly to her dad. Of course, I knew
she cooked for him, and did the housework too,
but I'd always imagined he supplied
the funds for their expenses. Kate denied
this with a laugh. 'His efforts on the journal
aren't salaried, you know.' 'What, not at all?'
'Well, hardly. You could say business affairs
are not his strongest suit. He only cares

for music, really. I love that about him.
The journal wouldn't have a life without him.
It's done for love, you see. Perhaps it's strange,
but I like funding him; he's such a change
from everybody else. Some of the guys
who work at Beston's seem to recognize
no other good – they're constantly obsessing
about money, it's really quite depressing.
I get it: they're well off, no one can doubt it;
I only wish they could relax about it.'

When I got home that night I told Louise,
'I feel I'm losing you. My darling, please
don't shut me out.' She answered, 'I suppose
in marriage you can't always feel so close
to someone, can you?' I let this go by,
and then after a moment said, 'Please try.
It used to be so good.' She said, 'It's just
there has to be a certain store of trust.
I keep imagining you with Loretta.'
'That's just destructive, and you should know better.
That whole thing's finished, in the past,' I said.
Now, like a bird, she cocked her lovely head
and glanced at me, then quickly turned away.
'Maybe I can trust you, as you say,
or maybe it's just in your character.
Whenever we're in bed I think of her.
It grosses me out, you can't imagine how.
Oh God, I wish I was in India now!'

A hotel room. While I was waiting there,
I watched TV, nervous, very aware
I'd never done this kind of thing before.
Before long, she arrived, and when I saw
her blond hair, for a moment then my brain
confused her with my boss's mistress, Jane,
though I could see this girl was nowhere near
as beautiful as Jane, and it was clear

she wasn't a blonde either. Her face was tired
with an unhealthy pallor which transpired
despite the heavy make-up, and a look
of desperate toughness in her eyes. She took
a drink, and tried to snuggle up as best
she could, putting her head against my chest,
making her skirt ride upwards with a squirm,
her feet up, though the sofa was too firm
for this position to be comfortable.
I saw her thigh was bruised, the vulnerable
nature of her calling was suggested.
It was very unsexy. Now I rested
my hand upon her hair, and I could see
her dark roots in the parting. Probably
the darkish brown suited her well enough
before she coloured it. A little dandruff
showed up there. For a minute we conversed
awkwardly, and then she said, 'Now first
let's get the payment done with, gorgeous boy,
and after that we'll kick back and enjoy
ourselves. You're gonna like this.' So I took
the crisp banknotes out of my pocket book
and, as I gave them, I was thinking, 'Wait,
can I really be this desperate
for sex? Can paying to make love be thrilling
in any way, or will it just be chilling?
Should I go now?' But even as I debated
what I should do, the girl anticipated:
already she was undressing as I watched,
her bra was coming off, I saw her crotch,
with slick gestures she now began to flaunt her
nakedness, and I began to want her.

Status

Back in the car, our friend the President
sat at the wheel again, and off we went
towards a rainbow bridge linking the next
attraction on our way. On the apex
the car slowed to a halt, and we looked down
towards a golden gate shaped like a crown.
He said, 'Sometimes my enemies suggested
I wished to see America invested
with monarchy again. It was a lie
without foundation. No, the reason why
you have me with you here is that I stated
that Man is most of all things motivated
by a passion for distinction, a desire
to be observed, considered, praised, admired.
It seems to me no other urge is quite
as keen, nor is there any appetite
of human character more universal
than that for winning honour, no reversal
more keenly felt than losing honour is.
It marshals all our other energies:
the love of learning and desire of fame
are really little other than this same
passion for honour, praise, and admiration.
You see, our fundamental motivation
is that we need the world to validate us.
Nowadays you people call it "status"
or else "respect". It is a commonplace
that Homo sapiens is a social race.
What is the glue which binds us to this herd?
the answer can be given in a word:

respect. 'For this, we'll cause ourselves to be
false to our feelings, slaves to drudgery
or chastity, or something just as vile.
Respect will make it all appear worthwhile,
its pull is almost irresistible.
Clever folk are as susceptible
as stupid ones in this: the intellect's
no barrier to it. It's a bit like sex,
that way. Respect is everything: you'll see,
if you ever get some, believe me.
The good Lord said, "Where benefits abound
I will bestow more." And that's what I found
respect was like. When first I moved to France,
intellectual women looked askance
at me; I couldn't bring myself to speak
in their presence, I felt myself so weak
and defective. In Europe I didn't have *it* –
the breeding, allure, charisma, and the wit,
which everyone required in large supply
to win the admiration of Versailles.
But when I was elected President
I was the paragon and ornament
of all America. Now that was status:
the bankers were as toadying as waiters.'

At this juncture the bug-eyed actor dropped
his acted role a moment to adopt
a confidential tone with us. 'Can you,'
he asked, 'accept the Adams point of view
that status is a basic motivation
for humankind, not just dissimulation
of something sexual? Couldn't there be
a force which binds us to society,
another natural urge, which isn't sex?'
The question was quite obviously addressed
more to my guide than me, but he appeared
neither to see the actor nor to hear.

The actor, who I saw was clearly used
to being ignored or even at times abused
by his public, took no offence at this.
He went on, 'I've become convinced there is.
The mechanism of status, in my view,
is what keeps groups together. It's the glue
binding our social structures, the strong claim
society holds against us in the name
of the herd. Isn't this the social law
the President was really groping for
when he said, "Every man should know his place and be made
   to keep it"?'

The King said to his daughter, 'Behaving differently
to stereotype is rarely a good plan.
It jars with people's notions of what royalty should be
and undermines respect for our whole clan.
But quite apart from that, you have to understand
you won't find happiness yourself through deviance of that sort.
Try to find friends within the circle of the court.

'I know it's limiting. But looking anywhere
outside your natural milieu is something you'll regret
in due course – if not sooner. Above all, have a care
for what you say in front of staff. Try to restrict
your conversation to the most banal subjects
which couldn't cause offence, even when spread around
in cafés and in bars all over town.'

The girl goes to her bedroom. She brushes out her hair,
samples her subtle perfumes, and picks a favourite dress
from her corridor of cupboards. Notice at once her care
to choose one any commoner might possess.
Going to the window of the oriel recess,
she calls down to the street sweeper beneath her in the square,
'Tell me, sweeper, is life among the populace
as dull as it is here, inside the palace?'

Our cicerone, the President, restarted the car. He let it glide
across the rainbow bridge's other side
and drove on through that crown-shaped entrance-way
onto a smaller-than-life-sized freeway.
Leaving this almost straight away, we parked
inside a drive-in theatre. All was dark
in here until, upon the giant screen,
we saw a presidential limousine
driving across the vast African plain.
'A vile despot,' the voice near me explained.
'He killed opponents with an unsurpassed
brutality, and got himself a vast
fortune, and by his bloody and corrupt
government, the nation was bankrupt.'
I watched the limo covering the ground
in eerie silence with no ambient sound.
Out of the bush there surged up nine or ten
ragged children and half-naked men
running towards it, waving to the car,
drawn on towards the glint of this lodestar,
each one delighted, laughing as he races,
a lovely, guileless joy upon their faces,
just happy to be near the limousine.
I thought, 'But what can this possibly mean?
Why are the boys made happy by this car,
what makes them wave, what draws them from afar
just to be near it?' And as though he heard
my thoughts, the President said, 'They are stirred
by that same driving force which animates
most of mankind. We want to emulate
the people who have status and success,
or work for them, or even just witness
their presence. Yes, even proximity
to status gives us pleasure. Just to see
the limo makes these boys happy today,
and happy in exactly the same way

as crowds outside the Oscars, or the throng
waiting for the President along
his route, excited now, their arms held high
to be glad-handed as he passes by.
This natural love of high status supports
a social order, and is largely thought
to be benign. When it's strongly allied
to ambition, you might be criticized
as pushy, or when it remains steadfast
to status of an order which has passed,
that's known as snobbishness. But behind both the status
    urge is driving.'

She said, 'He stands up there among the Emperor's kin.
His robes attract the eye of every girl.
It's not just me who notices. Can you imagine –
the belt is made of gold, studded with pearls?

'He has to hold the ritual fly-switch –
he does it so well! With such grace and poise!
And though it's true that he's extremely rich,
he just seems nicer than the other boys.

'That gold is hard to wear, heavier by far than cloth;
the costume is stiff and scratchy, and not a proper fit:
he says he's always happy when he finally takes it off.
Isn't that an amusing thing? Well, isn't it?'

We abandoned our sports car in the theatre parking lot
and walked along an alley. Soon we found
some spotlit waxworks on a piece of ground
raised like a stage. And now the President
said, 'Look at these two here who represent
a duel with pistols. Hamilton fought Burr
and died to keep his honour – since a slur
on someone's good name had to be retracted
or else defended with one's life. He acted

to save his status as a gentleman
and died in doing so. Now this young man –'
he pointed to a fellow on the floor,
his throat slit open, in a pool of gore –
'his crime was stepping on somebody's shoes,
which in the barrio code implied he'd lose
respect and status.'
                    The next tableau
was set outside an elegant chateau.
Two men were grabbing at each other's clothing:
waxworks, but with a desperate look of loathing
upon their faces. 'See these dukes of France
disputing which of them should have the chance
to hand the King his hat. Here at Versailles
a fairly trivial act could signify
a man's standing. The truth is, we ascribe
most status in accordance with our tribe;
but other social groups exert their sway
at the same moment, rather in the way
that gravity acts to varying degree
from different bodies simultaneously;
and resolution of their different forces
is what defines the planets' various courses.
Status gives pleasure, wholly genuine,
but also wields a dreaded discipline,
policing our activity far more
than do the sacred scriptures, or the law.
Its stern enforcers are esteem and blame.
There is no way out of the status game –
unless you leave society altogether,
like sadhus do. But even they can't sever
the social bond entirely, and you'll find
they do enjoy a status of a kind.'
Now, as if in reverie, my guide
began to speak: 'Didn't you once describe
Hamilton as a man whose fierce ambitions
sprang from a superabundance of secretions

which he could never find sufficient whores
to draw off? Surely that suggests you saw
status as from a different origin.'
But then he turned to me and said, 'Begin
by saying how it felt when you first started
your banking job. What pleasure was imparted
then, or at the time you were promoted?
Was there a special happiness connoted
by higher status?' I said, 'Well, I guess
it did feel good. I liked the friendliness
which certain people showed me, not the least
my own bank manager, and the increased
respect, which seemed to distance them from me,
as well as acting as a guarantee
of good behaviour. And it felt all right
not to appear a dud and parasite,
at least to people like Louise's mother.'

Striding towards us now, I saw another
performer in a wig, who I presumed
to be a clergyman from his costume.
His eyes sparkled with humour and mischief.
'Although I took the cloth,' he said, 'my chief
concern was the economy of land
and crops; and then I also set my hand
to the role of neutral countries in a war,
the dialect of Naples, and many more
topics, too numerous to mention here.
I wrote satire, and my public career
found me both minister and diplomat.
But I'm not here because of all of that.
I'm here because when I was young I wrote
a monograph on money, and devote
a section to what wealth and poverty
might be. I was the first person to see
that being rich is purely relative:
it almost doesn't matter how you live,

provided you are better off than those
around you. From this principle it follows
that you can say the same of poverty.
In fact, when you examine history
you see that in the Bronze Age even kings
could not aspire to the material things
an ordinary person has today.
My great contemporary did not gainsay
this thought; in fact he went further than me
and showed our concept of necessity
also to be relatively drawn.
The labourer who at one time would have worn
a skin to keep him from the cold and dirt
was now persuaded that a linen shirt
was a necessity. And in your day
haven't economists begun to say
that schools and running water constitute
necessities of life?
                    'Absolute
wealth does not exist. How else explain
this paradox: that rich people sustain
a higher rate of saving than the poor
and yet, as states are blessed with ever more
prosperity, their savings rates don't rise?
And yet they don't. You have to recognize
that wealth is really just about comparing
ourselves with other people, how we're faring,
and how they are, establishing a rank,
a relative position. So the bank
account, the good address, the works of art,
are sought less for themselves than for the part
they play in giving rise to some respect.
Status is the name for this effect.'

Little child with curls of gold,
dispatched to school with brush and comb,
though you are only four years old,
what do you do when you come home?

'I go and hide under the table.
I am angry with my ma.
She has to work so we are able
to have a nice house and a car.'

With this the cleric gave a little bow
and took his leave. The President said, 'Now
come here and look at this.' I saw a dome
of glass, which held a model of our home
and all the roofs around it, with the church
steeple in the distance. From our perch
outside the flat we saw everything here
just as portrayed; and, as I leaned to peer
more closely at the so-familiar view,
my guide said, 'What does all this mean to you?
What thought is conjured in your mind by these?'
I said, 'A conversation with Louise
when we sat out here on the night of Hew's
house-warming. Recently he'd sold his mews
and moved to a prestigious new address.
That night Louise put on her newest dress;
she waxed her legs and put her hair up too.
Arriving at the party, we found Hew
in bluff and genial form. He seemed excited
to see us, and immediately invited
the two of us to tour the house with him,
showing us round the indoor pool and gym,
and all the rest of it. Dinner was seated –
business people mainly, but completed
by just a smattering of slightly arty
types, vaguely familiar from the parties
at Louise's gallery. I guessed
there must have been fifteen or twenty guests
present, and there seemed to be almost
as many catering staff. I saw our host
had put Louise beside him; she was making
him laugh repeatedly – there's no mistaking

Louise's charm, the spell she could exert
so easily on men. With those alert
movements of her head, her coffee eyes
aglitter, she could almost hypnotize;
and with her hair tied up, her slender neck
was elegantly freed, and the effect
was heightened by the odd lock curling free.
Hew was entranced by her. Who wouldn't be?
Meanwhile, with less fluency, at my table
I talked fashion, as well as I was able,
with the designer Wilhelmina Fleiss.
Mannish, cropped hair, with eyes of muddied ice,
she wore a suit and looked like a cliché
lesbian, though I'd heard people say
she had no lovers, whether girl or man.
Whatever her leanings, she now began
by telling me how beautiful Louise
was looking, hinted with practised ease
that she would like to dress her, then she paused
before she asked me how Loretta was.
I said I hadn't seen her, which was true.
She said, "I often used to see you two
around together." It seemed like an appeal
to speak in confidence, and made me feel
very uneasy.

   'True, without a doubt
a lot of people seemed to know about
our love affair, and yet that didn't mean
I wanted to confide in Wilhelmine,
and all the less since she was known to be
a gossip-monger of the first degree.
She seemed to get the message. Now she moved
on to a topic I felt she approved
more than almost any, listing with pleasure
the actresses and ladies of leisure
whom she had dressed. And yet, for all her chatter
about celebrity, I felt what really mattered

to everybody here, including her –
the mark of tribal status as it were –
was purely money, and the things it bought
were picked at random, almost an afterthought:
the trophy wives, contemporary art,
desired less for themselves than for their part
in demonstrating it. It made me feel
disreputable, rather down-at-heel,
and suddenly I experienced an aching
to earn far more money than I was making.

'Over coffee, I felt my phone vibrate:
a text sent by my secretary, Kate,
who was our babysitter for that night.
Jack had been sick and, though he was all right,
the message seemed to offer me a way
to make myself an early getaway –
a chance I was happy enough to seize.
I said goodbye to Hew and told Louise
I'd deal with it and she was not to hurry:
for sure, there wasn't any cause to worry.
At home I let Kate go, and for a spell
sat at Jack's bedside, sang to him as well,
until I sensed a soothing sleep descend
upon him in the darkness. In the end
Louise came home, we went outside to chat,
sitting on the roof outside our flat,
talking about the party, drinking beer,
and looking at the roofs which you see here.'
I gestured to the model, and my guide
said nothing, but by nodding testified
that he was listening. I felt impelled
to go on with the story and to tell
the things we said that night.

                                    'The moon rose higher
into the sky, above the church's spire,
and glinted on the slate roofs and the tiles
like silver dust; Louise was tetchy, riled

by some resentment which she left unstated.
I wondered if she might be irritated
that I had left the dinner, and confessed
how little I'd enjoyed it. I tried to express,
not too revealingly, the slight unease
I felt around those people. But Louise
was having none of it: "I don't agree.
I took them as I found them, and to me
they seemed pretty good-natured. In the end
those guys want to have fun and be your friend
like anybody else, really."
                          I thought
how women always end up being caught
unawares by their own beauty. Then
I thought of how she'd said, time and again,
when we got married, how much more she liked
the company of Raoul, Joe, and Mike,
and my musician friends, than all the rich
kids she had met at private school. She'd ditched
her parents' milieu easily enough –
but had she already come to miss that stuff:
her parents' world, the happy childhood days
in the long garden, by the shining Bay?
Almost as if she'd read my thoughts, she now
began to talk about her dad and how
she had misjudged him. I observed her bright
staccato movements in the silver light,
and also the intelligent dark eyes,
as black as olives. Now she recognized
with hindsight what she'd hated as their wealth
was really their control over herself.
She cocked her head. "But now I'm over that,
and looking back I feel I've been a prat.
Of course no one needs money when they're young,
but once you have your children, once you're hung
with some responsibility, you start
to find it useful, it can play a part.

And if you have some, what's wrong with a lot?
And that reminds me, Hew has bought the yacht
he always wanted, he was telling me
tonight at dinner, and if you agree
he wants to take us to the Hebrides."
I said, "What has become of the Louise
who ran away and lived with the sadhu?
In Goa, when I fell in love with you,
I certainly never proposed myself
as someone who could hope to bring you wealth."
"I know," she said, impatiently. "Your wife
is never going to have that kind of life.
And I don't care. But I admit I'd find
it fun to do a voyage of that kind.
I can't see any reason to eschew it,
and personally I'm looking forward to it."
I felt lacking. And yet, when I compared
myself with how my grandfather had fared,
or my father, I was far better off,
though both of them would certainly have scoffed
to think that they had lacked for anything.
In the Navy, money was never the main thing.'

If you can set your thoughts aside,
it is said in the East
that perfect consciousness will dawn
when mental life has ceased.

Sex is ruled by power and rank,
by riches and applause,
and clothed by them according to
their sumptuary laws.

Your gloves are cast aside, my love,
your coat lies by the door,
your dress, discarded hurriedly,
is crumpled on the floor.

You have unclasped the jewellery
which so few could afford,
admired by most, despised by some,
but never quite ignored.

The night is yours, my love, all yours;
the sun sets in the west.
Who now can see this naked form
and not count himself blessed?

We left behind the scale model of our rooftop demesne,
and as we walked, the President explained:
'For people today, money in large amounts
is almost the universal thing that counts
for status, but it wasn't always so.
Before the money economy, long ago,
the priests and warriors were privileged
as least as much as the wealthy personage
is in industrial economies.
Look over there: you see the ceremonies
of priestly Brahmins being carried out.
Their ancient scriptures leave no room for doubt
about the ranking of society.
The thing was based on ritual purity:
the Brahmins first, of course, and after them
the warriors and military men,
with merchants coming in a feeble third –
such was the order which their rules conferred.
When I spoke of a passion for esteem
a moment since, I certainly didn't mean
a lust for money. No, that was a view
which I despised wholly as much as you –'
he nodded at my guide – 'who always hated
the notion that success could be equated
with lucre: an intolerable idea
to which you gave the name of "dollaria".'

We left the Brahmins now and made our way
along a passage, to the next display,
consisting of a pair of robed Chinese
who sat upon the floor taking their ease
with scrolls of painting and calligraphy.
The President observed, 'These two you see
are from the Yuan period – gentlemen,
or chun tzu, who adopt the way of jen,
or humane-ness. That fellow over there
has painted those; his friend's a millionaire,
a landlord, and a connoisseur, who buys
the painting from him. Both men would despise
the thought of any money changing hands.
A gift is offered, each one understands
that this is valuable, and yet no slur
upon the artist's status is inferred.'

As we walked on, a man came into view,
attired in not much more than some tattoos,
who greeted us. 'My home is in a land
of plenty, where the timber-bearing stands
of spruce and cedar grow profuse and tall,
promoted by a plentiful rainfall.
The mountains give us military seclusion,
the sea its hordes of fish in such profusion,
starvation is unknown. We are the tribes
of the potlatch, our status is ascribed
according to the sum of property
which we can give away or cause to be
destroyed. My people are the Koskimo,
a proud tribe from Prince Rupert who don't know
what it is to suffer a rebuttal.
We used to make war on the Kwakiutl
with bows and arrows, heavy clubs, and daggers,
but now we fight with property. We stagger
our rival nations with the sheer amount
of fish oil at the feast, and by the count

of blankets and canoes we give away
and numbers of potlatches we defray.'
And now he drew a curtain to reveal
upon a plinth a blackish metal shield
upon the face of which was figured out
a crude engraving of a brown bear's snout.
'My people call this a "copper",' he said,
'although the front is covered in black lead.
From an artistic point of view you'll see
it's nothing too unique, and certainly
the value of the metal isn't great,
and yet the price of coppers can inflate
vertiginously. The way that works
is one of our society's strangest quirks:
when one of these coppers comes to be sold,
the buyer of it must outdo the old
value which was paid for it before,
and so the copper's valued ever more
expensively, each time it changes hands.
They are the pure expression of a man's
status, and anyone with real ambition
may well be beggared by an acquisition.'
I thought of Louise and the sumptuous home
in San Francisco, and the time I'd flown
from India to find her. In the hall,
those giant paintings hanging on the wall –
Rothko, Pollock, Warhol, Lichtenstein –
and then the basement gallery, a shrine
to Art. An ordinary boy like me
never imagined that he'd get to see
artists this famous outside the confines
of a museum. Certainly, Yves Kleins
had never been referred to by Louise
at any point when in the Goanese
café she did a doodle of a ship
and wrote my name on it. I bit my lip,

keeping whatever cool that I could feign
as Candy went round, saying artists' names
by way of commentary. If I felt cowed
by that display, well, they were all gone now.

The portly President, my guide, and I
took up our way again, saying goodbye
to our friend the Koskimo. And as we went,
and neither colleague ventured a comment,
I found myself telling them, 'Pretty soon
after we had the talk beneath the moon
out on the rooftop, Louise went away
to Spain, to an art fair, for a few days.
Unluckily for me, just at this time
I woke up, sneezed abruptly, and my spine
locked up. So there I was, hobbling about,
trying to cope with work and Jack. I doubt
I could have managed were it not for Kate,
who came over and helped to put things straight.
This plain girl, with the always-about-to-laugh
expression, who in some ways still seemed half
a child, came in and cooked for me and Jack,
bathed him, and even massaged my sore back.
And it was after one of these sessions
that suddenly I felt the soft impression
of her lips, just below my nape, and then
she said, "I'm away now; I'll come again
tomorrow morning before work. Goodbye."
My brain stopped; I was powerless to reply.
I felt a rush, not so much of desire
as of pure happiness. After the dire
months without sex, this blotchily complexioned
girl made me a gesture of affection
and suddenly my spirits rose. I laughed
and took some Disprin, soaked in a hot bath,
and then went through to hustle Jack to bed.
There I found her under the bedspread

with Jack, upon the sofa, side by side
in front of the TV, preoccupied
with a computer game. To be truthful,
seeing her like that, she seemed too youthful
for me to sleep with now, even supposing
that I had been prepared to risk proposing
such a thing. Which I was not. My main,
in fact my only, wish was to regain
Louise's confidence. I was haunted
by my betrayal: in my heart I wanted
to run the movie backwards, from the sour
fruit I had cultivated to the flower
from which it had grown in so little time.
It seemed such a short sequence to rewind.'

Rounding a bend, the three of us now came
to an arch of bunting with the headline 'FAME!'
which we passed underneath, and here we found
an AstroTurf laid out upon the ground.
A score of naked men stood on this sward
with shrivelled genitals, preparing swords,
strapping on armour, combing their long hair,
as they waited for battle. 'Now, look there,'
the President advised. 'The Spartan hoplites wait
for death or triumph. Nothing is so great
an honour for them as to give their lives
in combat. The mentality derives
from one of humankind's strangest conceits:
the clearly false conception that you cheat
on death by winning durable renown –
you die, but not quite, since, though you go down
to Hades, still your name survives on earth
immortally.'
                         Across the AstroTurf
we saw a man approaching now, without
a spear or shield, and clad in robes, a stout

fellow who addressed us in this way:
'I didn't state my views, but had my say
by letting truth emerge from dialectic,
and gave the arguments to an eclectic
group of characters, real or fictitious.
I thought the role of family was pernicious,
believed that on the whole women were fettered
by motherhood, and kept back from the better,
more active life that was enjoyed by men;
but once my own Republic happened, then
women would be able to excel
as warriors and philosophers as well.
As for having children, for my part
I thought that virtue, literature, and art
were better things by far to procreate
than sons or daughters. Anyone would rate
them so, and look with envy at Homer
and Hesiod; anyone would prefer
to have this sort of offspring if they could,
which brings them glory and which has withstood
the longest test of time.'
                    He hesitated,
then, in a more informal manner, stated,
'Well, yes, OK, it's nonsense, I agree.
How could it be of benefit to me
once I am dead? How could anything?
What benefit will folk remembering
my name bring me? It's claptrap, even dafter
than the one about the life hereafter.
And yet . . . and yet the notion is seductive.
Why is it? Do you have any instructive
insight in the matter? Is it just
that death's so terrifying that we must
seek out whatever comfort we can find,
even when it's a deluded kind?'

He looked at my companion, but this last
was not listening, in fact was looking past
him at a fellow who was hanging round
rather shyly, staring at the ground.
He was a small man with an elvish look,
a little portly, carrying a book,
and wore a hood and cassock-like costume.
He said, 'I lived at Aldgate in some rooms
over the gate itself. I ran the wool
customs at the time, my days were full
of weighing, and of merchants trying to shirk
their taxes. Then at night I set to work
writing my book. But though I sat up late,
my head was full of tariffs, fines, and weights,
and on my days of rest I had my boys,
Lewis and Tom, with all their games and noise,
who hung around my desk, such was their need
for Daddy, like a pair of hounds whose feed
is overdue. I never did complete
that story. The intention was to treat
of fame, so I recounted how an eagle
had swept me up and flew me to a regal
mansion in the heavens. There I found
that beautiful woman who gives renown
to mortals, and I witnessed then how random
she was, dispensing fame with wild abandon
to people who'd done nothing to deserve,
as much as those who did. And I observed
how randomly she withheld it as well
from those with real merit, and repelled
deserving suitors so their names would be
snuffed out, forgotten for eternity.'

When fish swim in an ordered school,
their predators select
the one not perfectly aligned –
the 'oddity effect',

the leadership illusion,
is not a case of rule:
they keep place by adjusting to
the others in the school,

and when the group adopts a new
direction for a spell,
a new front one's established who
can lead them just as well.

Charles the King of England
thought fashion was a shame,
he thought its fickle wastefulness
was something he could tame.

He used his royal status,
he used his royal guile;
decided to make a fashion that
would always be in style.

He made up the design himself,
called it the Persian vest –
of course it soon went out of date
just like all the rest.

As we walked on, I said to my two companions,
'About this time, the bank resolved to send
my boss to the Far East and have him spend
a month there, setting up a partnership.
I noticed his assistant, Jane, let slip
some of her old aloofness now, maybe
because in Clint's absence she felt more free
to be one of the gang, or else perhaps
she just had less to do, and longer gaps
between his calls from China and Japan.
Whatever the reason, I now began
to see her, in her high-neck tops and pearls,
chatting away with all the other girls.

So after work I took her for a drink
and she confided, "I usually think
there's too much on and wish he'd go away
but now it's been so long I have to say
I'm kind of bored." Like everyone at the bank,
I knew that they were lovers, but I shrank
from mentioning it openly. Instead
I tried to be ambiguous, and said,
"I'm sure he's missing you out there." But Jane
made no pretence. "Men are all the same.
They tell their lovers that they're more important
than their wives, but really women oughtn't
to fall for this, and when they say they'll leave them,
a lover would be crazy to believe them.
They say it just to keep us hanging on.
Few of them really cross that Rubicon,
as Clint calls it. You're probably the same."
"But I don't have a lover." "Really?" said Jane.
She looked conspiratorial and smirked.
I raised a hand in protest. I was irked
that everybody knew I'd had a thing
with Loretta; it was enough to bring
about a guilty look, even a blush.
Jane said, "I think that Kate has got a crush
on you." I said, "I'm sure you're wrong." She raised
her eyebrows. "Really? I wouldn't be amazed.
She seems to be always around your flat –
isn't there something telling about that?"
"Not really. She just comes to babysit."
"Are you sure you don't fancy her a bit?"
"No. I do like Kate, but in the end
she's just a little girl, a family friend,
delightful in many ways, I can agree,
but not someone desirable to me.
Not in that way. It may sound shameful, Jane,
the truth is, I'm just not turned on by plain

women." She said, "You mean the blotchy skin?"
"What I mean is, the girls who really win
my notice, and the ones that I pursue,
are the great beauties." Then I said: "Like you."

'We went to her apartment. In the hall
a pair of skis was propped against the wall;
in fact, the whole place spoke her love of sports:
photos of kayaking and ski resorts,
the yellow Three Peaks Challenge baseball cap,
and swimming goggles hanging from a tap.
A picture of her father in the loo
was evidence he'd been athletic too,
holding a silver cup, a champion
at university for pentathlon.
Jane lit the pebble gas fire. First she found
some lager in the fridge, then hunted round
to find an opener. She was self-possessed
and full of modesty, as usual dressed
in a long skirt and with a high-necked sweater.
I remembered how sarcastically Loretta
had spoken of her, saying she'd make a good
Englishwoman in a Hollywood
movie, the way she dressed. But that was small
wonder: she was competitive with all
women, and especially in Jane's case,
whose beauty was much more than commonplace.
I thought, "Dear God, what am I doing here?"
and, walking over to the window, peered
down into the street. It seemed insane
of me to let this happen, since if Jane
was indiscreet, even to a single friend,
soon everyone would know, and in the end
Louise would get to hear, and she would be
incensed, and even more estranged from me.
Too late. Jane was already at my side,
and now I felt my arm begin to glide

all of its own accord, and draw her near.
I felt her little waist through the cashmere
sweater, felt my heart career, felt guilt
for what was happening; I saw her tilt
her face to mine, looked into those grey eyes,
tasted the wide mouth. It's no surprise,
after the many months of chastity,
that I was drunk with happiness to see
her clothes come off, the whiteness of her skin,
the little hazel triangle; begin
with her that awkward, ancient pantomime;
and find her role as unreserved as mine.'

And now we had arrived before a bank
of TV screens. Although they all stood blank
to start with, one by one they now began
to light up with the portrait of a man.
He said, 'We had more fame than anyone.
OK, OK, I'll grant we had some fun
at first, but to be honest, later on
we were too much of a phenomenon.
For me, the best bit was the time before
we got famous. Listen, I know the score:
photographers chasing your car, the crowd
outside the hotel, everything allowed,
and every pretty girl wanting to date us.
Yes, I know a thing or two 'bout status,
but it was never paramount for me;
my issue was spirituality.
Think for yourself: what the world thinks of you
is an illusion you may come to rue.
The nicest thing's to open the newspaper
and not find yourself in it. All that caper
with press and television goes away
if you're lucky, but in a deeper way

I'm not sure you can totally eschew
the stuff society demands of you.
In my case I suppose that was the songs.'

The image froze up and, among those throngs
of TVs, one displayed a bobbing green
pointer which moved across its blackened screen:
the cardiac monitor of hospitals.
And now a thick black rain began to fall
across my vision, I started to black out,
and clung to that screen as a last redoubt
against unconsciousness. I lost the track
of everything, I found I was on my back,
lying in bed, a vile nausea gripped
my whole body, and tubes of plastic slipped,
Medusa-like, out of my arms and head.
I wondered if I was already dead
or maybe just dying; and then the rain
thinned, and I was on my feet again:
the tubes had vanished. Now, my vision cleared,
the President's plump figure reappeared,
comfortingly solid, and at his side
the reassuring figure of my guide,
who sucked on his cigar, and looked at me
with some concern. He said, 'It seems to me
true that the joys of status are alluring;
true, too, that few passions are so enduring;
and yet the satisfaction we have there
is like sweeties for children as compared
with that of love.'

In the great house a kind of rent:
the small talk which incessantly
alludes to the social ornament
and prestige of the company.

But on the attic floor, distraint
of clothing, inhibition, show;
in that breathless moment how faint
the sound of voices down below.

If we could stay, my darling girl,
in that pained urgency of lovers,
careless of rent, of the whole world,
I think then we would live forever.

But years go by, and now we hear
the voices louder than before,
and now we have to go downstairs
and we must join the talk once more,

and if you see me now resigned
to speak of property or pearls,
remember there was that other time,
though it seems like another world.

My companions and I left the bank of screens now, and progressed
to where a young man waited for us, dressed
in ornate yellow robes, standing erect,
and spoke this discourse: 'I did not expect
to rule my empire. A single family,
pre-eminent in the nobility,
had taken charge of that. They had control
of my army and government; my role
was ceremonial, just a puppet who
had no deals and no politics to do.
I never made, but only signed, the law;
and yet my status held the world in awe.
You have to understand that my Japan
was an empire where every noble man
who owned a shinden near the palace quarter
burned with ambition to present a daughter –
often enough a pre-pubescent girl –
to the supposed ruler of the world.

Because of this, Heian society
had grown, like crystals, a variety
of different relationships with women
for the Emperor to have: beginning
with the Empress at the top, descending
through various categories of wife, and ending
with the concubines. And so you see
liaisons of all kinds were forced on me.
It wasn't that I specially desired
these well-born girls; more, that it was required
by my high-ranking nobles of their liege
that I should make imperial prestige
widely available.'

          This solemn-faced
young man now slipped away, and was replaced
by another, cheerier fellow, wreathed about
with violets and ivy. And no doubt
he had been drinking, too, because his face
was flushed. 'The man I love doesn't embrace
status,' he told us. 'His priorities
were very different from society's.
Any advantage which can be possessed
for which a person might be thought as blessed,
and which the world admires, you can be sure
that, for my teacher, this has no allure:
not money, with its helicopter rides,
or trophy real estate, or trophy brides,
not great talent in music or the arts,
not even great intelligence which charts
new frontiers of knowledge – none of these
weigh very much at all with Socrates.
I am a general and a politician
but, acting to fulfil either position,
I have to turn aside from all the things
the world admires, and when the siren sings
I plug my ears with wax, and steer my course
closer to what my teacher will endorse.

I'm always conscious that in leaving him
I'm passing up the best, and giving in
to my desire for those honours which come
from ordinary people; I succumb
to what the world admires, and eschew
what I feel to be right and good and true.
Whereas, for him, status doesn't intrude
upon his life at all. This attitude,
for which in our day people thought him odd,
was later on attributed to God,
before Whom all the princes, popes, and kings
were no more worthy than their underlings.'

Green seas and islands of no worth,
country where sugar failed to grow,
forgotten corner of the earth,
without a godown or silo –
why would a person want to go
where there's no metal to be won,
where nothing shines except the sun?

No one then wanted to frazzle
on a beach of coral sand;
rather to dress in silk or dazzle
London with a four-in-hand,
or perhaps a palace on the Strand.
A few miles of somewhere like Kent
would also be money well spent.

But then a sudden change of fashion
brings the city to the coast.
Society finds a new passion
for lying in the sun. The most
forgotten island can now boast
champagne and liquor by the crate,
prestigious shops, and real estate.

Forgotten isle, forgotten isle,
where you and I walked hand in hand
along the empty beaches while
the sandpipers fed in the sand;
forgotten now, your moment spanned
millennia, then in a trice
became everyone's paradise.

Custom

Taking our leave now of the President,
we found the Status gift shop, where we spent
our money on some famous brands, and then
passed out into the Park's main street again.
My guide lit a cigar. And as we strode
along the traffic-free and well-washed road,
I said to him, 'Though Jane and I were lovers,
at work we still behaved to one another
as if nothing had changed. I lunched alone
and after work I often headed home –
Louise was out of town – to check on Jack.
But after the briefest time there, I'd be back
outside, headed for Jane's. On other days,
unable to endure any delay,
I went straight to her, staying until late
and only heading homewards because Kate
(who was my babysitter) had to go.
During those days she earned a lot of dough.
Even Louise, out in the USA,
became aware how much I was away
from the apartment. Jane and I both knew
how little time was left us to pursue
this love affair, since both Louise and Clint
would soon be coming back, and then our stint
would be used up. I think somehow we found
this deadline set us free: since we were bound
to part in any case, until that day
it felt as if we didn't have to weigh
the consequences. As you might have guessed,
there was a downside to this recklessness.

One day (it was her birthday) we both skived
off work, got in the car and took a drive
southwards out of London. Our idea
was to have lunch in Brighton, see the pier,
and maybe walk up on the Downs as well.
But then it rained. We went to a hotel
instead. Here, on the grand staircase,
some kind of fashion shoot was taking place.
As I signed in with an invented name,
I saw the models scrutinizing Jane.
Just then a voice said, "Hello, Pat, how nice,
and what a surprise!" – Wilhelmina Fleiss.
She didn't say, "What are you doing here?" –
she didn't have to; the answer was clear
for anyone to see. But even so
I should at least have made a better show;
perhaps going for coffee and then leaving
for everyone to see, at least achieving
some kind of arguably innocent
performance, which later I could invent
a story round which wasn't simply fucking
Jane upstairs.

        'But now, instead of ducking,
I did something utterly unambiguous:
I walked to the lift with Jane. It was a fatuous
error to make: where else could one assume
we were headed, other than to a room?
What other explanation could there be?
I wanted Jane just then to a degree
where no more sane objective could defer
the one of getting into bed with her,
feeling her skin, her hair, her woman's touch –
yes, in all truth, I wanted her that much.
As soon as she and I were in the lift
I said, "Oh, crap." And she, catching my drift,
said, "Who was she?" "An acquaintance of mine,
and someone I suspect will talk, big time."

"Couldn't you ask her just to be discreet?"
"I don't know her so well. We sometimes meet
at parties. Well, I've met her once or twice.
Perhaps she'll keep her big mouth shut. Oh, Christ."
Once in our room we straight away had sex
for a long time, and afterwards we slept,
and then drank tea in bed.

                 'Although this girl
was exquisite, truly Venus in pearls,
up to this point in our relationship
she didn't have that painful, nagging grip
she had on me later. Sometimes I thought
that sex for her was something like a sport
and that if I played tennis, or could ski,
or ride, she would as soon do that with me
as lie here on my shoulder while the rain
flurried and dribbled on the window panes.
Sex is an ideal sport for English weather,
and since, until that afternoon, I never
found very much to talk about with Jane,
I was just thinking, "Maybe once again . . ."
when suddenly she started telling me
how her mother had died when she was three,
and how she had no memory of her, and how
she felt an emptiness about that now.
I said, "Like me, only mine didn't die:
she got a better job and said goodbye,
sent me to Ballyclare to my grandmother,
and went off to Nigeria with her lover."
And now we started telling and comparing
childhood memories, and in this sharing
I found, perhaps for the first time between us,
a discourse which felt properly spontaneous.
After this, Jane was different. I sensed
she wanted something urgent, more intense,
between us; and this made me feel at best
uneasy, and at worst not quite honest.

That weekend we went out to a Chinese
restaurant (chosen because Louise
and I had never been there). As we ate
our prawns, she started to elaborate
a fantasy about how she and I
could spend some time together, how we'd fly
to a deserted coast and find a beach
with no hotel on it, and she would teach
me how to scuba dive, and we'd explore
the reefs which stood off from the circling shore,
and photograph together schools of bright
yellow and purple fishes, and at night
sleep in a straw cabana by the bay.
Of course I knew that such a holiday,
however much it might be to my taste,
could never in reality take place
because Louise would learn about the trip,
and anyway my whole relationship
with Jane couldn't have possibly survived
beyond next Friday when Louise arrived
back from America. And I could tell
that Jane must have been thinking this as well,
because she said, "What's going to happen when
Clint re-appears?" I said, "You'll start again
where you left off with him." "What just like that?
D'you really think it's so straightforward, Pat?"
She pouted, and her face took on a stern
aspect, and she came over taciturn.
Later that evening, lying in the bed
at her apartment, suddenly she said,
"I really like this, Pat. What about you?"
"For sure." She said, "I wonder if that's true.
This really means something to me, you know."
There was a long silence. I let it go.
At last she spoke again: "And does Louise
love you?" "I think she does, but by degrees
we've grown more distant. I'm no longer sure.
She doesn't want to have sex any more."

"What, not at all? Never?" "Well, hardly ever.
It does make it a strain living together."
"Why don't you leave her then?" I said, "I guess
I am committed to the marriage. Yes."
"I think you're still in love with her, that's why."
To this I found I hadn't a reply.
She said, "I know that Clint won't leave his wife,
and I'm fed up with it. It's not a life.
We're always hiding, always circumspect.
He doesn't put me first, but he expects
that I should always keep myself for him,
available when he can fit me in.
Perhaps I should leave him." I said, "Perhaps."
This is so non-committal that she snaps:
"You're not even trying to understand!"
I looked at her, taking her by the hand:
her blonde hair was all tangled at the back;
between her soft grey eyes a tiny crack
of displeasure was etched upon her brow.
I said, "I'm being honest with you now:
what are you doing having these affairs
with married men? You're beautiful, who cares
what married men want? Sweetie, there are scores
of single men out there who would adore
to love you, marry you, give you a child,
anything you want. You are beguiled
by something in yourself. The thing is, Jane,
it's always very easy to complain
that Clint, and even I myself, are using
you – but Jane, you are the one who's choosing
married men."'

     I added, to my guide,
'Tell me, my friend, was I not justified?
Human emotions are like social custom:
once formed, it isn't easy to adjust them.
We favour what's familiar. I can see
you're thinking this applies as much to me

as her – and yes, of course I am aware
of that as well. Haven't we all been there?
It's easier to advise than to take action.'

We were advancing on the next attraction:
its façade was a Queen Anne country seat,
half life-size, and constructed in concrete,
but painted out to look like brick. The door
was open, and a sign against it bore
the title 'Conservation – National Trust'.
Below, in smaller letters, was discussed
the restoration which had taken place:
all later supplements had been effaced,
and rooms put back to their initial state;
the colours of the walls were accurate
to ancient hues which had been overpainted,
and period furniture supplied, untainted
by modern gilt and like anachronisms.
Likewise a thoroughgoing exorcism
of later bow windows and a French door
was made, and the originals restored.
All in all, it was a striking tale
of know-how and attention to detail
which spared no pains to keep the past intact.
As we went in, a man gave us a tract
condemning Darwin's theory, which we took.

Ahead of us, inside a spotlit nook,
I saw a waxwork which I scrutinized
for a moment, and seemed to recognize:
the fine patrician features, the cheroot,
the military moustache, and linen suit.
I said, 'He is the king with whom I stayed
in India that time, the one who made
a guest-house of his palace. It was he
whose marriage had turned out so happily
in spite of being arranged, the one whose queen
had made that courtyard garden of supreme

loveliness, unaided. And while she
had tended to her plants so lovingly,
the raja acted as my cicerone,
showing me round his erstwhile patrimony.
"If it was all still ours, you wouldn't see
this kind of a modern monstrosity,"
he said, pointing to an enormous villa.
"That one was built by our local distiller.
These jumped-up fellows always want to be
bigger than everybody else. To me,
all of that marble's inappropriate –
quite vulgar, actually. It violates
the architectural integrity
of the whole town." The raja honestly
was unable to see that this distiller,
in building his enormous marble villa,
was doing what his ancestors had done
when, centuries ago, they had begun
his own big marble house. And, strange to say,
a part of me could share in this dismay
at novelty.'

        My guide said, 'In the end,
we like what is familiar, and we tend
to be suspicious of whatever's new.
Custom is a consoling social glue
which binds us solidly to other folk.'
I could make out behind him as he spoke
a figure shambling down the corridor
towards us. We had seen the guy before:
tall, sandy-haired, with an intelligent
demeanour, one of two past Presidents
we'd met in the White House.

        He saw us now
and pitched right in: 'My friends, you must allow
that even revolutionaries can be
conservative, and this applies to me
as much as any. Looking at the span
of human history, it's clear that Man

as a species is switching habitat
from something agricultural to that
of cities made of asphalt and of glass,
where, sheltered and protected, he can pass
a cosy life. Half our population
already lives inside these conurbations,
and clearly in the future all men will.
Yet in my heart I much preferred to till
the soil, and hoped my country could retain
the old economy of beasts and grain
as much as possible. For, in my view,
a durable and genuine virtue
was to be found in farming folk alone,
since no people in history had shown
a case of corrupt morals in the mass
of cultivators. If I look an ass
in hindsight, I can say in my defence
that all men hold custom in reverence
to some degree. And if I didn't see
the future of our great economy,
I'm not the only rebel to combine
my revolution with an anodyne
conservatism. Many who decry
the power of capital are fighting shy
of change; and eco-warriors seem to think
that no species need ever go extinct,
as if a revolution in Man's will
might order evolution to stand still:
the ultimate conservative position.
Mankind likes what it knows, it likes tradition.
All changes in habits of life and thought
are irksome to us, usually wrought
reluctantly, or made with reservation.
I said it clearly in my Declaration
when I wrote, "All experience has shown
that humankind is more disposed to groan
and suffer evil when it is a norm
they're used to than they are to seek reform

or overturn the cause of their oppression."
Our love of the familiar finds expression
in all custom, and every neighbourhood.
Whatever is familiar, feels good.'

We left him, and went forward in the gloom
until the passage gave into a room
with just a single exhibit inside
a glass display case. I said to my guide,
'I recognize that mug. Look, there's the crest
of West Ham on the side. At the request
of Peter Marsh, from Personnel, I went
to see him in his office. He was bent,
head down over his desk, and when he spoke
at last, his voice sounded high-pitched and choked,
his eyes were shifty, looking up to me
from where his hands cradled this mug of tea
upon the desk. "Patrick," he said, "the news
isn't good. But I cannot refuse
to do my duty, even when it ends
by putting me at loggerheads with friends."
We weren't friends. But it wasn't hard to see
this wasn't going to end up well for me.
"Patrick, I want to be open and frank.
You know that our objective at the bank
is to create a team. For this we must
communicate and have each other's trust.
Bonding is helpful to our corporate goals –
it's why we did the 'walk on burning coals'
weekend. Can you remember how resistant
some people were ? But Clint, he was insistent
that everybody came. He really cares
about this bonding thing. But, Patrick, there's
the point. Clint . . . well, he doesn't seem
to feel that you are really on the team.
That doesn't necessarily reflect
my own views, but I do have to respect

my boss's judgement call. Look, I know
this may seem harsh: we have to let you go."
I said, "So Clint's back then." Peter said, "Right.
He flew in from Osaka late last night."

'That evening I rang Jane. She sounded tired
and drunk. She said, "I'm sorry you were fired.
That's really terrible." I said, "So why'd
you have to tell Clint, then?" She said, "I tried
not to, but it wasn't any good.
As soon as he saw me, he understood
something was up. It just didn't make sense,
he said, for us to nourish a pretence.
It wasn't that kind of relationship.
And I agreed, really." I bit my lip,
and stared down at the phone. "I see . . . And then
you told him." "Yes I did, and that was when
he said he'd fire you. It was a surprise
to me; of course, I didn't realize
he'd take it like that." "No. Of course." I felt
exasperated. How could she have dealt
me such a blow with such insouciance?
But I was starting to experience
another feeling, as yet vague and dim:
a consciousness that she was choosing him.
This was an unexpected bit of news;
to put it in the terms Jane might have used,
it was like snorkelling off a precipice:
suddenly beneath me an abyss
had opened up, but I just kept on swimming,
'cause after all, we'd known from the beginning
this thing between us couldn't last for long . . .
hadn't we? And yet I had a strong
sense of unease arriving at the crunch.
I found myself saying, "Shall we have lunch?"
and she said, "We can't do that any more."
I said, "Well, yeah . . . I guess you're right . . . for sure."

But now that Jane no longer wanted me,
to my surprise I found she haunted me,
and as I went about trying to find
a new job, she was always on my mind.
Really, I thought of nothing but this girl –
her blouses buttoned to the neck, her pearls,
her lovely grey eyes.

                'Now I thought of it,
my feelings were precisely opposite
to what they'd been that rainy afternoon
we parleyed in the Brighton hotel room.
Then I'd insisted she return to Clint
when he came back. But now, after a stint
of being robbed of her, I was insane
to get her back. And now I couldn't gain
the least favour: she wouldn't take my calls,
and, as for emails, she ignored them all.
Eventually I got her on the phone
by subterfuge, and, hoping I had thrown
her off her guard, suggested we could meet
when she got out from work in a discreet
organic café which I knew nearby.
"What would be the point?" was her reply.
"Well, just to chat. Besides, I really miss
you, Jane." She answered, without emphasis,
"I miss you too. But I don't want to cheat
on Clint again." I said, "So we just meet
and have coffee together. Nothing more."
She said, "No, no, I can't. Don't be a bore."
That night I dreamed of Jane and the sadhu
in Goa, in the café. They were due
to leave together – "Just a little fling,"
Jane said. The sadhu'd given her a ring,
and she in turn agreed to be his bride.'

And now I heard the accents of my guide
beside me saying softly, 'When I saw
soldiers traumatized in the Great War,

I found many of those I came to treat
exhibited compulsion to repeat
unpleasant, even horrific, events in dreams.'

The yogi stretches on the lawn,
but still his pupil cannot follow.
A rigid joint will not perform
and go where it is asked to go.
Men stick to actions that they know;
and hands bitten by dogs before
are offered to the dogs once more.

And that is how the past persists;
it lives because mankind harks back:
the pilgrims in the Mayflower list
the princes in the Almanach
de Gotha; all their portraits track
with glaring eyes your passing through
this life. What do they want of you?

Like ancestors, your childhood past
has laid its own destructive spoor.
A sickening enthusiast,
it whines and scratches at the door,
dog-like, to run amok once more.
The girl who loved you yesterday –
how have you driven her away?

My child, everyone descends
from people in the past, but you
owe them nothing; and in the end
the clan, the god, the food taboo,
can have no special claim on you.
Those muscle memories of pain
make havoc where they come again.

Upon the lawn the bent fakir
performs his drills day after day.
Patient adjustments engineer

the posture of his protégé.
Even a heart is changed this way:
the limbs will move at your command,
the dog will bring your sticks to hand.

At home Louise was changing. She had started work full time
down at the gallery, where she combined
her usual duties with curating Hew's
mushrooming collection. And in view
of all his business, they were very pleased
to give him the assistance of Louise,
and there was even talk of him taking
a stake in the gallery. All this was making
Louise much busier than she'd been before,
so now with Jack at school I felt much more
alone than in the past. I spent my days
applying for jobs and writing résumés.
I looked for work in archaeology
as well as banking, since a part of me
still toyed with the idea of going back
to my first love; but still a total lack
of success greeted every application.
Day by day, this programme of frustration
started to get to me, and, for the sake
of getting out, I now began to take
walks around the city. Spring was just
turning to early summer; the robust
green of new leaves stood out against the black
polluted tree trunks; summer clothes were back
in all the shops; and in the parks the sour
and haunting perfume of hawthorn in flower.

Jane obsessed me now. A head of blond
hair like hers, spotted beside a pond
on Hampstead Heath, or else a herringbone
jacket like hers, crossing the Marylebone

High Street – glimpses like these were all it took
to make me think I'd seen her, and to look
again, and find I hadn't. I remember well,
walking along the Edgware Road, the smell
of fatty meat drifting from a kebab
parlour, I saw her step out of a cab
and go into a café, and I raced
across the road and rushed into that place,
calling her name. But it wasn't her.
Jane had been very clear that she'd prefer
me not to call, or visit her again,
and up to now I'd been pretty restrained,
though it was hard to fight against the urge.
But this encounter gave me such a surge
of new excitement, I could not suppress
my need to talk to her. The call was less
successful than I'd hoped. Jane sounded cold,
with no desire at all to be cajoled,
and eager just to end the conversation.

The weeks dragged onward in acute frustration.
Although I didn't want to be a pest,
the truth was I was getting too obsessed,
and kept on finding reasons to assail her
with online offerings, and to email her,
though she never replied. I can't pretend
I had much self-control. And in the end,
in spite of being told to stay away,
I drove to see her, found a parking bay
outside her house, and waited to confront
her on the pavement – just the kind of stunt
Loretta might have pulled. Oddly, it worked.
I saw her come towards me as I lurked
inside the car, and when she crossed the road
I clambered out and casually strode
into her path. 'My God!' she said. 'It's you.'
I said, 'Just happened to be passing through,

and thought I'd ring your bell . . .' (an idiotic
lie, but I was dazed by her hypnotic
grey eyes, and in fact could hardly speak).
She leaned forward and kissed me on the cheek,
and laughed. I could see from the get-go
she was happy to see me. And although
she'd told me not to call her or email,
now we were face to face she didn't fail
to usher me upstairs. And once in here,
my heart began to race, the atmosphere
between us was electric, suffocating;
some unexpected force was operating:
she seemed far lovelier than the girl I'd missed.
I put my arms round her, and when we kissed
to my surprise she was extremely willing,
and we went straight to bed. There was a thrilling
urgency about it, as her dress
came off, and now again her nakedness
seemed better than the image in my mind.
And afterwards, while we remained entwined
upon the bed, I told her, 'Jane, I've missed
you lots.' But Jane made no reply to this.
I said, 'These last few weeks I've understood
that you and I have something very good.'
She said, 'It makes me feel very bad.
Pat, we shouldn't be doing this, I'm sad,
I'm very sad to say it, in a way,
but Pat, I've promised Clint I'm going to stay
faithful to him from now.' I said, 'You've got
to be kidding. Because for sure he's not
faithful to you. He's married.' 'So are you.'
Well, there was no denying this was true.
I said, 'You know, when all is said and done,
my love life with Louise is moribund.'
Jane looked me in the eye; she said, 'You know
Clint's going to leave his wife quite soon, although

he wants the children to be more mature
before he takes that step.' I thought, 'Yeah, sure
he does.' But what I heard my own voice say
was, 'Listen, Jane, I can't go on this way.
I think I'm going to have to leave Louise.'
'Really? Then I'm confused. I thought that she's
the big commitment you would never chuck,
no matter what other women you fuck.'
'Well, I don't think that now. You know, it's strange,
just recently I've seen the need to change
my life; I understand I need to break
with Louise now, really, for both our sakes.'
I said it, and maybe it seemed half true
at that moment, but coming home I knew
it was a lie.
        I found Louise and Jack
ensconced together, with a popcorn snack
in front of the TV. At this humdrum
display I was completely overcome
with regret. Later, when we went to bed,
I took Louise's hand in mine and said,
'We managed to be close on holiday;
couldn't we try to make it more that way
during our ordinary lives as well?'
Her hand gave no response, and I could tell
that this appeal had little force with her.
She said, 'You mean the outing to Big Sur?
But Pat, you know, when all is said and done,
it's difficult to feel close to someone
when they're unfaithful to you.' In her voice
something was clenched. She said, 'I'd have no choice
but to walk out if you did that again.'
Now, as I listened to the light refrain
of her snoring beside me, I reflected
whether by some sixth sense she had detected
that I had spent the evening having sex with Jane Day.

My love, remember this: dreams fade.
Though you call them to mind at first,
as time moves on they're overlaid
with a new logic and dispersed.
You can't summon them back. The worst
and best of them soon come to be
forgotten as our infancy.

Sometimes if you write them down,
that can evoke a recollection;
but weakened, like a hand-me-down
folk costume, which has lost connection
to its origin. Reflection
cannot discover in the words
a music which the dreamer heard.

Incense burnt to a residue,
the frescoes of the temples fade.
Woodworm attacked the gods' statues,
their shrines decayed at the roadside.
Eventually the old faith died,
there was no Bacchus or Silenus
now. Something was lost between us.

From here there can be no way back:
a single legion, last of many,
waits the barbarian attack
upon our ancient patrimony.
Look down on me, goddess Athene,
allow me one more deluded sleep
where that legion camps with no escape.

'If you can only stick with what you know, you won't get lost;
preserve the status quo at any cost
both in your self and in the universe.
Remember this: all change is for the worse.'
The speaker bore a tilak on his head,
a Brahmin sikha, and a sacred thread

slung across his shoulder. Beside him lay
a fire pit, water, ghee, and an array
of powders, a pressing-stone, and rice:
whatever was needed for the sacrifice.
'In the beginning, the ritual was done
to keep the world in order: for the sun
and rain to do their office as they should,
even for institutions to hold good,
like vows and contracts. In a congruous way,
cosmic disorder could be kept at bay
by ordering one's life in the correct
manner. This meant you must respect
the station you were born to, know your place,
and play your allotted role in every case
according to the sacred texts. Your caste
defined your occupation and would last
your whole lifetime; for there was no escape,
no cutting through that burdensome red tape
of duty, or "own-dharma"; though it's true
you could come back next lifetime with a new
identity. Till then you had to show
complete obedience to the status quo.
Be what you were born. You can't deny,
by any standards this must qualify
as socially conservative; and in the light
of how things are today, it seems the height
of reaction. But it is not my task
to condemn it. I would rather ask:
what did the system have that it endured
through the millennia? What was procured
by having social roles so well defined
and so immutable? Is humankind
disposed by nature to this kind of thing?
And does a tyranny of custom cling
like clothes on every nakedness?'

He takes his leave. The woman lies
heartsick on the hotel divan.
Frustrated love inside her cries,
and cried since the affair began,
but not for him. Whatever man
she takes on brings her something less
than what she might call happiness.

She sees the dhobi hunkered down
beside the river, hears the blow
his paddle makes upon the mound
of clothes. A century ago
the caste laws wouldn't let him know
anything else, and he was fated
to do the work his birth dictated.

Not any more. The time is past
when destiny found no relief.
The saddest moment for the caste
system is now, when the belief
in it is dying, but its fief
remains intact, and misery
is our own failure to be free.

She rises, and at the bedside
puts on her sari thoughtfully.
Vagina sore, unsatisfied,
she wonders how she came to be
in this place again. To free
yourself amounts to something more
than knowing what you were before

Aggression

We came to the gift shop and, passing through,
went out onto a sunny avenue
and strolled along it, carried by the crowds.
Occasionally a grotesque head stood proud
above this human river: in the Park,
while smaller-than-life-size was the hallmark
of real estate, the opposite was true
for actors in the 'streetmosphere' crew,
who typically had costumes which inflated,
or walked on stilts, or wore exaggerated
hands and heads as part of their disguise
to make them visible. I recognized
one of them now, not really in this case
a cartoon figure, but an actual face
from my own life: my secretary Kate's
father, his giant papier mâché pate
bobbing towards us now above the throng.
I told my colleague as we walked along,
'When I heard he'd died, I went around
to see if I could help. For once I found
Kate's cheerfulness muted, her glad eyes grave
and ringed by sleeplessness, and when I gave
a hug, she clung to me. We went upstairs
into her father's book-lined bedroom where
his corpse was laid upon the bed, the skin
waxy, the wrinkles on his face filled in
by death's belated plastic surgery:
he seemed a piece of sculpted ivory.
I saw at once that Kate found nothing horrid
about the corpse. She kissed him on the forehead,

remarking how his face looked strangely youthful,
which in a way it did, though to be truthful
it didn't seem like him at all. She replaced
the linen lovingly across his face,
and we descended to the kitchen.

                                        'Here
she had already laid up wine and beer
for after the cremation. She uncorked
one of the bottles, and we sat and talked,
the budgies fluttering round us in their cages
as she explained about the various stages
of settling his affairs. Her older brother
was seeing to the creditors and other
money matters (which weren't very great)
and had applied to deal with the estate –
the old man, typically, had left no will,
so there were special duties to fulfil.
After that she started reminiscing
about her father, saying how she'd miss him;
and during this conversation, from nowhere,
she asked if I'd restarted my affair
with Jane Day. I didn't bother trying
to deny it. With her father's body lying
stretched out upstairs beneath a linen sheet,
it seemed somehow pointless to use deceit.
She said, "The office definitely suspects
she's shagging you again." She seemed to reflect
for a moment, then said, "Would you say
your marriage is unhappy?" "In a way
it's going better than it was before,"
I said, with steadfast cheerfulness. I saw
from her expression that she was confounded
by this; even to me the statement sounded
unlikely. I believe her innocence
seduced me into trying to make sense
of it for her, and I went on: "You see,
in truth, Louise no longer wanted me;

we had no sex life; getting into bed
was every night a torture, and instead
of loving feelings bringing happiness,
a rock of anger formed inside my chest
and pressed on me till I could hardly breathe.
I couldn't sleep at all, I'd have to leave
the bedroom, even get out of the flat
to calm myself; but always worse than that
was the obscure depression that would seize
my insides then, crumbling like a disease
the bones of confidence within me. How
was I to dissipate the gloom which now
came drifting down in silent flakes to lay
across my spirit? Well, I found a way;
and since I've been with Jane the fury's ceased,
I feel more like myself, I'm more at ease –
more confident as well."'

*The traitor to his country, who's secretly disloyal
to all his friends, is bound to feel alone,
even if not exposed. And the end of all betrayal
will be this isolation in your home.*

*Louise takes off her dress. Unsettling as always,
her body is indifferent to your glances.
She turns towards the mirror, her curving back displays
lines of a cello, and to your advances*

*is equally unyielding. Now, however late
the hour, you'll never sleep. And in your mind
you feel the nausea rising, the sentences of hate,
one on the other. You would like to find*

*the most insulting verdict, the most hurtful attack.
So ask yourself: what kind of love is this?
This is a child's love; passion which must exact
a punishment for loving gone amiss.*

You go down to the car. And as you race
across the empty city your soul is in uproar.
Already you see a blond head, and feel the live embrace
of earnest eyes behind that other door.

A phantom summoned by the knocker's clangour,
she opens, wrapped about in the bedclothing.
A man is loyal to his country. Yours is the anger
which fills your head with sentences of loathing.

Kate sat back and her eyes widened. She said, 'Hold it right there.
You're telling me you need a love affair
just to feel normal about your life?
But in that case why don't you leave your wife?'
Why was I confiding in a child?
I said, 'I still want to be reconciled
with Louise. This may only be a blip
in our marriage, and the relationship
is still more valuable than anything –
certainly more than any passing fling.
Our child, our home, my whole life's history
comes out of her. It's really not a mystery
that I should want to hang on if I can
and rescue something of what we began.'
'Still,' she said, 'to me it does seem sad
if the person you're with makes you feel bad.'

She and her brother paid her father's debts
and sold the house. She soon managed to get
the leasehold of a rental flat nearby;
it lacked a coat of paint, which she and I
did one weekend. I also gave a hand
to move the furniture, borrowed a van –
because of the dimensions, she let go
the music library and grand piano
which bore Sir Edward Elgar's signature –
but all the birds came, and such furniture

as she was able to accommodate.
I always relished doing things with Kate.
One night, after Louise put Jack to bed,
quite out of nowhere, suddenly she said,
'You're not sleeping with Kate, are you?' I blinked.
'Dear God, Louise, whatever makes you think
of that?' 'You're not? Well then, that's all right.
It's only that you went out every night
when I was gone. And now you're operating
as her removals man, and decorating
her flat.' 'Louise, don't be ridiculous.'
It aided me to sound incredulous
that she had got it wrong, but all the same,
how long could my relationship with Jane
remain unknown to her, now we had been
spotted in the hotel by Wilhelmine?
Her powers of intuition on their own
had already picked up some undertone,
some inkling of betrayal in my actions.

We had arrived now at the next attraction.
Here a group of people clustered round
what seemed to be a large army compound
with gun turrets, tangles of razor wire,
and men in camouflage. Sounds of gunfire
crackled from loudspeakers, all along
the snaking queue, to entertain the throng,
some waxworks had been placed portraying fights
with foils, or boxing gloves, or jousting knights –
encounters that could decorously suggest
aggression and destruction and conquest.
Above these tableaux, on a giant screen,
scenes from a wildlife programme could be seen.
My guide said, 'What you see are killer whales
toying with seal pups; first they use their tails
to club them in the air, and when they splash
back in the ocean, then the whales thrash

them time and time again, while they are still
alive. Is it because they get a thrill
from this torture? Or is there some arcane
purpose in their play? We can't explain,
any more than we can understand
why cats play with a mouse. A vicious strand
in human nature certainly exists
as well, and cannot simply be dismissed.
What is this urge to hurt and terrify
what we can dominate? For my part, I
was never frightened of hypothesizing,
regardless of how wacky or surprising
the theory was. At first I thought aggression
might constitute sadistical expression
of sexual urges. Later I contrived
a stranger notion still: that it derived
from an entirely different drive, which all
living things exhibit. This I called
the "death instinct" because its sole volition
is to conduct all life to the condition
of inorganic matter. Yet this theory of mine does seem a
    curious one in retrospect . . .'

Hypotheses of science replace
each other like the world's empires.
A triumph morphs into disgrace,
a love arises and expires,
our vows corrupt, and all our prior
convictions vanish. Looking back,
we understand the cup was cracked.

Nothing seems what it was before.
Perhaps some version of the truth
has to be nailed to the church door:
St James's bones, the Buddha's tooth,
the hot caresses of our youth:
like prayer flags flapping in the wind,
the stories slowly fade and thin.

We hear in ancient Chinese lore,
when crops had failed and famine pressed,
with no money for tea, the poor
served boiled water to their guests,
poured it, sipped it, and all the rest,
just as they used to in the times
of real tea and easy minds.

It's said they christened it 'white tea'.
My love, we can agree on this,
at least: to say that you love me
and I have kept our promises.
Let's make that the hypothesis,
can't we? And say we do believe
that we can see a future in the leaves.

My companion seemed to lose the thread of what he had
    been saying;
or else perhaps he couldn't tolerate
the prospect of the queue; at any rate
he broke off now and took my arm and steered
me over to a side entrance. Through here
a line of vehicles dressed up as tanks
was drawn up at a kerbside, like a rank
of taxis, each provided with a gun
which pointed forwards. Now we mounted one,
and in a moment we were on our way,
threading between exhibits on display:
a model aircraft carrier, and toys
of every kind beloved of little boys
(missiles and rockets, tanks and fighter planes,
an armoury of guns worthy of *Jane's*),
and here and there among them, the fantastic
warriors of fiction, cast in plastic –
Action Man, oblivious to dangers,
Jedi and Pokémon and Power Rangers.

Our tank slowed to a halt, and now we saw
a man like Gulliver crossing the floor
among the toys. He wore a dapper suit
and shortish beard, the gaze was resolute
and friendly, and his manner was appealing.
I guessed at once that he was used to dealing
with people, and most likely also used
to getting his own way. He introduced
himself in these terms: 'I'm a man of letters –
founded a magazine – there was none better –
an author, oenophile, and gastronome,
a lover of opera, I feel at home
with the good things in life. But, though I rated
refinement, I was also fascinated
by thuggish violence, and wrote a book
on football hooligans, even partook
in their assemblies and their rampages,
and shared their drinking and their outrages.
What I learned soon enough was that these mobs
were very often people with good jobs
as plumbers, or on City trading floors,
or schoolteachers, and so on. There was more
social variety than I had thought;
in fact there were people of every sort.
When I first went with them, they didn't admit
they wanted violence, but they wanted it.
Our bus stopped on the highway at a store:
the thugs went in there, able to ignore
the storekeeper, walking round the shelves
and taking what they wanted for themselves.
Nobody could stop them. So I saw
how gangs can easily defy the law;
but more than that: I saw how crowds transform,
the way that bees can turn into a swarm,
and how mysteriously they coalesce
and get a group identity. And yes,

once there's a crowd, the violence can erupt
like everybody wanted, an abrupt
transition into mayhem, which they named
"going off". I heard a man exclaim,
"It's going off, it's going off," and they
were all about me; nothing can convey
the charge it carried, every man and boy
infused with sheer emotion – it was joy,
it was beyond joy, it was ecstasy –
it was impossible even for me
not to experience something of the thrill.
Above the mayhem I could hear the shrill
sound of a woman screaming, and the row
of sirens. One man said, "I'm happy now,
happier than I've ever been." I saw
another heave a bin through a glass door,
and then a group trashing a family car,
whacking the father with an iron bar,
throwing his teenage son onto the ground,
and half a dozen men gathered around
to kick him. As their heavy boots drove in,
the sound was different when they struck skin
from how it sounded when they struck clothing.
It was like that. And there was no self-loathing
afterwards, and no regrets. The thugs
spoke of it then like others speak of drugs,
as something special which they need to get,
which once they've had, they don't want to forget –
no, never. And in fact they're not
so distant from the mark, because the shot
of frenzied hormones which the body makes
does get us high: it's all as if it takes
place in slower time, and you can see
every detail in perfect clarity
and nothing else impinges – you are caught
within that moment with no other thought
inside your head. It's that intense and pure.'

We left him there and drove on, but our tour
of the attraction wasn't over yet.
In front of us a little stage was set
with a projection screen, and here we paused
a moment, while some unseen sensor caused
the light level to fall; and then the screen
flickered into life: a roadside scene,
shot jerkily, hand-held, two youthful dudes
in view, striking aggressive attitudes.
Their arms are raised, we see their fingers stabbing
the air; and in a moment one is grabbing
a fistful of the other fellow's vest;
jostling follows, and shoving in the chest.
My guide pronounced, 'We have already seen
how violence is akin to kerosene:
it goes up with a whoosh from groups of men,
transmutes the everyday into mayhem;
and though the perpetrators may be coy
about admitting it, it is a joy,
an ecstasy even. Make no mistake:
people want violence for its own sake.
But that isn't the only motivation.
Another reason for participation
in these affairs is to defend our status
when someone wishes to humiliate us.
It seems that killing on a point of pride
is sadly quite a common homicide,
and every day young men go to their deaths
for stepping on someone's foot, or coat, or less.
The least affront often exacts this price;
even an innuendo may suffice
to raise that homicidal IOU.'
He pointed at the men on screen. 'These two
are quarrelling about a parking place.
Ridiculous. But rather than lose face –
look what happens.' As he spoke the words,
we saw one of them stumble on the kerb;

as soon as his opponent saw him laid
upon the ground, swiftly he pulls a blade
and stabs him in the stomach, and the gore
pumps from the opening, pooling on the floor
in dark puddles as we observe him die;
the life ahead of him slips quickly by.
My guide said, 'So you see what desperate acts
are done for a mere nothing, though in fact
nothings are everything in loss of face;
and pride, which balks at swallowing disgrace,
prefers to die. But there's another ground
for violence, which waits for us around
the corner. Come.'
                          The little tank rolled on
towards a dais, where a spotlight shone
upon a man and woman, stark naked,
their sweating faces twisted up in hatred,
their fists flying, their fingers locked in bunches
of hair, or landing vicious kicks and punches
upon the face, the body, anywhere.
In all the brutal gestures of this pair,
the theme of aggression was plain to see,
and yet, despite its choreography,
the acting of the combatants was way
too wooden, and too burdened with cliché
to look realistic. (There was no denial:
this hammy acting was the Park's house style.)
My colleague gestured to the scene and said,
'This is the amity which loving bred,
for no human emotion gives us less
repose than sexual possessiveness.
Aggression is its genie, savagery
its patient, ever-willing devotee.
Look on this pair and tell me what the scene
suggests to you.' 'But, guide, to me it means
nothing at all.' 'Really? Well then, instead
tell me the thought that first enters your head.'

I let my mind go blank as he advised
and let the first suggested thought arise.
Then, with a measure of embarrassment
I said, 'In truth, it is an incident
which didn't do my good sense any credit –
in fact, something I'd far prefer to edit
out if I could. I should really explain
that when I started seeing Jane again
she told me she was breaking up with Clint.
I had my doubts – there was always a hint
of something going on: one time a date
cancelled, for no clear reason, very late;
another time she had borrowed his car;
but the most telling evidence by far
was that he hadn't sacked her. She had said
he was hiring a new girl in her stead
and moving her to the assistants' pool,
but that hadn't happened. I felt a fool
and very jealous, though I did my best
not to show this to Jane. For the rest,
I had no work to go to at this stage
so I'd plenty of leisure to engage
in jealous fantasy and speculation
as I wrote out umpteen job applications.
So when Jane stood me up one Saturday
(yet again Louise had gone away
for work), I did something I must have known
was very stupid. I picked up the phone
and called Loretta Ashe just one more time.
The silky voice came lightly down the line.
"Oh hello, babe," she said, "it's been a while.
You sound solemn. What's up? It's not your style
to be gloomy. What's that? You got the sack?
That's tough. But don't forget, when things look black,
the darkest hour is just before the dawn.
You'll find something, 'cause you're a Capricorn.

Come over here, Pat; we can have a cup
of tea, and chat, and I will cheer you up.'
I went.
      'Loretta didn't offer tea
in the event, but still she did make free
with the champagne. She had a cavalier
attitude to earning and careers,
in fact to everything that wasn't art
or pleasure; this also made me start
to feel better about having been fired,
and not having a job. Soon we retired
to bed, but at a fairly early stage
I realized I just couldn't engage
with what was happening: it was plain
that what I wanted was to be with Jane;
the nexus with Loretta had been lost.
I got out of the bed and walked across
to the sash window, which was open wide,
and stuck my head out. The sunshine outside
was hot, and the communal garden smelled
of new-mown grass. A pair of lovers held
each other closely on the banded lawn,
lilac was flowering and the hawthorn
spilling its petals on the gravel walk.
Loretta said, "What's happening? Can't you talk?"
The words I wanted failed to arise:
this scene before me seemed a paradise
from which I was excluded; it should have been
Jane and myself in that Arcadian scene
down there upon the lawn, but I was trapped
inside Loretta's house. I let my rapt
attention linger on a moment more
before I turned and picked up from the floor
my shirt and pants, and started to get dressed.
I said, "I'm really sorry. But it's best
if I leave now. I never should have come."
She said, "What's wrong? You suddenly turn glum,

and then without a single word of comment
you say you're leaving. Pat, it's fraudulent
behaviour. At the very least you owe
some kind of explanation. Surely we know
each other well enough for that." These words
sounded so reasonable I was stirred
to a moment of deluded honesty.
Did I expect some kind of amnesty,
or did I think she wouldn't mind being dumped
by coitus interruptus? Like a chump
I was saying, "It's come as a surprise,
Loretta, but I have to recognize
we're through." She said, "What do you mean, 'we're through'?"
I said, "I guess I have somebody new."
Well yes, of course I should have known better:
this was the kind of drama that Loretta
liked more than anything. She said, "I see.
and who is it?" I said, "An employee
of Beston's Bank. It's no one that you know.
Her name is Jane." Loretta said, "Oh no,
for God's sake, please, don't tell me it's the thick
secretary that sucks the boss's dick,
the one I met, the little peroxide tart
who couldn't understand conceptual art."
I hoped perhaps she'd finished, but Loretta
was just hitting her stride; I had to let her
rant on, as she scrambled to her feet,
her freckled skin flushing up in the heat
of her outrage. "You really are a creep.
I can't believe that you can be that cheap.
Any bit of skirt can have you, Pat,
you're so predictable, and worse than that,
you're shallow."
    'Now, without warning, she threw
a heavy jade ashtray at me. It flew
spinning past my head and brusquely crashed
through both halves of the fully open sash

window. I thought, "This time the maniac
has gone and killed someone." I turned my back
on her for an instant, to have a look
out of the window, but that was all it took
for her to leap behind me from the bed
and break the bedside lamp across my head.
I staggered away from her, but she came on,
stark naked, like a red-haired amazon
in some baroque cartoon, swinging her fists
wildly at me. I caught her by the wrists
but tripped among the bedclothes on the floor
and fell, still holding her. And then I saw
blood on the sheets. I thought, "She's cut my head
open," and, still restraining her, I said,
"I'm bleeding, look." But it was her, not me
that was bleeding. Now we both could see
her foot was pumping blood out from a gash
made by a shard of window which had slashed
The inside of her heel.

                'At once I bound
the wound up with a scarf, but quickly found
the bleeding wouldn't stop. Loretta panicked,
babbling she was fainting in a manic,
breathless voice. I got her dressed, applied
a tourniquet and carrying her outside,
drove to the hospital. I understood
the need to arrive as quickly as we could,
for her sake, but throughout the drive Loretta
was saying, "Pat, I need to write a letter
to Anton . . . Pat, I feel I'm going to die.
Stop the car at once, I want to buy
a notepad and pencil, I need to write my will, Pat, stop the
    car . . ."'

In the days of the insurgency, and ethnic turbulence,
it was then that making love became suddenly so intense.
Tell me, when the bombs fell and I held you in my arms,
had we not understood till then the power of our charms?

With a brace of big explosions everyone will vote for you:
it might be worth an airstrike, or a cannonade or two.
An affair can seem lacklustre when the drug of wartime ends,
so if enemies can do it, after all, why shouldn't friends?

Our tank began to move on now, leaving the wrestling pair,
and looking back, I saw them standing there,
chatting away as they recuperated
from the exertion of their act, and waited
for their next customers. Now at my side
I heard the measured accents of my guide:
'And so. Sexual jealousy ignites
aggression easily; the sort of fights
you and your girlfriend had are typical
except in this: most of the physical
violence is carried out by men
on women – yes, by far the most.'
                                        Just then
I saw a woman, straddling the rail
our tank ran on; we really couldn't fail
to see her, or for that matter to stop.
She wore a long skirt and a short-sleeved top
which hugged her body. Clearly she had been
beautiful once: that much could be seen
in her cheekbones and in her slender arms
where you could still discern those dying charms.
She spoke up now: 'When Troy fell, all of us
women were captured. Neoptolemus
took Andromache (he'd killed her son –
doubtless he felt she'd want another one,
fathered by him); hateful Odysseus got
my saintly mother; while I fell to the lot

of Agamemnon, King of Mycenae
(I was raped in the Temple of Athene
before that, by another loathsome Greek:
Locrian Ajax). So you see, I speak
with pretty good credentials when I say
that the heroic culture of my day
considered women as the spoils of war.
Moses certainly knew what we were for
and told the Jews after they'd won the fight
to take the virgins of the Midianites;
and Sabine girls were seized and violated.
The centuries have passed, but not abated
what has been taking place since time began:
men have made use of violence when they can
to kidnap women. Nothing could be more
certain to bring rapine about than war.
I wasn't first, nor will I be the last.'
She ceased, and standing back to let us pass,
she pointed to an opening in the wall
in front of us. Our tank began to crawl
towards it and, passing the threshold, trundled
along a dimly lighted subway tunnel
into an empty station where it coasted
to a standstill.

        Here, the walls were posted
with bills of women's faces, and my guide
explained, 'Whether a virgin or a bride,
whether in cocktail dress or mourning crêpe,
everyone here's the victim of a rape.
I tell you that for every one displayed
there are a thousand others.' I surveyed
this tragic gallery, and saw each face
bore a stencilled inscription of the place
in which the crime had happened, and the date.
There was Nanjing, in 1938,
a score of Prussian and Silesian towns
in 1945, with girls in gowns

or filthy rags, or shawls or rabbit skin;
I saw women of Danzig and Berlin,
the Bosnians of 1992
held by the Serbs in camps. Then I saw too
a pitiful string of Tutsi, overrun
by Hutu mobs, the 1971
Bengalis, and the women of Darfur,
the comfort women, slaves, and many more
women from wars too numerous to name.
My guide said, 'Wars surely promote this shame
and make a breeding ground for its increase,
but on these hoardings rapes in times of peace
feature as well. In nearly all of those
a girl is raped by somebody she knows,
sometimes quite well, even a former flame.'
And then he said, 'Remember when I came
to your rescue during that confrontation
show, your wife had made an accusation.'

The moment flashed before my mind: the crowd
angry and out to do me harm, then cowed
by the innate charisma of my guide.
He takes me by the arm with dignified
assurance, and as one we make our way
between that mob, into the light of day.
'I do remember. But I can say this:
I forced nothing on her, and not a kiss
or fondle did she ever have from me
but what she gathered wholly willingly.
I don't know why she said that thing. Although
I have to say – if I stay with the flow
of my thoughts – that sometimes, having sex,
it almost felt like it. Though she said yes,
her body's instinct seemed to contradict
what she was doing, making it a mixed
kind of dance performed without brio.
I hated that. She must have done, also.

Who had done this to us? What obscure
infection now inhabited our pure
cells, and in its unobserved abode
was gobbling and unravelling our codes
against our wishes? Somehow, this disease
had got a hold of us, and by degrees
Louise and I were drifting to a stance
of setting ourselves up at variance
on everything. And though much of the time
this was a steady-burning though malign
species of thing, at other times it flared
to mystifying quarrels, and we aired
a fury which was surely out of scale.
Our good intentions were of no avail.
How did these incidents arise? They rose
on any pretext, all the time, imposed
themselves, like tax, on any bit of fun,
recalled us always to the starting gun.
When I proposed booking a restaurant
for her birthday, she countered, "But I want
a big party." "But we don't have space
for that, Louise." "Well, Hew's offered his place."
"But Louise, I don't want to give a bash
for you in Hew's house. Yes, it would be flash,
but I don't want to be receiving favours
from Hew all of the time; to me it savours
of sponging." She said, "You're being a prig.
Just because I happen to want a big
party for once, and Hew offers his place,
you get all touchy about loss of face.
I only want to entertain my friends,
I'm not trying to be flash, so don't pretend
I'm some kind of materialist princess
wanting to show off. No one is less
that way than I am. Since I was at school
I've never thought it specially smart or cool
to show off in the world. What counts for me
are simple things: my work, our family,

yoga and meditation, things like that.
You make me out to be a spoiled brat
but really my desires are very few."
I said, "Here's the real story about you:
when you were wealthy you chose to ignore
the fact, while it amused you to explore
the lifestyle of a sadhu or to know
something of how an ordinary Joe
like me lives, and even become my wife
and get to live an ordinary life.
But once your family lost their money, hey,
you pretty soon reverted to the way
most women are, the way your mother was.
You're fascinated now by Hew because
Hew has the dough, the power, the access,
whatever it is society calls success.
All this impresses you. But even so
it isn't right for you and me to go
accepting favours which we can't repay."
At first she seemed to have nothing to say
to this attack, but then in weary tones
she said, "Look, Pat, we'll have the thing at home
if that's what you insist. But, about Hew,
you're really being unfair. It isn't true
that I am either sponging or impressed
by his money. I notice his success
tends to be enviable to other chaps
around him, even daunting, which perhaps
is understandable, but not a feeling
which I share. After all, we're dealing
with an old family friend who I have known
since I was little, and who's always shown
himself to be benign and open-handed
with us and with my mother. To be candid,
the one in this marriage who seems most prone
to fascinations is yourself." Her tone
was so intelligent when she explained
herself in these terms that I felt ashamed

of what I'd said and tried to see it her way.
It was no use: the bonds of yesterday
were loosening their hold; and though I tried,
we were so lined up on opposing sides,
it seemed as if our contrary positions
were prior to thought, almost like politicians'.
Demoralizing. And to make things worse,
I didn't have a job I could immerse
myself in doing, I was unconnected
with the wider world, and not respected
by people; and the well-meant sympathizing
of helpful friends seemed vaguely patronizing.
An empty time. And in this cul-de-sac
only my relationship with Jack
sustained me, and I was – I'm bound to say –
happiest when Louise had gone away
for work, which she did often at this time:
her presence left me feeling undermined.
But at this low point, just when I most needed,
I found another job, one which exceeded
my previous one, both in its salary
and also in its seniority.
It wasn't just a job, it was promotion.
I felt like I had drunk a thrilling potion
causing all my doubts to disappear.
It banished my depression, and my fears
about how I was going to find the rent,
and what we would live on once we had spent
the payoff from my last job.
                              'And this, too:
when people asked me "So, what do you do?"
as often happens, I could now detect
for my reply a measure of respect.
But if the new job made me confident,
Louise appeared strangely indifferent
to everything. In general, I was learning,
it wasn't just a question of my earnings:

nothing I did made very much impression
on her these days. Her utter self-possession
frustrated me – and it was only one
aspect of her evasion. She would shun
intimacy in every way, invite
friends whenever we went out at night,
and also any time we went away
for weekends or a family holiday.
At home, when Jack had gone to bed, she shirked
my company, and plunged herself in work
until at last she took herself to bed
and, laying down her beautiful dark head,
passed into unconsciousness.'

         I ceased.
Our vehicle gave a little jerk, and eased
forward on its rail, leaving the grim
station with its posters of women
abused in war and peace, into a zone
of combat scenes, portrayed in polychrome,
which showed those medieval jousting fights
when martial combat was a game for knights
performed before spectators of the court –
a martial forerunner of modern sport.
And as we drove between these sublimated
murderers, my colleague indicated
one who was lying injured on the ground,
attended by some ladies gathered round,
and said, 'Finish the story of your friend
who cut her foot. How did the rescue end?'
'For her, with several stitches and a plaster –
and, for me, personally, in disaster.
It happened a few days later.

         'On that day,
I'd done another interview. My way
homewards enticed me by an indirection
to Jane's place and that feminine affection
which I craved, but which also made me late
in getting home. It's painful to relate

what happened then. At once I had a strong
impression something had gone very wrong:
Louise was in the kitchen at the sink.
She looks angry, and also on the brink
of tears. I say hello. Louise doesn't reply
but only stares at me. Her darting eye
flicking towards the table draws my gaze
downwards, and as my worried glance surveys
its surface, I'm appalled to see a letter
which I can tell at once is from Loretta
by all the ink-blots and the different-sized
writing. I pick it up and scrutinize
its message. It begins, "Disgusting prick,
I'm finally finished with your tacky tricks.
You tried to kill me. It's only by luck
I'm still alive. But now could you just fuck
off out of my existence, frauding creep?
As far as I'm concerned that little cheap
bitch is welcome to you. In my view
she got what she deserved when she got you.
I feel sorry for her. I do. Women
are always all too quickly taken in
by fraudulent and shallow men like you.
No doubt you'll soon be doing her in too.
Murderer – that's what you'd like to be.
I'm only lucky that it wasn't me.
You're vile, Pat, I despise you. Loretta."
In all respects this wasn't quite the letter
you'd choose your wife to open.

                                    'But in fact
Loretta had shown an unintended tact
in writing "little bitch" instead of "Jane".
I saw it gave me much less to explain:
the way the note read now, the suggestion
might be that Louise was the bitch in question.
I took advantage of this and repressed
my whole affair with Jane, only confessed

that I had gone round to Loretta's place,
and then, when I rejected her embrace,
she lost control and in a fit of rage
threw things at me, going on a rampage,
and cutting her foot. I acknowledge missing
some of the detail: that we'd just been kissing,
were naked in her bed, and just about
to have sex. It was easier without.
In any case, Louise gave little credence
to my pathetic pleas of innocence,
though literally speaking they were true.
She said, "Last time you promised you were through
with her as well. I trusted you on that.
But how can I ever really trust you, Pat?
How can I? So you tell me you weren't screwing.
OK, in that event, what were you doing
in her house at all? You promised me a
dozen times that you weren't going to see her
any more. But look at this." She let her
lovely eyes fall downwards to the letter,
then raised them once again, her gaze alert
and still accusatory, despite the hurt
which it expressed. "Look," she said, "I know
that our love life has been a little slow,
in fact more than a little. And I grant
it's not been easy for you. But I can't
accept because of this you go with other
women. If you have to take a lover,
Patrick, be very sure that you will lose
me. You're going to have to choose."
And I believed her. But I'd no conception
that fatal evening of the new direction
her life would take, and what she held in store
for me as she flung out, slamming the door.
I only learned that later, when I found
her laptop diary. Knowing I was bound
by common decency not to intrude
on these files, which were private, I subdued

the urge to read it for at least a minute.
I should have waited longer. I found in it
those words which told what pastime she'd been at
that evening when she slammed out of the flat.
I read: "Is Patrick's infidelity
the reason for it? In reality
the two of us could always get along
well enough, and though he did me wrong
I don't hate him; I'm even pretty sure
I still love him, and yet I can't endure
the thought of sex. But now the strangest thing
has happened. When I told him that his fling
with Loretta must end, I couldn't stay
inside the flat, I had to get away
for a few hours at least, to go somewhere,
anywhere really. I set off downstairs
and drove to Hew's place in a kind of trance,
without reflecting, merely on the chance
that I might find him in. He looked surprised
but also pleased I'd come. I saw his eyes
were slightly puffy, and his thick white hair
tousled; I was suddenly aware
I'd woken him. We went into his snug,
he took an armchair, I sat on the rug
in front of the gas fire, and for a spell
we drank some wine and talked. I didn't tell
him anything about Pat and Loretta,
but just being with him made me feel better.
I felt the anguish start to drain away
and in its place the intoxicating sway
of power, a sudden feeling I could do
anything I chose without taboo
or hindrance. I was like a jailbird
released into the world. Without a word
I rose and pulled Hew to his feet as well,
entirely confident I could compel
whatever I desired of him, and led
him up the flight of stairs to his own bed.

Here at once, contrary to my fears
and everything I'd felt in recent years,
I now experienced such fierce onslaught
of sexual craving as I had long thought
I was dead to, cascading through my limbs
as Hew undresses me, my brain swims,
I never felt so flooded and connected
with sex, the thing was wholly unexpected.
Where did that come from?"

                'Yes, when I read
this narrative, I wished that they were dead
and me too – dead, and free of the nightmare.
Such were the joys of being made aware.
But that was all much later on. For now,
I only knew that we had had a row
and she had left the flat, and that I might
lose her. I didn't sleep at all that night.
At dawn I went into Jack's room to sit
and have the calm his presence would transmit
in my confusion. Everything she said
was tumbling over and over in my head
as I weighed up the future, how it stood
with her and me. At once I understood
that, from now on, if I was going to mend
my marriage with Louise, I was condemned
to live in total sexual abstinence.
Was there meaning in such an existence?
I thought how lots of people renounce sex
and live happy, not just those who elect
the priesthood, or a Trappist monastery,
but old folks, and perhaps more ordinary
married couples than we might suppose.
My parents seemed to figure among those;
and I recalled my father once had said
that even when the sexual side is dead,
marriage is still a boon for happiness.
Surely no boon could have beguiled me less.

It seemed outlandish to renounce an active
love life. And Jane was sexy and attractive
to me – very. Giving up this squeeze
for some kind of chaste friendship with Louise
seemed like a pretty poor exchange to make;
but sitting here I felt that, for Jack's sake
and also for Louise's, I should try.

'Next day, I left the office and stopped by
Jane's flat. Of course, I wanted to explain
it all to her in person. As I came
towards her doorway, everything I'd planned
to say was simple, clear to understand,
but from the moment that she let me in
I dithered, at a loss how to begin.
I felt dazed by this place, which was the source
of stirring memories, and by the force
of her beauty. Even the furnishings
recalled to me our private skirmishings:
the bedcover, the rug upon the floor,
the sofa, all these objects were a store
of memory; I saw her naked there,
the willing waist, the wanton derrière,
the whiteness of her limbs, the cloud-grey bruise
of her ingenuous eyes, hard to refuse.
I saw she was still dressed for her commute:
a pair of low-heeled shoes, a business suit,
a chaste grey sweater, buttoned at the neck.
I mumbled greetings, giving her a peck
and moved away. This didn't do for Jane,
who still suspected nothing. Now she came
and stood closer, taking me by the wrists
and turned her face upwards. We could have kissed
so easily, and for a moment now
the butter-coloured fringe across her brow,
the faultless mouth, the fluttering grey eyes
uttered their spell and I was paralysed;

but with a pang I turned away instead
and braced myself for what must be, and said,
"Jane, we have to talk."

'I told her then
I wanted to bring our friendship to an end
and that I'd settled for the sake of Jack
to try and get my marriage back on track.
These things are never easy. As I spoke,
I thought of the obsession she awoke,
not when I loved her first, since that had been
an unextravagant, almost routine
affair, but once she'd given me the slip
and I discovered I was in the grip
of the most violent possible passion, and paced about, seeing
her everywhere in the streets.'

*The Christian boy declared, 'The earliest signs
are often horses tethered along the highway's verge.
Soon you see the encampment with its caravans, sometimes
the smoke of campfires; then the gypsy women emerge –
lissom and captivating, a proof you can live free
under the wheeling stars, belonging to no country.*

*'That is a life a man can dream about:
they have no eyes for you, their glances range abroad,
seeking no terminus, their journey paramount.
A girl who doesn't love you is like the winding road:
an endlessly receding promise to fulfil.
Don't call it love unless you feel this thrill.'*

*– 'Gajo, your kind of longing is a cheat.
Our women find no freedom aboard the caravans,
the rousing road you speak of is a fetter for their feet.
And in the marching orders which govern Romany clans,
its wanderings are dull as a parade-ground drill,
those wheeling constellations a treadmill.*

*'Love where you are loved. Gajo, if you cannot,
you are condemned because you will surely follow*

the vans unhappily. It is your people's lot
to find the gypsy woman's promise hollow.
For them this is a home, and not a bivouac:
don't call it love, unless she loves you back.'

The little tank slowed down, and came to rest beside an actor
with a commanding air, though short of stature.
He wore a uniform with epaulettes,
and several rows of medals on his chest,
and an embroidered eagle on his hat.
He had the bearing of an autocrat
and in his face I seemed to recognize
the cold expression and mesmeric eyes,
the big mouth that was slightly pointed down
on either side, and seemed to make him frown
although he wasn't frowning. He intoned:
'To me, peace is depressing. War alone
brings to its highest pitch vitality
in men, and sets a true nobility
upon a people. Fighting in a war
fulfils a man; it's what a man is for;
it validates him like having a child
validates a woman. I reviled
the state of peace, and not just for a man
but also for a nation. I began
aggressive wars, and liked to get involved
in other people's conflicts. I resolved
to bring my country back into manhood
by martial valour, since the way things stood
it was degenerate. And don't suppose,
even a minute, I was one of those
who sent others to war but never fought
themselves. No, I was never that sort.
I struggled in the trenches with the rest,
an excellent soldier, one of the best,
and came away with shrapnel in my side
which stayed with me until the day I died.'

The actor broke off there, and coming out
of role went on, 'There isn't any doubt
that nowadays this attitude to war
is out of style. And yet it's very sure
that in the history of humankind
fighting has generally been held a fine
employment for an honourable caste,
and people mainly were enthusiasts
for making war – not just the well-to-do
and noble, but the common people too:
think of the multitudes who took delight in
volunteering for the trenches. Fighting
has always been adjudged a glorious task.
But, acting in this role, I'm bound to ask
what was the special satisfaction brought
by such a dangerous work? At first I thought
that reading history might make this clear;
but history's more opaque than it appears
and, in my view, we tend to patronize
people from the past; I realized
I'd do better to ask people I've known
personally who've been in combat zones.
I did. Although a fair few hated it,
yet there were many too who rated it
and kept on going back. These on the whole
were ones who'd volunteered in their role
as soldiers or reporters. With some misgivings,
they spoke of an intensity of living
which, though scary, can also be a thrill;
and many said that love affairs fulfilled
them better during war. It's like a drug
for some of these people. Death's ghoulish mug
looming in front of them makes everyday
problems vanish, an auto-da-fé
of inner angst and psychological
impediments. It's not what I would call

a very tempting prospect, but for some
there's no doubt that the holy bonfire comes
as their solution.'

                Now he stepped aside
to let our tank move on. And now the ride
continued through a polyester jungle
where fluffy chimpanzees squatted and dangled
among the branches, hooting to their mates.
My guide said, 'In my lifetime these primates
were not thought to be violent, but we know
from subsequent studies that they are so.
Their pacifism was a fairy tale.
Like chimps, in human beings the young males
comprise the social group who figure here.
We find women kill women nowhere near
as much as men kill men. But nothing kills
like war. Of all humanity's warped thrills
this is the costliest and deadliest;
and sadly too, one of the most impressed
upon our nature.'

                As he spoke, our tank
was slowing and we passed out of that rank,
synthetic jungle, coming to a stop
beside a kind of film-set coffee shop
where, in among some waxwork figures, sat
a pair of actors. One of them was fat
with trainers on his feet, open-necked shirt,
sitting beside a plateful of dessert;
his wife was dark, and with a fiery air.
She said, 'Come and sit down, pull up a chair,'
and so I did. Her husband left his spoon
of éclair, Chantilly, and macaroon
waving in the air, and launched upon
a précis of research that they had done
together. 'We both wanted to explore
the question of why men should go to war.
The risks are obvious, but what's the gain?
Well, booty for starters, whether grain

or lowing cattle, minerals or gold,
or fertile plains and trading routes controlled,
all these are clear advantages. But we –
my wife and I, that is – began to see
that women were a more important clue
in terms of an evolutionary view.
In war, you either kill or else enslave
your enemies, but usually you save
their women for yourselves. What we showed
was that in ancient times a war bestowed
a hugely better probability
on average, and despite the jeopardy,
of extra women; and for men this brings
an increase in your number of offspring.
But girls are more restricted by the term
of pregnancy than by the source of sperm
available to them, so lack of males
on hand is almost never what curtails
a woman's family. And that is why
women don't band together and supply
themselves with extra men by making raids
on neighbouring villages. These ambuscades
in other animals are rare –' his dessert spoon
was still poised in the air. 'Although baboons
and other primates are belligerent,
and like humans go in for ravishment
of females, yet it's only among chimps
and dolphins that we really have a glimpse
of what you'd call an organized warfare . . .'
He hadn't finished, but we left him there
still brandishing his spoonful of Chantilly
in front of him, and heard him willy-nilly
expatiating as we drew away.

Already I could see the next display
just up ahead and, as our tank drew nearer,
the detail of the spectacle came clearer

and I made out a warhorse, richly decked
in gold caparison, and round its neck
a garland of roses, and at its side
a statue with a spear. I asked my guide,
'So what's all this about?' He pointed then
and I became aware of two young men
I hadn't seen at first, standing abreast
of the display. One of them was dressed
in an embroidered tunic and chain mail,
the other made up to look deathly pale,
his clothes covered in blood, his boyish neck
festooned with bloodstains by special effects
to give the look of a long open gash.
I noticed that his wrists were also slashed.
He grinned and raised his hand in a salute.
Now his companion spoke – a handsome brute,
though thuggish-looking, carrying a knife:
'I was the one who launched the toxic strife
which plagued our city. My companion here –
my enemy when living – made a clear
promise of marriage to a girl. The dope
was unaware a wealthy widow hoped
to get him for her daughter. Then one day
this widow saw him coming; straight away
she goes down to the street and "Hello, boy,"
she says, "I'd like to wish you every joy
on your engagement, which I heard about.
You will be very happy, I don't doubt."
As if speaking a pious orison,
the woman's voice now drops, and she goes on,
"Although in another way I'm sorry too,
since I was keeping my daughter for you."
With that she pushes open her front door,
revealing the girl. Now, there is one thing more
which you should know: this shut-away temptress
was a miracle of sexiness

and beauty. Our princeling takes one glance
at her, and she immediately supplants
his other paramour. He says, "OK,
I'll marry her." So now the Amidei
are up in arms, affronted by this slight
to their honour. I was with them that night
inside St Stephen's Church when they debated
how to avenge it. Someone advocated
cutting him up to spoil his pretty face
and brand him with a visible disgrace.
I said, "That's not the way to right this wrong.
Scarring the culprit would only prolong
the shame on all of us. No, my friend,
the dude must die, and that'll be an end
of it." A fatal counsel.

                        'Easter Day,
1215. The bridegroom's on his way
to his wedding, apparelled all in white,
a garland of flowers on his head, upright
in the saddle, riding the grey horse
you see before you. Suddenly a force
of enemies irrupts into the street
and pulls him from his charger. He retreats
across the bridge of butchers' shops, but they
catch him again, and with their daggers slay
him there upon the bridge; and then they slash
his throat and wrists and let his lifeblood splash
down into the river. After this,
everyone in our metropolis
took sides; suddenly every Florentine
became either a Guelph or Ghibelline,
and even the poor were caught up in the feud
between us, and the carnage which ensued.
How quickly that happens; for the allure of being on a side is
    very strong.'

Tides *always obey the hidden*
gravity of the moon,
rising and falling when they're bidden,
no one is immune.

The heavy hulls the water frees
are lifted from the dirt,
and tons of wood can drift at ease
across an unknown earth.

Our ships are beached along the bight
and waiting on the tide,
and I am sleepless through the night
and you sleep at my side.

We quarrel about womankind
or someone else's marriage,
and what the other loves, we find
a reason to disparage.

We quarrel about politics
and God and history,
it seems there isn't anything
on which we can agree.

I'm gazing through the window,
the day is coming soon,
the ships are on the beach below,
there isn't any moon.

My guide now said, 'The years since my death have seen a host
of social psychologists investigating
the difficulties groups have in relating
to each other. When these guys divide
people randomly into two sides,
both teams at once begin to deprecate
the other, to dislike or even hate

its members. They'll withhold a benefit
even when there is quite a definite
cost to their own group of doing so.
And these are random groups! From this we know
that when for whatever reason groups arise,
just being part of one of them implies
enmity to the other. Yes, it seems
that people don't form groups because they mean
aggressive acts and stand in need of troops:
they get aggressive 'cause they're in a group.'

We now arrived beside a paling, posted
with advertising bills, and as we coasted
along beside them in our tank, my guide
explained, 'Mostly advertisements provide
promise of women of childbearing age –
the copywriters looking to engage
the urge to reproduce. Nothing can match
that drive. But there exists a smaller batch
of ads, though still important, which relate
to something else which we can isolate:
we hanker to be on a winning team.
I myself made little of this theme,
not counting it as primal, but the guys
who made the Park have seen it otherwise.
Their intuition is that at its core
all team sport is a substitute for war.'
He pointed, and I saw posters displayed
of footballers and cricketers portrayed
punching the air, or with their arms held up
in triumph, showing off a streamered cup,
and racing drivers spraying their champagne.
And as we passed these winning scenes there came
a throng of memories of Jack's obsession
with football, and the endless weekend sessions

we played together in the park. I knew
that what really attracted him and drew
him to the sport was not so much the game
itself, as the excitement and acclaim
of winning, and of being on a side.

'Psychology of groups,' went on my guide,
'is ineluctable. I'd say a law
exists for all communities: the more
hostility and conflict are suppressed
inside a group, the more they are addressed
towards the outside world. Every creed's
a religion of love if you accede
to its precepts; but equally they're all
cruel and intolerant to those who fall
outside the brotherhood. And, since I died,
I came to see this principle applied
not just to love and hate, but ethics too.
It's hard to admit, but seems to be true:
morality is something we subscribe
to willingly enough within our tribe.
The closer knit the group, the more we feel
its rules bind us, the less we cheat and steal;
but when we deal with one who stands outside
the group, often the rules are not applied
so rigorously. What would be a shame
among those of our ilk hasn't the same
stigma at all when it is acted out
on an outsider we can think about
as alien, heathen, foreign, or the like.'

'It's true,' a voice said. 'I witnessed the strike
of cavalry against that camp.' We saw
a moustached military man. He wore
his stained and braided jacket with its brass
buttons open down the front, and grasped
a pipe with a long stem. He said, 'You might
have thought it was impossible for white

people to butcher and to mutilate
humans like those men did. But I can state
only the truth, observed with my own eyes.
I saw the scalpings and I heard the cries,
witnessed the women and the old men seized
and sabred down, the children on their knees,
their brains clubbed out of them by men who deemed
themselves civilized Christians. It seemed
the thing would never stop. And then a squaw,
not twenty years old, beautiful, I saw
the cutlass slit her belly like a hare,
her child pulled out of her and scalped right there
before my eyes. I was a mere bystander.
But later, when the cavalry commander
who ordered the attack was called before
committee on the conduct of the war
(the outrage never even came to trial),
I testified against him and his vile
comrades – for which they shot me through the head.
But since then, in the long while I've been dead,
I've come to realize many things, and one
is that if you convince yourself someone
is on the other side, if you regard
someone as alien, then it isn't hard
to hold them less than human. It's germane
that officer had proved himself humane
opposing slavery, made it his mission
to campaign boldly for its abolition.
When threats against his life were commonplace,
he mounted his pulpit, and said, "By grace
of God and these two pistols, I will preach
today." Both in his actions and his speech
he could be ethical; yet in this case
of the Cheyenne he showed a different face,
as I was witness on that day of shame at Sand Creek.'

The herd runs together, and the rules of the herd will run
as far as its outliers. Beyond that mental line
between our crowd and theirs we lose the habit
of recognizing humans, and after that is begun
the looting of houses, and the girls casually seized,
the joy of battle, its frenzy in the sunshine,
the child calmly knocked on the head like a rabbit,
punctilious burnings at the stake, and other pieties.

But friends, surely such killers are of a different stamp
to people like ourselves; and surely for our part
such savageries are something we would shun.
Nor could we tolerate those concentration camps,
as cold and ordered as the metal shelves
of butcher's shops. Americans, take heart
with this consoling thought: only the Huns
could do such things. Cambodians, comfort yourselves.

Religion

In ancient times before the Bible
or the Rig Veda had been
written down, the gods were tribal
and partisan, and intervened
in human lives, were clearly seen
to multiply or blight the cattle,
determine victory in battle.

They made the sun rise every day,
threw thunderbolts, caused crops to grow,
the male peacock to display,
the dormant volcano to blow,
the Northern Lights to stage their show,
told man what virtue was, and crime,
eclipsed the sun from time to time.

Like a migrating population
from an original beachhead,
the hordes of a godless explanation
establish on the coast, then spread
inland from homestead to homestead.
One by one their answers meet
with those of God, and God retreats.

Louise, can anything exist
for which there is no evidence?
Doctrine of love we once professed
lives only in its utterance;
and the dominions of the sense
pay tribute elsewhere, or are glossed
as scriptural allegory, or lost.

And so, my love, there was a time
when God hung on, to fill the gaps
where science failed, maybe as prime
mover, whose active powers then lapse;
perhaps he'd made the world, perhaps
just the Big Bang. There might remain
things only Jahweh could explain.

Unhappy time for gods: to live
on in a crumbling palace, to play
a role in ceremony, give
out medals. On the grand allée
leaves of the maples fall away
like provinces of empire. Fate
no longer loves the gods. They wait.

Clatter of falling tiles at night,
the mushroom odour of dry rot.
In our decay the ancient rite
of man and woman has been lost.
In the roofless harem a frost
of glittering indifference lies:
this is the way religion dies.

'Welcome to God, welcome to heaven and hell,
welcome to heightened consciousness as well,
miracles, angels, demons, avatars,
the soul and the eternal life, blah, blah . . .'
The speaker of this greeting was a pandit
robed in white and bearded like a bandit.
Before my guide or I could well respond,
he gave a gap-toothed grin and carried on:
'In all religious talk there's not a scrap
of truth or usefulness. It's utter crap,
which never did anyone any good,
made up by priests to get a livelihood
from those who have no manliness or sense.
Do yourself a favour and dispense

with it entirely, for it won't progress
either your welfare or your happiness
in any way. If I had a dollar
for every mystic and religious wallah,
now that would make me happy. Or a girl
for every fib about the other world,
yes, I could go for that. The truth is this:
that all religion's born of cowardice
about dying. Millennia ago,
my friends and I were trying to overthrow
religion and remake philosophy
without an afterlife, rationally,
on a materialistic, godless model.
India, home of all religious twaddle,
was our country, and so we had our work
cut out. I'm proud to say we didn't shirk
the difficult issue: How can one live
without the hope an afterlife can give?
But our philosophy was not without
its tempting side: our brotherhood allowed
a role for sensual appetite, in fact
we saw enjoyment as a rational act.
You might assume that this would be appealing
to humankind. But what I found revealing
was that most people opted to neglect
pleasure and keep God, and so our sect
never really caught on with the masses.
That's how much the fear of death surpasses
other desires of man.'
                              Now with a wave
he motioned to a reproduction grave
set up nearby, complete with AstroTurf,
a plastic headstone, and a jar of earth
containing a bunch of artificial flowers.
'This terror has conscripted all our powers,
religion is an ally in its war –
which is inevitably lost. For sure,

it's comforting what the religions say:
that there is going to be a Judgement Day
when we will live again, that some supposed
essence of us will live on as a ghost
or persist in a purer, better land.
It isn't at all hard to understand
why the closer we come to death, the more is
our urge to focus on these fairy stories.'
He paused now; and it seemed that he had stopped
playing the role, because his voice then dropped
and, in a confidential tone, went on:
'I must admit that sometimes I am drawn,
in spite of all my atheism, to these
delusions, to these childish fantasies.
But first I should explain. I'm not a stooge
or unemployed actor like the huge
preponderance of my fellow 'streetmosphere'
performers who have found employment here.
No, I'm actually the architect,
the one who came up with the whole concept
for this section. Perhaps you think it's odd
they chose someone who doesn't worship God,
or own religious faith of any sort,
to be in charge here? Think again; it ought
to be self-evident.

              'Religious folk detest
other people's creeds. At the very best
they privately disparage them; at worst
they actually consider them accursed.
Whatever they say, the reality
is that they'll show a partiality
for their own faith. For this reason the Park
felt it would be more balanced to embark
on this project with somebody like me,
who could treat all religions equally.
It happened, then, that at an early stage
the company posted on their web page

an open competition for ideas
for this attraction. As an engineer
I thought it would be something of a lark
to put my own proposal to the Park.
And so I did. And rather to my terror –
quite possibly by bureaucratic error –
I was selected. Now I had to give a
proper detailed project – and deliver.
I did my homework conscientiously
but study as I might, I couldn't see
what point there was in trying to portray
what all the different religions say.
The many creeds were a phenomenon
in themselves, but not a prolegomenon
to anything useful. So I left out
the doctrines and instead I set about
designing an attraction which would show
some typical features and maybe throw
some light on why it is that humans need
to have a god and a religious creed.'

He led us down a leafy promenade
towards a pair of doors in the façade
of a lofty marble temple. Passing inside,
we found an aisle, not so very wide
but long, stretching away towards a raised
tribune, on which an idol had been placed.
'There was so much I needed to cram in,'
he said, 'and I decided to begin
with a display about religious ritual.
Rites are such a primary and habitual
feature of religion, that I took
a lot of trouble with them. If you look
along the walls, you'll see we've put in bays
at intervals, for ritual displays
taken from every creed.'
                                    We made our way
along the aisle, inspecting the display

which he'd 'imagineered', and as we went
he commented. We saw the ash of Lent
being distributed; unleavened bread
blessed at the Passover; we saw the dead
burning on holy Manikarnika.
Here, too, the plate of money which the vicar
raises before the altar, here the sweet
offerings of prasad at Ganesha's feet;
the hooded processant bearing a verge,
the zealot at Ashura with his scourge,
a prayer wheel, the beating of a gong,
all this and more we saw, passing along.
Here were the baptism and ordination,
upanayana and a commination,
the mikvah, and the churching of the wife,
the circumciser with the ritual knife,
and a dozen other deeds bizarre to me
but charged with meaning for the devotee.
My guide and I were led by our new friend
past all these installations to the end,
where on the stage the idol had its place –
a life-size statue with a painted face
and nylon robes, the colours bright and kitsch.
'Go on,' the engineer said, 'push the switch.'
I did as he advised, and right away
a harsh recorded voice began to play.
'Greetings,' it said, 'to all who venture here.
I was a son of Chao, who learned to steer
an honourable and quiet course in times
of killing, chaos, pillage, and rapine.
For, though the times were violent and bloody,
I spent my life in teaching and in study.
I was among the first who clearly saw
things of this world are bound by natural law.
Know this: there are no ghostly beings, no sprites.
I'm telling you, in ceremonies and rites

nothing supernatural takes place:
that was my insight for the human race.
Praying for health or rain is wasted breath.
You won't avoid disease or stave off death
that way, no intervention will occur.
And yet, despite this, rituals do confer
subjective benefits on those who take
a part in them: the fact is that they make
people feel good – that much seems to be
a given of human psychology.
Part of our satisfaction is the fact
of bonding with our fellows in the act;
but even performed alone, the enterprise
brings its reward: a ritual satisfies.'

The statue seemed to have no more to say
and so the engineer showed us the way
down from the platform and along the hall
into a smaller chamber. Here the wall
was covered by a huge photo which showed
a pinnacle of rock, piebald with snow,
on which a massive ruined fortress sprawled
against the sky. The stonework seemed to fall
sheer with the cliff face so the fort was moated
by deep chasms of air, and eagles floated
around its near-impregnable position.
In front of this there rose an apparition:
a hologram, hooded and robed in black,
who spoke these words: 'We came under attack
from the besieging armies all that winter,
shivering in our fortress on its splinter
of frosty mountaintop – the final place
on earth we owned – determined to outface
our enemies below. And I recall
the wind howling at night around the wall,
the watch prowling about, stamping and clapping
their sides to warm themselves, our banner flapping

upon those icy gusts, its cloth whipped ragged,
and on the eaves the icicles as jagged
and uneven as sharks' teeth. Down below
our enemies patrolled. Our food ran low,
then it was finished. Now we couldn't wait:
our leaders went out to negotiate.
The terms they got were these: people like me,
the ordinary believers, would be free
to go. But for the true initiates,
the ones we called "Perfect", another fate
was ordered. These would all be burned alive
and not a man or woman to survive,
for they had made an immutable vow.
A new conviction came upon me now:
with only three more days to the deadline,
some twenty of us understood the time
had come for us to take that vow as well.
We had Consolamentum, said farewell,
distributing our worldly goods to those
who we would leave behind us. With the snows
at last melting away on the hillside,
we made our way down in a dignified
procession by that pathway and the stair
cut in the rock face, to the bottom where
the people of the Roman Church had made
a giant bonfire, walled with a stockade.
We climbed the ladders, stepped onto that bier,
and though we naturally did feel fear,
we were content, since we were all aware
that we would soon be freed from matter's snare:
the cycle of incarnation.'

                    Now he ceased,
and now his hologram folded and creased,
like whipped cream when it starts to grow thicker,
before the image gave a final flicker
and disappeared. Our friend the engineer
turned to us and spread his hands. 'So here

you see religion lightening the load
of a condemned man. But the episode
raises the more important question: why
did this believer volunteer to die
when he was just about to get away?
What does his action mean? What does it say
about us human beings and our creeds?
The truth is, people have an urgent need
to cling to something. A credo fulfils us,
it comforts us in some way, even thrills us,
gives us a sense of purpose in the world.
Beliefs are as mysterious as girls:
I can't explain them to you or say why
some are aggressive, others mild and shy;
I only see that there exists attraction.
There is a love of creeds, and satisfaction
in them, which I observe and note.
There doesn't seem to be an antidote.'

He motioned us to follow, and the next
feature he had to show in this complex
was a gold stupa on a shotcrete mound.
In front of it, scattered upon the ground,
were flowers and photos left by devotees.
Our friend the engineer explained, 'To me,
an atheist, it's hard not to deplore
crusades, jihads, and other holy wars,
the pogroms and religious persecutions,
the ghettos, deprivations, and exclusions
religion brings. And yet, in all the lies
the priests have told us, we must recognize
that God has helped promote the social order,
both as a punisher and a rewarder,
and as authority's authority.
Under this stupa, in a treasury,
there lie a thousand scrolls which are inscribed
with rules of conduct for a thousand tribes,

with laws of nations and their moral codes,
grown up by tradition, or else bestowed
suddenly by a prophet or a saviour
to regulate society's behaviour.
Lawyers and kings pore over them, of course,
but in reality they're not enforced
so much by kings (who in a subtle way
are always somehow servants in the pay
of their subjects) as by the bonds between
us and our fellow men, by which I mean
that drive to social status which connects
humans, and is the counterpart of sex
within a group, a nation, or a tribe.'

He seemed to have concluded; and my guide
letting this pass in silence, we pressed on
into the gloom. Ahead of us there shone
a spotlight pinpointing a golden dress
upon a tailor's dummy. I could guess
what my colleague was going to ask me now
so I forestalled him, saying, 'Please allow
me to explain what this exhibit means.
That gold dress is the one that Wilhelmine
made for Louise, and caused her to discover
at last that Jane and I had been lovers.
I can't forget the feeling of despair
when one morning I heard Louise declare,
"I just heard Wilhelmina Fleiss is showing
her new winter collection, and I'm going.
I want something to wear on my birthday."
The simple statement filled me with dismay:
the mere mention of Wilhelmina's name
conjured for me my own regret and shame
in Brighton on that rainy afternoon
when Jane and I, proceeding to our room,
stumbled upon her doing a fashion shoot.
Her power over me now was absolute;

she could destroy my marriage with a word,
even though – and this was the absurd
part of it – I'd long ago stopped seeing
Jane. I started off by disagreeing,
as if on grounds of taste: I told Louise,
"Choose anything you like, my love, but please
don't go to Wilhelmine, her stuff is hideous."
Perhaps I should have been a touch insidious,
because she said, "It's really not like you
to have strong views on a fashion issue."
I said, "I sat by her the other day
at Hew's housewarming, and I have to say
I took against her." Louise looked at me
suspiciously. "Patrick, I fail to see
why liking her's important. It's a dress
I'm looking for, not spiritual closeness."
I said, "This may sound stupid but, Louise,
don't get a dress from Wilhelmina, please.
I'd always look at it and see a trace
of that soulless and calculating face."
Louise looked skeptical. Though it was plain
that I was hiding something, she remained
silent.'

My guide said, 'Well? And did she go?'
'I couldn't stop her. But she made no show
of having learned anything untoward
when she returned – just sounded mildly bored
when I asked how it went. And so I thought
that maybe Wilhelmina had stopped short
of telling her about my escapade.
Maybe some shred of decency had played
in my favour. Perhaps she liked me, perhaps
she'd never tell a soul about my lapse.'
'Such is the human tendency to mould
reality to its own desires, and hold
illusion to be truth,' my guide opined.
'It's also the way religion works, I find.'

He paused, as if he expected to hear
a rejoinder, but neither the engineer
nor I spoke, and his words hung in the air
as we walked onwards, down a gloomy stair
and then along an ample corridor,
our footfalls clacking on its concrete floor;
and all the way his gaze was straight ahead.
At length I spoke: 'I've often heard it said
that in a marriage when a spouse betrays
their spouse, the cheated partner is always
the last to know it. I was unaware
that she and Hew were having an affair,
but even so I sensed something was shifting
within our life together; I felt her drifting
further away from me; I never knew
what she was getting up to or with who.
All of the normal marital exchange –
where plans are worked out, where they're weighed and
    changed –
had been abandoned. She was constantly
away in New York for the gallery.
Business trips. One day she let me know
the party we'd decided we would throw
for her birthday was going to be at Hew's
house after all. I said, "Now I'm confused.
I thought we agreed to give it here, at home."
"I've changed my mind," she said, and now her tone
became silky-vicious. "You see, my dear,
I've found out that you're having an affair
with Jane Day, and although of course I do
see the obvious attractions there for you,
some things have had to change. I realize –
and this can hardly come as a surprise –
I don't have to go on putting you first."
In every way this speech sounded rehearsed.
I understood I needed to explain
the situation frankly. "As for Jane,"

I said, "it's finished between her and me."
She gave a grim look. "Surely you can see
that I don't trust you any more. You shit
in the bed; now you must sleep in it."'

I ceased, because I now saw up ahead
a group of waxwork gods exhibited:
images of Jesus and the Buddha,
Shangdi, and Olorun, and Thor, and Rudra,
and many others from around the globe,
with weapons, or halos, or wearing robes,
and, as a strange exception to this norm,
my father, in his naval uniform.
I said, 'That one seems underqualified
for this posse.' The engineer replied,
'When I did my researches it was clear
that all religions both address our fear
of dying, and supply a moral law;
but these were not the only things I saw.
It also became evident to me
that the advantage for the devotee
goes further than this: that he feels supported
in other ways as well, as if escorted
through life by some higher authority.'
My guide said, 'Here I claim priority.
My point, made apropos of lots of things,
is that the first experience life brings
marks us forever: the relationships
with our mother and father write the script
which shapes our feelings through the rest of life,
whether towards employer, child, or wife.
Religion certainly is no exception,
and even a very cursory inspection
of our religious language will confirm
an ample lexicon of kinship terms:
God is the father, Meera is the mother,
adults are children, and the monk's a brother,

the nun's a sister with a wedding ring,
and so on; family's in everything –
so much so that sometimes religion seems
to be the maintenance by other means
of family life.'
             Coming up ahead
an ancient temple was exhibited
with gaping doors, and going in we found
animatronic figures gathered round
a broad-browed heifer, tethered with a halter,
its shins hobbled, and standing on an altar.
The priest intones a few words of devotion
and then lets fall his heavy axe. The motion
is jerky, slightly unconvincing. Blood
spurts out as scarlet paint and floods
the 'stone' gutters. Next, the priest
and his assistants flay and cut the beast,
and light bundles of sticks, and lay the meat
upon the griddle, so the gods can eat.
Smoke is pumped out, and an added smell
of roasting fat is mingled in as well
by an ingenious special effect –
a technical triumph of the project
of which the engineer was justly proud.

Pay nothing for a month, and see
if you are satisfied. There's no
commitment. And receive for free
this lavish book on French chateaux:
it's simply our way to show
our thanks to you for having tried.
You keep it, whatever you decide.

A doorway brought us out into the room of prayer. The
    engineer
 explained, 'It's next to sacrifice, since here

appeal to gods is also taking place;
and many scholars think that we can trace
the origin of prayer to sacrifice.
Who knows? My task was just to organize
the exhibition.' Now we saw the knight
at prayer in church from dusk until first light;
we saw the King before the battle kneel,
the monks chanting around the prayer wheel,
the girl in church, the child by the bed,
the old man in the mosque with lowered head,
the sailor in the storm talking aloud,
the tense supporter in the football crowd,
the beads told furtively beneath a coat.
'Since time began, we find people devote
themselves to this, and nothing is so odd
to those, like me, who don't believe in God.
I'm not the guy to offer insight there,
but what I *could* see was, these types of prayer
corresponded roughly to two kinds
of religion. And so, when I designed
the room of prayer, I distinguished between
religions where a god does intervene
in earthly matters – and resurrects
a dead man, say, or doggedly protects
a chosen people, or makes out with a girl
by wrapping himself up inside a swirl
of mist, or morphing to a Charolais –
between these, on the one hand, as I say,
and those religions where the deity
has no action or even velleity:
here I put the Buddhists and the Jains,
joint progeny of the Gangetic plains,
and also the Daoists. Now, to those
gods who intervened we could oppose
science's growing explanatory force.
What of the gods who took the other course?
What warrant can be offered in defence
of gods for whom there is no evidence –

who won't extend oracular advice,
answer a prayer, reward a sacrifice?'

'If you can say it, you can say it clearly.'
The words were spoken softly but severely
behind us. We turned around and saw
a figure where, only moments before,
there had been no one. For a hologram
it looked pretty solid. Here was a man
dressed casually, his lawless hair uncombed,
open-necked shirt, jacket of herringbone,
whose fierce imploring eyes appeared to blaze
with a concern for truth: the kind of gaze
which wins disciples, and inspires loyalty
among students, if not the faculty.
'And what cannot be said, we must consign
to silence. In other words, we must confine
ourselves to speaking of the propositions
of natural science, renounce any ambition
to talk about what cannot be expressed
by language. But then, when we've addressed
and answered every question science posed,
we find that life remains undiagnosed.
Its problem remains; it cannot be expressed
in words meaningfully – it manifests
itself. This quiddity's what's known as mystical . . .'

Loretta, I can only show
a jug with a florist's bouquet,
a dress of printed calico,
twisted and tossed on the parquet,
bedding in rumpled disarray,
the pale ungainly buttocks' rise
and fall, some moaning, and some cries.

And darling, I can only say
'emotional', 'physical', 'hot',
'excitement', 'a fantastic lay',

'feeling', 'urge', 'really a lot'.
No *words convey exactly what*
this thing consists of which infects
my being; so I just said 'sex'.

And now we saw another robed figure, who greeted us
in these terms: 'Hark, you seekers after truth!
I was a philosopher since earliest youth;
I wrote hundreds of books, immersed
myself in mysticism and conversed
in person with Jesus and with Moses,
wrote accounts of visions, wrote glozes,
met with Al-Khidr, saw him walk on water,
and was inspired by a sheikh's daughter
to write love poems of a spiritual kind.
You could say I had an eclectic mind.
I'd like to spend a day, a week, a year
talking to you, but your companion here
has given me instructions to be short.
And so I leave you with a single thought.
It's this: the water's colour on the whole
is nothing but the colour of the bowl,
and if the believer really understood
the meaning of this saying, then he would
admit the validity of all beliefs.'
He bowed, and we walked on, passing beneath
a copse of trees, emerging to survey
the next piece of the engineer's display.

A sunny vista lay before our eyes
which I immediately recognized
as Richmond Park, its groups of ancient trees
in creamy flower, the deer at their ease
recumbent in the long grass, the cars
dawdling between them, even a smell of tar
suggests the overheated road. This scene
is mainly back-projected on a screen,

but in the foreground there's some real grass;
also a stag made out of fibreglass
which turns its head to look this way and that.
Under that tree Louise and I had sat,
tripping on acid. I had thought, 'So this
is what the mystic scriptures meant by bliss:
not something difficult to apprehend
but something very easy, in the end
more real than ordinary reality
and much more lovely. Yet its quality
is more than loveliness: it feels holy,
as if the gods have leapt down into lowly
mortals in the way they used to do,
to help a protégé or to pursue
a lover. So Louise now seems to me
filled with divine essence; the chestnut tree
we sat beneath resembled Yggdrasil;
and even the ice-cream van on the hill
was holy as a temple. Yet I saw
no strange hallucination which the law
of nature has forbidden; just Louise,
an ice-cream van, some biggish chestnut trees.'

'So now you've met the mystics,' said our friend
the engineer. 'You've heard how they pretend
to special insight, special consciousness.
And yet they always struggle to express
the essence of it in words. Does that imply
the insights don't exist? Should we deny
that they are real? I feel that's up to you
to say or leave unanswered. My own view
is that there does exist some mystic state
which you can summon when you meditate,
by drugs, fasting, whipping yourself, or prayer,
whatever. I myself have not been there,
so I won't comment. People who have been
will say that they experience supreme

awareness, find out who they are really,
who in fact they've always been, quite clearly,
for the first time. Some of them maintain
they come out more receptive, more humane,
kinder, and so on. Honestly, I see
small evidence of it. It seems to me
their timeless understanding of God's grace
is transitory, leaving little trace
behind. They are like other people, yes.
Bliss can do little for our happiness.
If you must have it, have it and let it go,
because there's nothing more that you can know
about it, and it has no implication for living.'

'Seeing we don't live forever,
shouldn't we at least live true?'
   – My child, that task is altogether
   more than you and I can do.
   While truth is very fine,
   the whole truth is too strong for humankind.

'But I don't understand. The true
insight is given equally
to dunces as to scholars. Who
persuaded them they couldn't see?
How were they cajoled?
And why did they believe what they were told?'

   – My child, your words have no meaning;
   for what you see is what you see,
   there is no truer, direct seeing:
   no moment of eternity.
   All that is an illusion
   bred in the mind, a logical confusion.

'But no one dies. My father went
into the woods, into the dappled
clearings, the luxuriant
wild orchids, into the crab apple,

into the wild pear.'
      – Hush, my child. No one is living there.

      *

Look back upon transcendent things
as being, not so much misguided,
as mirages of mind which bring
nothing of consequence outside it,
and like a teen affair,
only a way-stop on the thoroughfare.

Girl that I loved at seventeen,
I wish we had possessed the store
of judgement, kindness, and esteem
we learned since. But I wish far more –
I wish, I wish in vain –
I could be in that troubled bed again.

Eventually her birthday came. Louise put on the yellow
gown which Wilhelmina Fleiss had made her.
In spite of all my efforts to dissuade her
from seeing Wilhelmine, I must admit
it suited her and was a perfect fit,
and said so; but her focus was elsewhere.
Inside the cab she said nothing and stared
pensively through the window. We arrived
at Hew's mansion. Now she came alive,
moving about the party, animated
and radiant. But for me what dominated
the evening was that moment which I see
even today with hated clarity,
an image that seemed to certify my doom:
Louise and Hew are entering the room
by the garden door; Louise clings to his arm,
she is smiling. I notice to my alarm
how everything about them speaks of trust
and intimacy; Louise is slightly flushed,

her hair forgotten in its disarray.
You see it in their ease, and in the way
their bodies seem to fit with one another;
and in a flash I realize they are lovers.

When we were getting into bed that night
I couldn't hold it back, I said outright:
'Are you having an affair with Hew?'
She said, 'No way. No way. And in my view
you're out of line even to ask me that.'
'I think you are. Not only from the fact
you spent almost the whole evening with him,
but from the way you were his Siamese twin;
you couldn't stop clinging to one another.
Everyone could see you are his lover,
you didn't give a damn. And as for Hew –
that awful grin upon his face – he knew
that everyone was watching, titillated.
I never felt quite so humiliated
in all my life.' Louise stared at me,
then barked a vicious laugh. She said, 'I see!
You've got a fucking nerve! You fuck Jane Day,
you fuck Loretta fucking Ashe, you lay
your secretary too, for all I know –
God only knows what other so-and-so
who flirts with you at work you haven't dated –
and you're the one feeling humiliated!
The truth is, you're disloyal in every cell
of your body, Patrick. I can tell
when we go out you're looking to get laid.
I always feel I'm going to be betrayed.'
I said, 'Honestly, what do you expect
when you're so cold?' (I failed to collect
my thoughts, they just came spilling out
– it was beyond me to be calm about
her coldness to me.) 'Hey, I'm not a priest
or old-aged pensioner. I haven't ceased

to have desires, or need for a sex life,
merely because I have a frigid wife.'
She said nothing. It wasn't hard to gauge
from her expression the candescent rage
this put her in. She glared at me and strode
into the bathroom, and though I followed,
the door was slammed and bolted in my face.
During this unsought-for breathing space
I understood I had contrived to say
all the wrong things, and this was not the way
for me to deal with her having a fling
with Hew, however upsetting
that was.

      I heard Louise taking a shower
and tried to calm myself. It seemed an hour
that she was locked in there, although in fact
it was more likely just a quarter of that.
When she came out I tried to speak again
in a more measured, sympathetic vein.
She wouldn't say a word. She got in bed
and lay down on her back; her lovely head
was on the pillow, and her eyes were closed;
she seemed almost a corpse, with the bedclothes
pulled up to her chin. I said, 'Louise,
if you won't talk to me at least do please
believe what I'm saying. You must know
I broke off with those girls ages ago.
I'm faithful to you now, I guarantee.
Nobody else means anything to me.'
She said flatly, 'You're very sweet. Goodnight,'
and then turned over and put out the light.
I don't think either of us slept at all.

Now we had come into another hall
of the attraction, and the engineer
was pointing out the main exhibit here:

in the centre of the room, a lofty column
rose up above us and, on top, a solemn
little saint sat cross-legged in the sun,
his long hair wound and tied up in a bun,
his grizzled beard lying upon his soles.
From where he sat, a couple of begging bowls,
suspended on a string, were hanging down.
The engineer ignored them. Passing round
this holy pedestal, he led the way
onwards, between a dozen more displays
where people lived outside the world in priories,
in lamaseries, in convents, and in friaries.
We saw munis, acharyas, and bhikkhus,
the desert fathers, anchorites, sadhus.
The engineer explained, 'Whatever rule
they lived under, whatever holy school
or order they belonged to, all this crowd
obeyed the rule which said "No sex allowed",
or tried to, as a part of their vocation.
Now, life is full of small renunciations
of sex, but these religious guys do seem
to have observed it at its most extreme.'
Such was the engineer's comment. And I
couldn't but be impressed as we passed by
with the variety of adepts there.
I saw celibacy was not a rare
choice for human beings through the ages.
I also saw that cenobites and sages
who take this path do not seem to be racked
with fierce frustration and regret. In fact,
most of them looked happy; and I asked
my guide whether, in his judgement, this masked
inner unhappiness. He answered me,
'I confess my patients tended not to be
people who chose a life of contemplation,
of abstinence and holy meditation;

but all my clinical experience
led me to think that sexual abstinence
usually bred neurosis of some kind,
and so unhappiness. Though bear in mind
my patients hadn't voluntarily contrived to live without sex . . .'

That night I dreamed Louise had taken vows. Her charms
still drew me on, despite the convent's discipline,
despite the strict routine of prayer which bored her,
despite that bag of a habit which hid her naked arms,
and motherhood considered as a sin.
I looked for love, despite the rules of the order.

She said, 'No sudden impulse or longing of my own
brought me to my confinement, here where no child cries,
to keep my maidenhead intact for my redeemer.
I didn't choose the gruel, the constricting walls of stone,
or to wear the metal cilice round my thighs.
You are the one who put me here, dreamer.'

A sage has self-control, and as he meditates
beneath the stars, his feelings are dismissed;
but we don't have his powers. When Capricorn and Saturn
wheel through the dark above, they demarcate our fate.
And, fixed as the stars are fixed,
our passions shift, but hold to their pattern.

The hologram of a girl sprang into life before us, arms extended
in greeting. She pronounced, 'I too transcended
our earthly consciousness. For there were times
when love's intensity was so sublime
I swooned with it. An angel would appear,
brandishing aloft a golden spear
whose iron tip glowed with an orange heat.
This beautiful creature stripped off the sheet
from my exposed, defenceless breast, and lunged
towards me with his lance. The weapon plunged

deep in my body, penetrating me
to my very entrails, prostrating me
in paroxysms of pain. When he withdrew,
he seemed to be tearing my guts out, too,
and then he stabbed it in again. The dire
agony of it set me afire
with love of God. Yes, strangely, this immense
pain brought on a sweetness so intense
that I for one could never wish to lose it.
These raptures didn't come when I could choose it,
but fell upon me even in a crowd,
making me swoon, or grunt and moan out loud;
so powerful that I couldn't resist,
but hugged my pain, enveloped in a bliss
sweeter than anything in all creation.
Such were the throes of my transverberation,
and if you want to see the marks it made
upon my heart, you can: it is displayed
in Alba. Alternatively, take a look
at my memoirs and my didactic books,
which give a full account of how the soul
ascends to union with God. This whole
progression is occult, antagonistic
to being explained in words. But countless mystics
often in practice have begun like me,
dismissing the world, the will, and memory,
and the imagination, all dissolved
in God, our very identity resolved
into sheer pain and rapture.' Silence fell
upon this speech, and for a while her spell
was on us all. Then with a flicker she was gone.

If I am conditioned to see in Jane's grey eyes
the monsoon clouds above the skies of Singapore;
and see that liner leaving, and the iron chains of its ties
swinging undone like a pearl necklace; to hear the roar

of a ship's hooter sounding as a tumult I can't subdue
within this human heart; then I am bound to take
my packet endlessly through that Malacca strait
where only love withheld will have value.
Leave me then, Jane, for your own sake,
and Jane, leave me for my sake, too.

I watched you getting ready. You lingered in the hall
to check the mirror, winding a scarf about your throat;
and if somewhere inside me I found you beautiful,
turning your back to leave me, and putting on your coat,
was that only the postcards of Africa made new?
And if the heavenly changes you had the power to make
in me, just being near, were no changes at all
but only that old flagellant ritual;
then leave with the sadhu for your own sake,
Louise, and say goodbye for my sake, too.

As if involuntarily now, I heard my voice as I began to speak
about the end, the agonizing weeks
and months when I knew she and Hew were lovers
but she had not confessed.

                     Only one other
time I challenged her: that trip which she
took to Manhattan, for the gallery,
when I discovered Hew had been there too.
Louise admitted nothing. And she knew
she didn't have to; she just played her part
as painstaking curator of his art:
it was a perfect screen for the affair.
She shrugged and said, 'Yes, and I saw him there.
He came into the gallery. So what?'
Her life began to strike me as the plot
of a detective novel. All her acts
bore multiple constructions, and the facts
were slippery, ambiguous in sense.
Neurotically, I looked for evidence

but dreaded finding it because I saw
that she and I were in a phoney war,
hoping the fighting wouldn't come, in spite
of knowing that it would. And then the night
I can never forget, the night she sat
quite calmly in the bedroom of our flat
and said, 'I'm having an affair with Hew.'
It was no more than I already knew,
but all was changed now that the words were spoken.
Our awkward tacit treaty had been broken:
a pistol shot, and suddenly renown
comes to a godforsaken Balkan town,
never to be forgotten.
                              Darling friend,
this was the end of all pretence, the end
of everything we shared, the plans, the home,
the happiness, gone to the hecatomb
of trench and Gatling gun, and Europe lost.
A line of demarcation had been crossed,
and what began with a kiss in a Goa street,
the tinny horns around us in the heat,
a buzz of waspish rickshaws spewing fumes,
was dying now in a London bedroom.
I felt its mortal soul slipping away
and was helpless; but rather in the way
the family of an aged millionaire,
almost despite themselves, are well prepared
for what the reading of his will might bring
without openly saying anything;
so I found Louise already primed
to hold this conversation, and her mind
made up with all the detail of arrangements
she wanted put in place for our estrangement
and the new life she was to have with Hew.
Nothing I could say seemed to get through:
her plan was too long plotted and well weighed;
in every glum particular she made

her hurt and her humiliation plain.
As at a séance, the ghosts of Loretta and Jane
raged into the room, the glass unstoppable
as it careered around the polished table.
Incidents I thought were safely hidden
spilled out relentlessly, unbidden,
in her account, like automatic writing
dashing across the page, each one indicting
me, and then convicting me afresh.
And now, in the supreme reproach made flesh,
Jack enters at the doorway of our room,
unconscious harbinger of his own doom,
clutching his blanket, his dishevelled hair
sticking up like feathers in the air,
saying he dreamed about a vampire bat.
If only it had been nothing but that.
We settled him back to sleep as day was dawning
behind the church steeple. Louise was yawning,
but I had never felt more wide awake.
I said to her, 'If only for Jack's sake
we ought to give this thing another try.'
But she rolled up her eyes and gave a sigh,
saying, 'But Patrick, can't you see, my dear,
that's just what I've been doing all these years?'

When I moved to this street,
a small shop ceased to trade;
it seemed unfortunate
but little odds was made.
Then slowly, lease by lease,
over a score of years
dismantled piece by piece,
the old street disappeared.
They put in a new mart,
the bric-a-brac made way
for contemporary art,
the diner had its day,

along with the model planes,
the wool, and the five-and-dime –
barely a store remains
from that original time.

My love, what I recall
is shuttered in my mind:
I hear its caterwaul
at the back of the metal blinds,
a scream which still persists
and a memory recast,
though the shops no longer exist
and the trades are things of the past.
The soul you brought alive
is breathing its final breath,
but something of it survives,
struggling, struggling with death.

In front of us now a monk arose from where he had been praying
beside a crucifix, and hailed us, saying,
'You seek enlightenment? You want salvation?
Pilgrims, the road goes by renunciation.
I am the dupe who grudgingly was bounced
into becoming Pope and then renounced
my holy office. Born the eleventh child
of twelve, at home I spent my juvenile
years working the fields; later I went
into a monastery, in which my bent
for abnegation could be exercised
more fully. Soon I recognized
that even here I'd not withdrawn enough.
I wanted isolation, and the rough
existence of an anchorite. I left
to live out on the mountain in a cleft
of the rock face, in harsh austerity
and prayer; and here the grim severity
of my existence won for me a fame
I hadn't sought. God knows I never claimed

position, let alone the papacy.
Resigning brought a bitter legacy
of censure; in the ages since I died
I've been condemned, and even vilified.'
He knelt down and resumed his prayers again.

As we walked on, the engineer explained:
'Here's the low-down about this holy friar:
renouncing privilege, to be admired,
must operate for greater social good.
Today this is often misunderstood.
A holy sage might do nothing but pray
yet still he was considered to convey
important benefits of holiness.
It was as if a holy man could bless
society merely by being present.
Essentially this was the argument
about Pope Celestine. While some set store
by his privations, others would deplore
that he resigned his See, and these maintained
it would have been more useful to sustain
humanity by working in the Church
than by that solitary and holy search
which he resumed.'
                              So spoke the engineer.
And now in front of us I saw appear
the General, wearing stockings and that blue
coat, his powdered hair tied in a queue,
a giant of a fellow, with an eagle
glare in the blue-grey eyes, and regal
bearing and dignity. The gait was sprightly,
despite his advancing years. He bowed politely
in the old manner, and I could see
in the line of his mouth that slight deformity
caused by his clumsy denture. 'Gentlemen,
it was my duty as a citizen

of our august republic, to renounce
what some would call advantage. Not an ounce
of regret have I ever felt about it.
Let me explain – in case any might doubt it –
the sort of man I was. I loved my home,
that farm beside the river where I'd grown
to be a man. Planting crops and trees,
farm animals and bee-keeping – these
were my enjoyments. I loved hunting too,
the breeding of dogs and horses was a true
passion and I always kept a pack
of my own hounds. By God, there was no lack
of chases in our country! All of these
were my pleasures – my solace and my ease
as well as my living. The public stage
on which I was the idol of my age
was duty, service, an opportunity
for a man to foster his community's
advantage, rather than to procure
graft and kickbacks, titles or sinecures
for himself. I don't believe that any
founder of our republic earned a penny
for his pains. And when I took command
of the continental army, I wouldn't stand
for any talk of salary or pay.
Things have changed a little since my day:
there seems to be a view, strongly entrenched,
that men in public life have an unquenched
desire for more and more power, and yes,
some do; but that's a folly and madness.
I tell you, when I thought I might assume
the Presidency, an ecliptic gloom
came over me and settled on my mind.
My first instinct was always to decline;
and when I took it on, it was with more
reluctance than I ever felt before

in my life. Later generations,
like yours, have looked on my disinclination
as counterfeit, a posture of the day
which meant nothing. But that was not my way.
Look at the record.

            'First it was requested
the government of Virginia be invested
in me personally. This I refused.
Next, my officers expressed their view
that I should be America's first king.
You see, people do want this sort of thing:
it doesn't take much anarchy to start
them calling for Cromwell or for Bonaparte;
and rebels often are the worst offenders.
Friends, my job was finished. I surrendered
my commission in the army and retired
to lead the life of a Virginia squire,
leaving civilian order paramount.
And later, in the same way, I renounced
the Presidency, though I could have had it
for life. You could say I made a habit
of renunciation. Perhaps. But I'm aware
that if by that my country has been spared
military juntas and dictators,
then maybe I have added to the greater
good something of lasting benefit.
Remember also, if you will permit
a word of caution from the afterlife,
that I was always faithful to my wife,
although I liked women and they liked me
well enough, I believe.' Delicacy
seemed to restrain him there. He bowed again,
in his courteous old-fashioned way, and then
walked stiffly, though erect and dignified,
towards the door and left. To either side
were windows and, inspired by a need
to see him one last time, I made all speed

to one of these and peered out. But no trace
of that blue coat or that determined face
was to be seen out there. Instead I saw
only that garden which I'd seen before
when I had visited the residence
and office of the US Presidents.
Now, as then, Louise was on the lawn,
wearing the same short dress that she had worn,
her scarlet hairgrip gleaming in her hair
like a bird's crest, and Jack was playing there
beside her on the grass. I turned around
to tell my two companions what I'd found
but as I did, a nausea gripped my gut,
a dense black rain began to fall and cut
across my field of vision. Now my two
companions seemed to thin, and now they grew
paler, and less substantial.
                                        As I blinked,
a different scene before me, quite distinct,
began to form as if superimposed.
I saw what looked like beds, standing in rows
around a room, which now solidified
just as the engineer and my guide
became more ghostly and faded away.
I lost my bearings in the disarray –
thought I was standing up, and was confused
to find myself horizontal, introduced
between the sheets of a hospital bed,
a drip stuck in me, but at least not dead,
and clearly I had woken from a dream.

Turning my head, I saw a magazine,
and, reading it, the acned face of Kate.
Her dress was stained, her hair was in a state,
she wore some strands of beads around her neck,
twisted together, and her wrists were decked
with festival bracelets. For a while
I couldn't work out how it was this child

was at my bedside. I recalled shaking
the sleeping pills into my palm and taking
a bunch of them, and later, I was sure,
confused but hardly caring, taking more,
only desiring the obliteration
of all feeling; and then the sharp sensation
of whisky in my nose and in my throat,
bracing me as I toyed with the remote,
switching between the channels on TV.
And then oblivion.

But now I see

Kate close her magazine. 'Awake at last,'
she says, and as so often in the past
she laughs for no reason, like young girls do,
in her infectious way, and I laugh too.
Throughout that day she sat with me and kept me
company until the doctor checked me
and, finding there was nothing much amiss,
gave me my discharge. Even after this
Kate was determined to escort me home
and get me settled in. Till now she'd shown
nothing but her usual cheerful guise
but now for once those brink-of-laughter eyes
looked serious; I saw a little frown
inscribe itself between her brows. 'I found
you here and couldn't move you so I called
an ambulance. Once in the hospital
you had tubes going in and out of you
everywhere, you started to turn blue.
I tell you, Patrick, it was terrifying
to watch, I was convinced that you were dying.
I rang Louise and she came down with Jack.
The doctor said you had a cardiac
arrest, but somehow they had reinstalled
the heartbeat. Fuck – I told Louise I'd call
as soon as you came round.'

I took the phone

and dialled that number which used to be home.

Louise answered, her voice sounding restrained
but not relaxed. To start with, it was plain
that she was angry. When I said as much,
she said, 'Of course I am. Can that be such
a big surprise? What did you think I'd feel?
Sometimes I think you are an imbecile.
Did you think Jack was going to find this fun?
Did you? Or did you forget you had a son?
How do you think he felt to see you lying
there, blue in the face and dying . . .'
Her voice tailed off a moment and then after
resumed in a much lower register,
'It was awful when Jack and I arrived.
D'you know, the doctors actually revived
you from the dead? It was horrible,
horrible!' I heard her voice tremble
and then it broke. I knew that she was crying
now, I heard the sobs intensifying,
and then there was nothing, the line went dead.
I waited for her a little time, then said,
'Louise? Louise . . .' but no answer came back.
But now she must have passed the phone to Jack;
I heard his tiny voice saying hello,
saying, when I was better, could we go
back to the Park, and do it all again?
And yes, hearing him now, I felt ashamed.

I also felt excited. Going to bed,
Louise's voice was playing in my head:
scathing perhaps, but now in recollection
I heard behind her anger the connection
she felt with me, I heard her voice falter
as she broke down in tears. And though it altered
nothing – and really nothing had been said –
the sound of it kept swirling round my head
like rags of washing churned in a machine
this way and that, an uneasy routine

which changed nothing but kept me in its thrall
most of the night. I hardly slept at all.

Next day was Sunday. Waking up, my head
was dully painful, and I lay in bed,
thinking I would be sick. At length I rose
and stumbled to the bathroom, took a dose
of Alka-Seltzer. Next time I woke
the nausea had gone. I drank a Coke
and cleaned my teeth. My muscles still felt sore,
but now my head was clearer than before.
I made some coffee. Later on that morning
Jane Day turned up without any warning
at my apartment. Kissing me hello,
she claimed she had a hangover, although
it seemed to me she'd never looked better;
she was wearing the usual high-necked sweater,
her blond hair in a straight line at her jaw,
her mouth so showy that, although she wore
no lipstick, it still looked as if she did.
No paltry hangover had ever hid
that girl's beauty.
               Sitting in an armchair,
she gave no sign at all of being aware
that I'd been in a coma on the brink
of death. She only said, 'I need a drink
just at this moment. Have you got a beer?'
I got us both one. Still it wasn't clear
to me why she had come, but I was pleased
to look at her again, and shoot the breeze,
and flirt a little like we used to do.
She said, 'I heard about Louise and Hew
getting engaged. That must be quite upsetting
for you.' I said, 'Jane, you are forgetting
Louise and I split up some months ago.'
'Yes,' she said, 'yes of course, I know
about that. All the same it must be hard.
I mean, some things in life you can discard,

others aren't dismissed so cavalierly.
I think you're still in love with her really,
aren't you?' At first I offered no reply
but she waited for one, and by and by
I said, 'Perhaps not so much.'

Her eyes,
which never left my face, betrayed surprise,
or puzzlement, at any rate. And then
she brightened, and said, 'I'm on my own again
myself, these days. That's right, Clint has chucked
me for a new girlfriend. Really I lucked
out because I never would have done it
myself. He met her at a bankers' summit
in Singapore last winter and it seems
he's found in her the mistress of his dreams –
I hope of *her* dreams too, because he'll never
leave his wife. Apparently she's clever
and pretty too, but has a withered thigh
and wears a brace. For her I prophesy
plenty of flowers, sexy underwear,
and taking second place. But why should I care?
Good luck to her. I've had enough of his
flattery and phoney promises.
You know what? As soon as he was through
with me as his girlfriend, he fired me too
as his assistant. I'm not trying to say
it was vindictive, because in a way
it was better for me as well, in fact
the only thing to do. So now he's sacked
us both.' She gave a laugh. 'I always felt
terrible about that, the way I dealt
with our affair and got you fired by Clint.'
'Don't let's drag up the past,' I said, a hint
of bitterness remaining from the lively
memories of that time. She went on blithely,
'I have decided to take your advice
and give up married men. I've had one twice

but that's enough, and now I'm really through.'
I said, 'It's not a good routine for you.'
'I know. But I've decided to change that.
You see, Patrick, I'm not a total prat,
though sometimes it seems that way. I can see
that, like it or not, there's a part of me
which is very turned on by the implicit
danger, and gets a thrill from the illicit
nature of those affairs. But equally
there's always been another part of me
which wanted a commitment way beyond
just fucking someone. Yes, and from now on
I'm siding with that part. Patrick, you know
I'm right about this, you even told me so
yourself one time, which was a lot straighter
than Clint ever was.'

                    A little later,
as she was leaving, she said, 'Patrick, hey,
remember we planned a diving holiday?
Perhaps we should do that trip together now;
we have to keep our spirits up somehow.'
She raised her grey eyes to me and I grew
restless at once. Certainly she knew
the power of her beauty. I thought of the weeks
I'd spent walking about the London streets
thinking obsessively about this girl –
her modest skirts and tops, her string of pearls,
and simple manner – desperate to have her.
I said, 'In a divorce, as you might gather,
there's always a lot of sorting out to do.
Right now, I'm really busy at work, too;
it's not the time to take a holiday.
Also, I don't want to be away
from Jack at all while we're getting divorced,
it wouldn't be right.' Jane said, 'Of course.'
Then she said, 'Are you really splitting
up with Louise or are you only sitting

tight and hoping she gets bored of Hew?'
'No, Louise and I are really through.'
'I wonder. Sometimes I think that you'd always
go back to her, whatever game she plays.'

But she was wrong. The past is wearisome
to live again. If anything had come
out of the theme park visit with my guide,
it was the fact that I could put aside
what made me unhappy. And in this sense
I had acquired a real independence.
For understanding is a powerful remedy to bondage.

In the Bahamas, when we anchored,
at first we thought we had found Japan,
and the route to spice for which we hankered
could now at last be drawn on the plan.
How wrong we were. Please understand
that what we found was better by far:
the continents of America.

Something of you remained unspoken.
You let me find a secret drawer
but one which I could never open,
like a nonsense poet's metaphor.
Darling, you always gave me more
than I expected; but always less
than I desired to possess.

And now, though I know the remedy
for that, something inside me still
would give a thousand maravedis
to be with you again, and feel
the sway of your frigid appeal,
and scrabble at drawers you locked away
and sail to Nippon and Cathay.

I went to visit Jack. Of course, his pleasure
at seeing me alive gave me a measure
of what a jerk I'd been. Louise as well
looked happy to see me, I could tell
at once, the way her coffee eyes met mine
instead of avoiding me. I felt a line
had been drawn under her hostility –
in fact it all felt like it used to be
when we had lived together. Jack said, 'Hey,
Dad, where are you taking me today?'
'Where do you want to go?' I said to him,
but now Louise surprised me, butting in,
'Don't go quite yet; we'll have a cup of tea.
Jack, why don't you finish your DVD
while Dad and I have tea?'
                                        Once he was gone,
she got busy putting the kettle on,
fussing with sugar, bits of washing-up,
the radio, and rinsing out a cup,
and so on. I didn't say a thing,
sensing she was silently rehearsing
what she was going to say. And sure enough,
once she was through with the tea-making stuff,
her eyes met mine and she began to speak.
'Patrick, when you and Jack came back last week
from Themeparkland, you asked me if I'd give
the marriage another go, at least to live
together, as a family again.
The whole suggestion struck me as insane.
But now I wonder, maybe you were right.
I can't describe quite how it felt that night
there at the hospital at your bedside,
the moment your breathing stopped, and you had died,
and not a heartbeat there on the machine.
I looked into Jack's eyes. I've never seen
anything like that. It kind of changed
my focal length, even in a strange

way changed my character. I saw we could
be reunited and in fact we should.'
I said, 'And Hew? Louise, what about him?'
She smiled. 'I guess I'll have to do without him.'
A stranger watching would surely have heard
the note of regret lingering in her words
and even in her smile. And I, who knew
her so well, understood at once the true
state of affairs: that she loved Hew, a thing
no choice was capable of banishing;
and that, on my side, I must turn away
from the cold loyalties of yesterday,
and, like Jane, pledge to found a new regime
and constitution. I had always seen
Jane as a simple soul, but she had been
ahead of me, I saw.

Is it that you can't recapture
the past? More that you endow
that past with another sense, a rupture
which makes it alien to us now.
The gladiator's net and lance,
the slaves of General Washington,
the breeding of the peers of France –
all tainted with opprobium.
My love, now we have grown apart,
it will seem poisoned from the start.

Something of history is severed;
something that will not revive,
and has been lost to us forever.
Where are the great churches alive
with worshippers, the epic stories
of the banquet hall, expression
of our bold ancestors' glories?
And where the passionate confession
told to each other in all truth
out of our bodies in our youth?

Heard no more. All those sublime
masses and oratorios
are music of another time.
And suffering you and I imposed
together, now looks mildly gruesome;
a bloodied face upon a cotton
shroud, a scourge in a museum,
and all theology forgotten.
People who once burned alive,
nothing but shreds of narrative.

I still had to collect my last possessions from the flat.
I chose a time when they were both away
for the weekend. Louise was quick to say,
'Take anything you want. Take everything
if you want.' She wasn't marrying
a pauper; clearly she had no need at all
for any of this stuff, though just a small
degree of sentimental attachment
to something from our marriage might have lent
a human touch. Still, I won't complain.
Kate came to help, and I was glad she came;
she lightened the mood; she could always get a
laugh out of me – I just felt better
for having her around. Despite her age
and high spirits there was a certain sage
realism about her. She knew the flat
from all the occasions she had babysat
for us, and as I wandered round she mused,
'This isn't really about things you'll use,
is it? It's about remembering.
Why don't you just pick out a few small things?'
I knew that she was right. I only took
a few photos of Jack, a picture book
I'd read him as a child, and from the bowl
beside my bed, the pebble with a hole
Louise had given me in the Parsees' hotel in Panjim.

Every keepsake's an addiction,
a relic of an ancient law.
And loyal to that jurisdiction,
the junkie waits outside the door
to have it, and then waits some more.

I waited there for you, my darling;
the cold was intense, and the sky
was black with congregating starlings:
behaviour will always testify
unconscious laws that we live by.

And where we have no recollection
behaviour's hardest to undo,
untouchable like a reflection
seen in the water. Like a fool
I waited too long beside that pool.

Ancient addiction, you endure
in things done for no evident
good reason, in self-harm, in pure
acts of aggression where we vent
shame and bitter bewilderment.

You speak to us not with the insistent
boom of a Nigeria-bound
liner, but maybe like a distant
nightmare of one, the howling sounds
of ghostly passengers, who went down.

An early spring weekend. It was my day for Jack.
We went for lunch at Dino's pizza shack,
and then to 'Vicky Park' to meet with Kate.
She hadn't arrived. We sat down to wait
and while Jack fiddled round with his Game Boy
I shut my eyes and started to enjoy
the feeble warming of the April sun
upon my face; my thoughts began to run

on Jane and on Louise. I heard Jack say,
'Here she is, Dad,' and there on the pathway
I saw Kate come towards us. She was wearing
trainers and a small backpack in glaring
rave patterns, and an old T-shirt,
and, as she walked, her long strides made her skirt
swing about her legs. In the pack
she'd brought a bag of stale bread for Jack
to feed the ducks, and so we made our way
towards the lake. Kate's skin looked grey
as well as acned after the long winter
but she was blithe as ever; not a hint of
the vulnerability and loneliness
of her position came to be expressed
in those young eyes. I saw her take Jack's hand
and laugh. Behind them both a heavy band
of raincloud had welled up and now encroached
upon the lower sky. As we approached
the lake, I saw its duplicate suffused
across the water, like a long black bruise
within the azure surface of the pond.
Against this dark background the new leaves shone
pale in the sunlight; jostling in its depths,
they seemed a cloud of vivid green insects.
Now Kate slipped off the straps of her backpack
and took out some baguette; and she and Jack
began to break bits off and throw them down;
and, as they did, the ducks came clustering round,
breaking the image up; and into the chopped
and rippled surface of the lake I dropped
the Goa pebble.

The war won, my ambitions granted.
Returning to my farm I find
the chestnuts and the oaks I planted
as whips, the soaring shafts of vine,
have measured out my own decline.

No lights downriver. My friends departed.
Sally, love of my youth, away
to England. I was so heavy-hearted
it was a year and a day
before I could bear to ride that way;

and when I did, the house I found
was gutted. Only some walls remained
and a chimney, while upon the ground
lay rafters, and the busted frame
of the mansion, ripped and charred by flame.

I thought of the many days I went there,
the friends most loved and close to me,
the sweetness of the hours spent there,
the happiest of my life: debris
and rubble consigned to memory.

I turned my horse and left those ruins,
feeling I'd looked upon her bones,
and rode home. What there's no undoing
needn't be dwelt on; but what I'd known
of love, and of being young, was gone.

They were my oldest friends. With them
they took the ties of colony,
ties that we too once loved but then
threw off; and in our mutiny
tore down the house and made men free.

* * * * *

A year later. Outside the school I waited,
with all the other parents congregated
to meet their children when the day was done.
A bird was singing: springtime had begun,
though icy gusts of wind blew down the street
and earlier, there'd been both hail and sleet.

I turned my collar up against the draught
and hunched my neck, wishing I'd brought a scarf.
Now Jack came running out. He saw me standing
and ran across, and he and I went hand-in-
hand around the corner to the car,
Jack skipping at my side. It wasn't far
to drive down to the garage, where I filled
the car, and then, out-bargained at the till,
added some sweets for Jack. Our route from here
took us past the apartment where last year
I stayed during the time Louise and I'd
lived separately, and where I'd nearly died.
As we drove by, I pointed it out to Jack;
but he was on his Game Boy in the back
not listening to me, maybe not inclined
to revisit the memory of that time,
frightened and nearly let down by his dad.
Kate had taken on the lease I'd had:
her old landlord was redeveloping
so she'd moved in here earlier this spring.
I thought how much she'd helped me, and in fact
had literally saved my life. And Jack
adored her too. I hoped one day she'd find
a guy worthy of her. A girl as kind
and capable as she was, and as fun,
does not come every day. He would be one
lucky dude.
            Arriving home I parked
the car outside the building, disembarked
Jack and our packages, and took the lift
up to our apartment on the fifth.
Fumbling with my keys I let us in
and, going through the hall to the kitchen,
put down my bags. I saw Louise was back
because she'd left her padded camera sack
and handbag on the countertop. Next door
we found her.

                She is sitting on the floor
in front of the TV. Her legs are drawn
up beside her, and her slender form
is propped against the sofa. At the sound
of the door opening she turns around
with a sudden bird-like movement, her long hair
black as a crow's wing, swinging in the air,
and gives a childlike wave and says, 'You're back.
Hello, Patrick darling. Hello Jack.'
In the hearth the gas fire is alight
and the whole room is wonderfully bright
and warm after the biting cold outside.
I stoop to kiss her and, smiling, dark-eyed,
she turns her face up to me. But her kiss
is cold, perfunctory; and riled by this
out of some bladder of my past the bile
of anger rises, and just for a while,
I taste the bitterness of that reflux.
But now, like venom of a serpent sucked,
it does no harm; I swallow, and the taste of loss slowly dissolves . . .

Kapellmeister Bach said, 'Think on this:
in youth and age I worked hard all my days.
Do likewise and you'll know equal success.'
Life is a kind of craft, and it repays
effort and practice with some happiness.

I went up to our room, to write that song.
At first my fickle mind drifted away
after distractions. Trivia have a strong
hold over us, it's easy to obey
their call, undisciplined and yet headstrong.

For these are claims the whole world understands:
adulterous affairs, their hectic thrills,
the pull of money, the prestige of brands
and works of art; yet none of these fulfils
deeper requirements of the artisan.

Beyond the window seagulls drift and ease
in random flight. At last my thinking clears,
I focus better. On the piano's keys
my fingers call out phrases, I can hear
the strands of music marrying by degrees.

For now in this hardest stage the truth is heard:
with utter clarity I am aware
of deepest instinct, how unseen it herds
and guides us like those warm updraughts of air
which govern the mysterious flight of birds.

This is the bass, my love, playing below
the prinky tunes put out by all the rest;
for though the soloists are played for show,
the humblest instrument is heard furthest
which in the band passes incognito.

Walk with me, darling, near that anchoring line
where all our intimacies are begun;
for it is not given to humankind
to find our happiness with more than one
companion on the road; and you are mine.

And when I go downstairs among the clatter
of other tasks, I only find them boring;
and long to turn my back upon that chatter
and come again to labour more absorbing,
a hundred times, my love, than any easier matter.

*

No lifetime lasts for long, but while I live,
I hope to have that labour in my head
and find its music with the primitive
bass line running within it like a thread,
and rise upon its current, pinions spread.
For though the notes fly by like time, the mode
is heard in every chord and every episode.

List of First Lines

Acknowledgements

My heartfelt thanks go to everyone who helped to produce this book, and especially to Andrew Barker, Fiona Carpenter, Georgina Difford, Jamie Keenan, Penelope Price, Jon Riley, Nick de Somogyi, Rose Tomaszewska and Corinna Zifko. Jon Riley was both generous with his time and judicious in his suggestions, and I feel very fortunate to have had the advice of such an outstanding editor. Several friends read the story and made helpful suggestions, among whom I am grateful to Guy Kennaway, Roc Sandford, and above all Fram Dinshaw. Many helped in other ways, among whom I would like to thank David Ekserdjian, Alan Jenkins, Rupert Merton, Matt Ridley, Felicity Rubinstein and Jason Shulman. I would also like to thank my agent, Caroline Dawnay, who believed in the book and was unwavering in her support when it was most needed. Special thanks are due to my children, Pandora, Sibylla, John and Tom, without whose enthusiasm for theme parks this book would never have arisen. Finally, I am grateful to my wife, Nicola Shulman, to whom this work is dedicated. Her wonderfully acute reading has been a touchstone for the clarity of meaning I sought, especially in the lyrics. She bears no responsibility for anything which may remain obscure. Far more important were her love and succour.